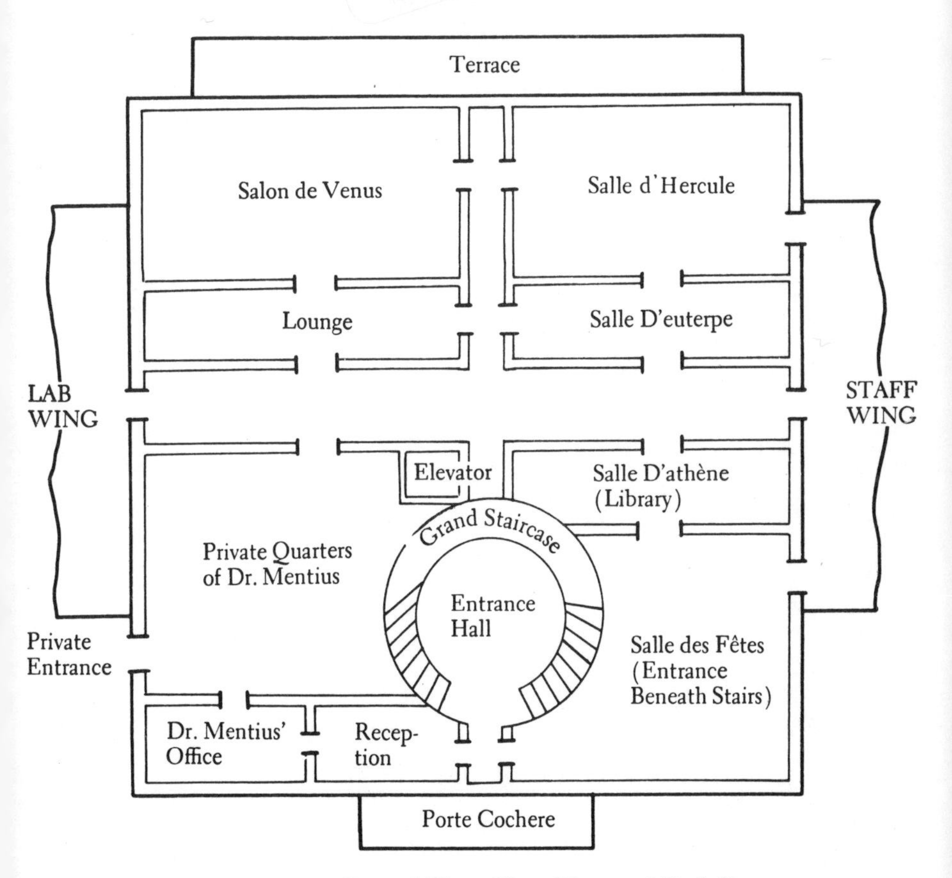

DIAGRAM B: *Ground Floor Plan, Chateau Mirabelle*

the methuselah enzyme

the methuselah enzyme

a novel by

Fred Mustard Stewart

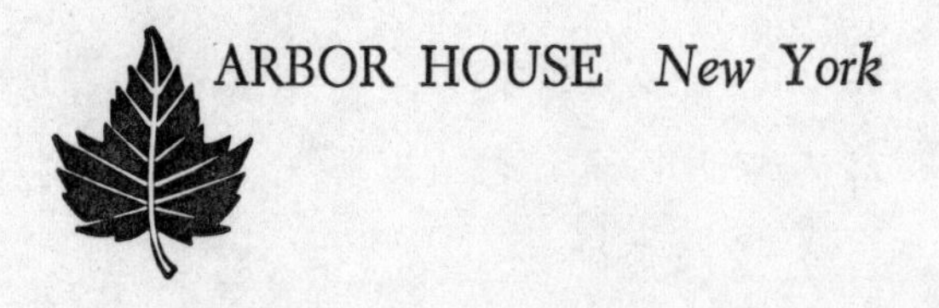

ARBOR HOUSE *New York*

 Published in the United States by Arbor House Publishing Co., Inc., New York, and simultaneously in Canada by Nelson, Foster & Scott, Ltd.

Manufactured in the United States of America

To my beloved wife, Joan

See dying vegetables life sustain,
See life dissolving vegetate again;
All forms that perish other forms supply;
(By turns we catch the vital breath and die)

Pope, *Essay on Man*

PART ONE

THE Bolshoi Ballet brought "Swan Lake" to a triumphant conclusion and the elegantly dressed first-night audience rose to its feet with applause. In one of the boxes, a beautiful girl—or, rather, young lady—was clapping enthusiastically, her blue eyes bright with excitement. She was tall, thin, and fragile, and could have been mistaken for a ballerina herself (which would not have been far from the truth: she had started studying ballet at the age of five in Shaker Heights, twenty years before). Her face was exquisitely molded, and her light blond hair hung straight down to her shoulders. She wore a blue Norman Norell gown that was simply cut and flatteringly unsophisticated. Her name was Ann Brandywine.

"Michael, I love them!" she said to the lean man with the graying hair standing next to her. "I love them almost as much as the home team."

Her husband smiled. He was a handsome man, more than twice her age, dressed in a well-cut dinner jacket. He seemed amused by his young wife's exuberance.

"You can have the home team. I'll take 'Swan Lake' over 'Astarte' any day."

"Here they come again! That's the third curtain call! I hope they get twenty."

"If they do, we'll miss dinner."

They got eight; and five minutes later, Michael Brandywine was putting the chinchilla shrug around his young wife's shoulders and leading her out of the box, down the red-carpeted stairs of the Metropolitan Opera House to the much-criticized foyer, then out onto the much-praised Lincoln Center Plaza. It was a cool May evening, and the fountain in the center of the plaza was shooting with intoxicated joy into the black sky. The dark blue Bentley was waiting at its accustomed place. As Louie, their chauffeur, saw them crossing the plaza, he hopped out and opened the back door. Louie knew his employer's fourth wife was a balletomane who dragged her husband to every performance in town. Louie was amused by the resigned way Michael Brandywine submitted to these ordeals. Although Michael, the president and chief stockholder of Brandywine Drugs, the fifth largest drug company in the world, was anything but a Babbitt—indeed, he was a worldly New Yorker who enjoyed the cultural banquet his city continually served—ballet was not his cultural cup of tea.

"How was it?" asked Louie as they reached the car.

"Wonderful!" said Ann. "But no one's as good as Jacques d'Amboise."

"She's never satisfied," said Michael as he climbed in the back seat behind her.

❧

"Happy first anniversary," he said twenty minutes later, touching his champagne glass to hers.

"Happy first anniversary, darling. It's been a beautiful year."

They sipped the Laurent Perrier that had been waiting for them at their table at the Baroque, their favorite restaurant on Fifty-third Street. Then, as they waited for their salmon to be sliced, Michael said, "I have a surprise for you."

She put her fingertips together and assumed a mock-thoughtful look. "Let me guess: you're going to buy me a wolfhound."

"Why in God's name would I buy you a wolfhound?"

"Because you know I want one. Then how about a German shepherd? He can protect me when I go to Gristede's."

"You don't need a dog to protect you at Gristede's: you need an accountant. No, the surprise is a trip to Switzerland."

She tried to look delighted. "To Switzerland? When?"

"Next month."

"In June?"

"I wasn't planning to ski. Did you ever hear of Dr. Herbert Mentius?"

"No."

"Dr. Mentius is a very brilliant man, from Brooklyn originally, whose father was an extremely successful furrier. Dr. Mentius sailed through Harvard and then went on to Columbia Medical School. And everyone said he was either going to be the greatest brain surgeon the world had ever seen, or the greatest biochemist, because he had degrees in both."

"He sounds awesome."

"He is. In fact, he's a genius. But instead of becoming the world's greatest brain surgeon or biochemist, Dr. Mentius became the world's greatest gerontologist."

Ann looked at her husband. Michael Brandywine was sixty-three: he could pass for fifty-five. He wasn't an ounce overweight, thanks to daily workouts at the Racquet and Tennis Club, and his handsome face, while wrinkled, had only the hint of a double chin. Nonetheless, though he rarely discussed it, she knew he was sensitive about his age. It was almost as if age were the one enemy this dynamic businessman could not defeat, and he resented it.

"So Dr. Mentius is an age doctor?"

"He's more a youth doctor. After much wrangling, I've managed to get a reservation for a two-month treatment at his youth clinic outside Lausanne. It's expensive as bloody hell, but his Alpha treatment is supposed to be the last word in rejuvenation. The clinic's in a chateau on the edge of a lake and it's deluxe all the way. If you'd come with me, I don't guarantee you'll have the best time of your life, but it might be interesting. And at the end of the two months, your husband will emerge looking like a new —and, hopefully, younger—man."

"Michael, this man isn't one of those crazy gland doctors the movie stars all go to?"

Michael shook his head. "No gland funny business and nothing crazy, though he gets his fair share of movie stars and the international crowd. But Mentius is quite respectable. I've heard a lot about him, and it's all favorable; the treatment is really worth the twenty-five thousand."

She looked surprised.

"Is *that* what it costs?"

He nodded. "Plus extra for you."

"Michael, it sounds to me as if Dr. Mentius is the world's greatest crook, not brain surgeon."

"He's honest, believe me. Will you come?"

She took his hand under the table.

"Of course, if you want me."

"I want you."

They finished the champagne as the captain took the salmon away.

Two hours later, they arrived home at their co-op at 813 Fifth Avenue; Ann went into her bedroom to undress while Michael poured himself a brandy. It was a magnificent apartment done in restrained taste, and Ann loved it, as she loved everything about the new life her marriage the year before had brought her. Why shouldn't she love it? She had been a $130-a-week secretary when her employer—the distant, rich, handsome Michael Brandywine—had swooped out of the executive suite, courted her for three weeks, then married her. It had been the ultimate Cinderella story as she moved from her third-floor walkup on Fourth Street to the rarefied, if polluted, air of Fifth Avenue.

Of course, it hadn't been quite that casual. Her family had known Michael for years. Her father, a successful doctor in Shaker Heights, had been the Brandywine family doctor before old Mr. Brandywine died and Michael moved the company headquarters to New York. Then, eighteen months ago, Ann's parents had both been killed in a plane crash. Thanks to her father's ruinous penchant for the commodities market, Ann and her brother Bob had been left the insurance, a pile of unpaid bills, and nothing else except the house. When the estate was settled, there was little left. Ann had moved to New York, written a letter to Michael applying for a job, and had received a courteous answer telling her there was a position available. Then, shortly after she started work, he had dropped by her desk to say hello. He had taken one look at her face and asked her to dinner. Michael was anything but shy.

She loved him, but she knew little about him. He was a secretive man who told her practically nothing about his business life and kept his thoughts very much to himself. In many ways, he treated her more like a daughter than a wife except, of course, sexually. In bed, he was all husband. He didn't want children, which Ann accepted; he had two children by previous marriages on whom he had settled handsome trusts and whom he saw infrequently, and they were all he wanted. But aside from that, her love life couldn't be improved upon.

But still, he was such a damned sphinx! This Switzerland business, for instance. How typical of him not to breathe a word about it until the reservations were made, then casually drop it in her lap. As she pulled off her pantyhose, noting there was a run in one leg, Ann found she slightly resented the way he had handled it. Then she shrugged it off. If that was the way he liked to operate, it was his privilege. She certainly had very little else to complain about.

She stood for a moment and looked at her naked reflection in a full-length mirror. Her body was almost too thin, thanks to constant weight-watching and regular exercise; but other than a tendency to gauntness, her figure was a beautiful one, lithe and well-proportioned. Her breasts would never put her in the Raquel Welch league: they were too small and pointed. But her legs were beautiful—her dancing fortunately had not made them muscular—and her belly had just the right hint of roundness. Physically, she was a thoroughbred.

"Playing Narcissus?" asked Michael, coming up behind her and kissing her neck. She smiled.

"Just taking inventory."

"I didn't know Vassar girls made a habit of standing naked in front of mirrors?"

"You'd be surprised what Vassar girls do."

"Nothing would surprise me about Vassar girls. But I have another surprise for you."

"Another clinic?"

"Not exactly."

She watched in the mirror as he pulled something out of his jacket pocket and held them up against her ears. They were two turquoise pendant earrings, the turquoises surrounded by large diamonds.

"Oh, Michael . . ." she whispered.

"Hold them."

She took the earrings and screwed them into her lobes. Then, as she watched in the mirror, he opened a large velvet box marked Cartier and pulled out a matching turquoise and diamond necklace which he draped around her neck and fastened.

"Happy first anniversary," he said.

"Michael," she whispered, staring at the jewels, "they're real, aren't they?"

"I hope to tell you they're real!"

"But they must have cost a fortune!"

"I got them on sale."

"Seriously: do you think you should? I mean, with all this money for the clinic, and what you lost on those oil leases. . . ." While he told her little of his business, she knew that recently he had dropped a considerable amount of capital in a syndicate that had bought millions of dollars worth of oil leases in Alaska and which, while everyone else was making fantastic finds, perversely enough had found nothing.

He turned her around and took her in his arms. "When a husband buys a wife goodies, if she's smart she'll say 'thank you' in the proper fashion and not worry about the bills."

She kissed him. "Michael, I love them. And I love you."

"You can wear them in Switzerland and show up Lady de Ross."

"Who's she?"

"She's going to be at the clinic too. She's a rich old bag who's got millions in numbered accounts."

"I'll wear my diamonds every day and make her green with envy."

"With no clothes on?"

"With no clothes. Just the necklace, the earrings, and me."

"You'll be the toast of the wheelchair set. Now, about thanking me properly . . ."

She smiled, took his hand, and led him gently to the bed.

❧

The young man had thick black hair that hung almost to his shoulders. He grabbed the blue tile gutter and hoisted himself out of the pool. His body, lean and tanned, glistened in the African sun as he scrambled to his feet, stretched, then leaned over to examine his hairy right thigh.

"I think I've got jock-itch," he complained.

Lady Kitty de Ross looked up at him over her dark glasses. "Occupational disease?" she said.

"Yeah," he grinned. "I caught it from you."

Lady Kitty returned her eyes to the latest issue of *Elle*. "Dear Hugh, your bovine wit is a bit much to take before breakfast. Why don't you go inside and spray yourself with fungicide, or whatever, then make me a Bloody Mary? And kindly wash your hands before you make the drink."

She was stretched on a deck chair beside the pool of her house in Tangier, overlooking the Straits of Gibraltar. The house had been designed three years before by a young London architect and had won two gold medals although, as Lady Kitty had sniffed, she was sure she'd seen the same house in a back issue of *Life*. It was all white stucco, glass walls, and gorgeous Portuguese tile, but the roof leaked and the guest bathroom continually overflowed. It had cost her one hundred and twenty thousand pounds, before devaluation.

Hugh Barstow was drying his long hair with a bath towel. "I thought you were taking the pledge until after breakfast," he said. "It would be kicky to try and stay sober till lunch."

Again she glared at him. "If I choose to get drunk before breakfast, after lunch, or by the light of the full moon, that, dear boy, is *my* business, not yours."

He is good-looking, thought Lady Kitty, but his manners leave a lot to be desired. Still, she supposed they were all one could expect from an ex-rock singer from Secaucus, New Jersey, whom she had picked up two weeks before at the Casino d'Afrique a half mile down the beach from her house. Besides, his crudeness was rather attractive. In her more candid moments, she would admit to herself that it was her own basic crudeness that responded to Hugh's. Lady Kitty had been born sixty-six years before, the daughter of a Liverpool veterinarian. But she had long since concealed most of her Liverpudlian heritage, replacing it with a secondhand Noel Coward brittleness that she had acquired in the thirties and forties when she had been the leading comedienne of the West End. Then, Kitty Beaufort, as she had called herself, was one of the most beautiful women in Europe, her face reducing even the most savage critics to rapture. Now, her skin was tough, her neck scrawny, and her golden hair stiff from a thousand expensive colorings. Still her figure was good. And when she was sober, she could be attractive. Since 1947, however, when she retired from the stage and married the immensely wealthy Lord Henry de Ross, she had been sober relatively infrequently. And when, five years before, Lord Henry had died, leaving her all of his South African mining fortune, she had stopped being sober at all except for rare occasions when, like today, she got up before noon. But already she was craving her first drink.

Hugh tossed the towel on a chair. "What's the big plan for today?" he asked. "Another all-day Mah-Jongg whoop-'em-up? Or another booze-'em-up with the fighting fags down the road?"

"Hugh, dear, I wish you wouldn't speak of Gerald and Archibald quite so crudely. Gerald is a very talented minor poet, and I'm not at all convinced Archibald is a faggot."

"Then why does he wear lipstick?"

"Well, at any rate, they don't fight. At least in public. And the plan for today is to pack."

"Pack? Where are we going?"

"To London for two weeks, then Paris for two more. Then we're going to Switzerland for two months."

"Christ, thanks for telling me so early! I mean, maybe I don't want to go?"

She lowered the magazine and looked at him. "Has somebody else offered you a job?"

He didn't answer.

"Well then. You're coming to Switzerland with me. It will be educational for you: you can learn to yodel."

"What are you going to do in Switzerland for two months?"

"Take a treatment. Now be a good boy and fix me that drink."

"Kitty baby, you really should cut down on the booze."

"Dear boy, a Bloody Mary is not a drink. It's a vitamin pill. Now stop being what I believe they call in Secaucus a 'pain in the ass,' and get me a drink."

Hugh gave her the finger, then went into the house.

❧

Martin Hirsch had no idea why his father wanted to see him. Martin had arrived the day before at the North Shore estate he laughingly called home, having concluded his second year at Williams. He rarely came home anymore. He hated the spacious pseudo-Georgian mansion overlooking Long Island Sound; his father had built it in 1932, spending over half a million depression dollars when the rest of the country had been starving. For that matter, he hated his father. The only reason he had come home at all was that he was flat broke, and he literally couldn't afford to go anywhere else until he could raise some scratch.

And now his father had called his bedroom on the house phone and asked him, with his usual chilly politeness, if he would come down to his study for a moment. Martin had said yes, then hastily put out the pipe of hash he had been smoking. It was the last of his hash, and he hated to see it go. But he couldn't very well stroll into his old man's study puffing hashish, particularly after what had happened last summer. Shuddering slightly at the memory of that, he hurried into the bathroom, gargled with mouthwash, washed his hands and slightly acned face, ran a comb through his thick sandy hair that was long, but not hippie-length; then he pulled on his spotted J. Press cord jacket and hurried into the hallway. Moving past the dark oil portrait of his great-grandfather, Albricht Hirsch, the German immigrant who had founded the underwriting firm of Hirsch, de-Bardeleben, and Co. in 1882, he ran down the graceful stair lined with more family portraits, then crossed the big hall to the study door, where he knocked.

"Come in."

He opened the door and entered the paneled room. Rich. Luxuriant. The lighted cabinets holding part of his father's famous collection of Chinese art. The antique English furniture. The tall windows looking out on the manicured lawns. It was an appropriate setting for Arnold Hirsch, senior partner of Hirsch, deBardeleben, and Co., one of the most powerful and respected men on Wall Street. Tall Arnold Hirsch, only an inch shorter than his son, whom he resembled physically except, of course, for the chasm of over half a century in their ages. Martin had been a product of Arnold's old age, and the generation gap that normally occurs between fathers and sons had been made a canyon by the fact that Arnold Hirsch, at seventy-five, was more like a grandfather. He was still a nice-looking old man, with a long Borzoi face like his son, but where once had been a thick crop of sandy hair like Martin's, there was now nothing but shining skin. He had a paunch, which his English tailor managed to minimize with carefully cut jackets and vests. But most impressive was his quiet air of authority which never failed to unnerve Martin. That, and the cunning gray eyes. When his father looked at him, Martin always felt he was looking right into his brain.

He was looking at him now.

"Sit down, Martin," he said, indicating a chair by the desk. He remained standing by the window. Typical, thought Martin, with disgust. He likes to stand: it gives him sort of an advantage. Oh well, screw him.

He sank into the chair, crossed his long legs, and looked sullenly at his father.

"What are your plans for the summer?" began Arnold.

"I wanted to go to Canada with Dick Grayson, but he got hepatitis last week."

"I see. That's too bad."

"So now I don't know what I'm going to do. I won't be here long, if that's what's bothering you."

Arnold could hardly miss the hostility in his tone.

"You know I enjoy having you here, Martin."

"Uh huh." You hate the sight of me, you phony.

"I do. I think you have a somewhat immature idea that I hold you responsible for the accident, and brood about it. I do hold you responsible, because you were. But I don't brood about it. Are you still smoking pot?"

"No." Damn him, he doesn't mince words, thought Martin, nervously. I wonder if he believes me? Judging from that look, I don't think he does.

"I'm glad you've stopped," said Arnold. "How are your finances?"

"Lousy." If he's going to be blunt, I'll be blunt. "Why can't I get *some* of the money out of Mother's trust? I don't think it's fair. I mean, the money is mine, after all."

"But you can't touch it till you're twenty-one. Meanwhile, it's earning six percent."

"What the hell good is that doing me? I need the money now! I mean, I'll be twenty-one next year, but meanwhile I have to beg off you. Why can't I borrow something against the trust, or use it for collateral, or whatever you do with trusts. I don't want a lot, just enough to . . ." He started to say, "to buy pot and hash," but caught himself in time. ". . . to have some pocket money. You know."

Arnold was watching him carefully. "Would you like three thousand dollars pocket money?"

Martin was taken completely by surprise. "Three thousand? You mean now?"

"Now. I'll write you the check this morning."

Martin looked at him suspiciously. "Father, you've never done anything like this before. Pardon me for being skeptical, but what's the gimmick?"

Arnold smiled as he sat down behind his Chippendale desk that he was pleased to have paid ten thousand dollars for in 1953 at Parke Bernet, but which was now worth conservatively ten times that amount.

"Martin, like all the young, you're much too cynical. But I'll admit there's a gimmick, as you call it."

"What is it?"

"Next week I'm going to a clinic owned by a brilliant man

named Herbert Mentius. The clinic's in Switzerland, and Dr. Mentius will be giving me a two-month rejuvenation treatment. I would like very much for you to go to the clinic with me. Realizing this may not be exactly your idea of fun, I'm prepared to give you three thousand dollars—as a gift, not a loan. Or call it a bribe, even. But since I'll be paying all your expenses as well, you'll come out ahead of the game."

Martin scratched his chin.

"Why are you bribing me?"

"I could say I want you at the clinic with me because I'd like to spend some time with you to try and get to know you better—to try and remove this hostility you obviously feel for me. But I doubt if you'd believe that, so I'll be blunt. Last summer, you killed your mother while driving a car under the influence of marijuana. Since then, I have reason to believe you have advanced to hashish and God knows what else. I want to take you to the clinic to keep an eye on you, to try and prevent you from taking drugs in any form at least for two months. If I can do that, I feel there's a chance you may give them up, although I'm really not too hopeful. I won't even extract a promise from you that you won't take any drugs at the clinic, because I know you'd break your word if you have the chance. My only hope is to prevent you from having the chance. The chateau is isolated, and Switzerland has very strict antinarcotics laws. Everything is illegal there, including marijuana, and they enforce the laws. So I think you'll have a hard time getting the stuff. At least, I'm willing to take the gamble. And, hopefully, if you can keep off it for two months, you may be able to keep off it the rest of your life—I don't know. But to me, it's worth a try." He paused. "Well, that's my reason. Are you interested?"

Martin shifted in his chair. Christ, what a crazy deal! he thought. Two months sealed up in some creepy clinic with a bunch of antiques and *him*. . . . But still, three thousand clear! That was a lot of hash, even at the new high prices. And even though Switzerland might be tough on heads, still in a clinic, with all the stuff they usually keep there . . . it should be possible to get something. . . .

"Well? How about it?" said Arnold quietly. "Shall I write you a check?" His hand was on the fountain pen that stuck out of the black marble base.

"What's the name of the clinic?"

"It's called the Chateau Mirabelle. It's on a small lake called Lake Windischgratz. It's a beautiful place, and there are all sorts of recreational facilities, so you shouldn't be too bored."

"Could I take my stereo?"

"Of course."

Again, Martin shifted. Two months with *him*. . . . Jesus. But still, he thought, I could hole up in my room, once I made a contact. I wouldn't have to see too much of him. And all that money.

"Well? Is it a deal?"

Martin slowly nodded. "It's a deal."

His father smiled his wintry smile, then began to write the check.

❦

Ann and Michael Brandywine enjoyed the flight from New York to Lausanne, with the stopover in London. When they landed at the Lausanne airport, they were met by Dieter, a chubby Swiss chauffeur sent by the clinic, who shepherded them through customs and then led them to a large black Daimler. En route, Ann stopped at a counter to buy several corny miniature chalets to send to her three nephews in Larchmont—she was godmother to the youngest of her brother Bob's children, and felt very close to them. Then she climbed in the back seat of the Daimler as Michael and Bill Bradshaw, his thirty-two-year-old assistant, brought along to ease some of Michael's business pressures, helped the chauffeur load the trunk with the luggage. Then Michael and Bill got in the back with Ann, Bill taking a jump seat, and Dieter started the drive to the Chateau Mirabelle.

"Bill, you're going to be living in the staff quarters," said Michael as the Daimler passed through Lausanne. "I'm sorry I couldn't arrange anything better, but frankly it would have cost me double to put you up in the guest quarters. I hope you don't mind?"

Ann was a bit shocked by Michael's blunt handling of a rather touchy situation. After all, Bill Bradshaw was a graduate of Harvard

Business School and had been with Michael for five years. He was a well-mannered, good-looking young man on the way up, and to put him in the staff quarters was, in her opinion, an insult. Bill's handsome Irish face reflected a confusion unusual for him. Then he said, "Well, no, of course I don't mind, Mr. Brandywine."

"Good. I'm sorry it had to be this way, but it's the best I could do. In fact, the last letter I got from Dr. Mentius said the guest quarters weren't even going to be open, which I didn't quite understand. All I know is, we're being put up in the chateau itself, and I'm going to be tied up with the doctor from nine to five each day. So you'll have to check in with the New York office each morning and be on tap in case of emergency calls. Then each afternoon, at five, you and I can meet in my suite and we can go over whatever correspondence there is, and you can fill me in on what's been happening. The rest of the time you can do pretty much what you like."

Ann was amused. The *rest* of the time? What was left except the nights? Poor Bill: Michael ran him a weary race. She often wondered why he put up with it.

An hour after leaving Lausanne, the Daimler arrived at the tiny town of Windischgratz, situated on the lake of the same name. They drove through the town, then took a rutty road around the lake until they arrived at a formal marble and wrought-iron gate, executed in the elaborate style of the French Second Empire. Pulling through the gate, the car entered a wooded park. The drive wound for almost a mile through the park, which was alive with rabbits, squirrels, and even an occasional deer. Then, as Ann and Michael watched through the windshield, the drive emerged from the woods into a wide expanse of green lawn. Here it separated into two forks which formed a huge circle, in the center of which was a fountain with a high, solitary jet. On the opposite perimeter of the circle was a truly beautiful sight: an elaborate white marble chateau designed, like the main gate, in the exuberant and slightly vulgar style of the 1860s, but nevertheless almost breathtaking in its green setting. Beyond it they could see the lake, several miles in diameter, whose shores were heavily wooded and whose waters were so deeply blue they were obviously fed by distant Alpine glaciers.

"The Chateau Mirabelle," announced Dieter as he started the

car slowly around the circular drive toward the porte cochere of the building. "It was put up a hundred years ago by a famous French prostitute."

Ann smiled. "Really? What was her name?"

"I forget, but that's what she was," said Dieter in his guttural accent. "She made a lot of money and retired here on Lake Windischgratz. Dr. Mentius and his wife bought the place eight years ago when it was rundown and empty, and they fixed it up. You see the new laboratory wing over there on the left? And here on the right is the kitchen and utility wing. The doctor built both of them, and kept them low and surrounded them with shrubbery so they wouldn't hurt the look of the old chateau."

It was true the two modern wings on either side of the square, two-storied chateau were as inconspicuous as possible, but Ann couldn't help feeling the place would have looked better without the additions. Still, the chateau was definitely splendid. Writhing, muscular gods supported the roof of the porte cochere (undoubtedly, thought Ann, the male caryatids were an inspiration of the "famous French prostitute"), and as the Daimler came to a halt at the steps that led to the double entrance doors flanked by heavy wrought-iron lanterns, three liveried footmen came out to unload the car.

"I see what you meant about deluxe," whispered Ann.

Michael nodded rather glumly. "Guess why the price is so high."

They were led into the entrance hall of the chateau, a huge round marble room extending through the second floor to a skylight in the roof, and, on the horizontal plane, extending all the way through the chateau to large terrace doors at the opposite end, through which the blue water of the lake distantly sparkled. On either side of the entrance hall an impressive double staircase swept to a rotunda on the second floor, and Ann could easily imagine the original owner of the building making her flamboyant entrances down the marble stairs to her guests below. The place was very much in the grand style; furthermore, it was immaculate. The marble stairs, the wrought-iron balustrades, the gilt carvings on the doors—everything was in mint condition; not only money but a great deal of love must have been expended to restore such a white elephant to its original glory.

There was a loud war whoop; then through a door to the left

ran a towheaded boy, about six, with an Indian war bonnet on his head. Behind him came another towhead, obviously the first boy's brother. Number Two carried a plastic tomahawk and was in full chase. The two sped across the entrance hall, narrowly missing Michael.

"Jeremy! Jeffrey!" shouted a thin woman in a plaid skirt and cashmere sweater who ran out of the door behind them. She was of medium height with dark hair cut in bangs and a thin, intelligent face with large eyes behind thick horn-rimmed glasses. She was about thirty and had the manner of a typical young Central Park West matron a few years out of Radcliffe or Barnard—in the case of Sally Mentius, Radcliffe. When she saw the Brandywines, she stopped chasing her children and introduced herself.

"I'm so sorry about the boys," she said, shaking Michael's hand. "But they've just come home from school and are impossible to handle. Well: welcome to the Chateau Mirabelle. Let's see . . . Henri." She turned to one of the footmen. "I think the Brandywines are in the Lake Suite across from Lady de Ross." She turned back to Michael and Ann and lowered her voice. "Lady de Ross got here this morning with her, um, I suppose 'gigolo' is the *polite* word, and she was completely smashed. At ten in the morning! Is she in for a shock when Herbie tells her no more booze! Herbie's my husband: you'll meet him later on. He's wonderful. Well, I shouldn't make you stand here, should I? Let's go upstairs and you can see your suite. There's an elevator, but I think you'll enjoy going up the grand staircase."

"The chateau is fantastic," said Ann. Sally glowed with pleasure.

"Do you like it?"

"How could you *not* like it? And you've done such a beautiful job restoring it."

As they were climbing the stairs, Sally said, "Herbie and I fell in love with it when we first walked in eight years ago. It was a *wreck* then! You couldn't believe the shape it was in. I know it's a bit much, architecturally, even a bit campy I suppose, though I'm so tired of that word, but we do love it. Of course, we thought of doing it in modern; but really, it would have ruined the place, wouldn't it? So we plunked for period and tried to furnish it exactly as it was a hundred years ago, which was a lot harder and quite a bit more expensive, believe me. Fortunately, we found some old tintypes of the interior that Léonide Leblanc had had taken . . . she was the woman who built the place . . ."

"The famous French prostitute?"

"Oh, did Dieter tell you that? He's supposed to say she was a 'courtesan'—that sounds a little better—but let's face it, she made her living on her back. Anyway, here's the upstairs corridor, and your suite's down here at the end, overlooking the lake. See that ceiling mural?" She pointed to a swarm of plump Bouguereau-esque nymphs and satyrs swirling over the entire ceiling of the long upstairs corridor. "It was painted by a hack German who, if you ask me, must have been a bit oversexed. We found out it's titled 'The Apotheosis of Fleshly Pleasure.' Isn't it simply awful?"

Ann and Michael craned their necks. "I think it's sort of sexy," said Michael. "Like being wallpapered in *Playboy* gatefolds."

Sally Mentius laughed. "I hadn't thought of it that way. Here's your suite."

They had reached the end of the hall where the footmen had opened the door to a huge living room. "I hope you like gilt," said Sally, leading them inside, "because there's a ton of it in here." In fact, the place was a riot of plaster cupids, rococo carvings, and Empire furniture. From the ceiling depended an enormous crystal chandelier. "We had a well-known architect here several years ago," continued Sally, "who took one look at this room and got literally sick. We had to move him out to the guest quarters down by the lake. I hope you won't want to move, because we've closed the guest quarters."

"Yes," said Michael, "your husband mentioned that in one of his letters. Why are they closed?"

"Well, usually we have twenty to thirty patients here taking the treatment. But this time, there's only six of you and we're putting all of you here in the chateau."

"Why are there only six?" asked Ann.

Sally hesitated. "Herbie will explain all of that later." She glanced at her watch. "Arnold Hirsch and his son are due here in an hour. You two rest and unpack, then come downstairs at seven o'clock to the Salon de Vénus. That's the big room on the lake directly underneath Lady de Ross's suite across the hall. Then we can all meet each other, and Herbie can tell you . . . well, he can talk to you." She headed for the door. "The bedroom and bath are through those double doors. If you need anything, just call the central switchboard: someone's on duty twenty-four hours a day. We really are so delighted to have you here, and I hope you enjoy your stay. See you at seven."

She smiled and left. Ann looked at Michael. "She's a talker, isn't she?"

"She certainly is." He went to the double doors and looked in at the bedroom. "My God, look at this bed!" he exclaimed. Ann came over and peered in at the bedroom, which was dominated by an enormous gilt bed crowned with a velvet canopy. The footmen had placed the luggage with the carefulness one seldom found in modern hotels. Then, as Michael tipped them, they left the suite. Ann took off her coat and put it on the bed. "I must say the rooms aren't going to be hard to take," she commented. "By the way, how did you know Lady de Ross was going to be here?"

Her husband looked at her rather oddly. "What do you mean?"

"Well, obviously something unusual's in the wind. I mean, Mrs. Mentius is going to let her husband spring it on us, but their only having six patients apparently means *something*. They didn't mention it in their letters?"

"No."

"But you told Bill in the car they *did* say something about closing the guest quarters?"

"They said that, but they didn't say why. And they said Lady de Ross would be here, but they didn't say anything about Arnold Hirsch."

"I wonder why? And who's Arnold Hirsch?"

"Head of a big underwriting firm on Wall Street."

She dropped the subject and began unpacking. But she had the odd feeling Michael was holding something back from her.

But then, she reflected, he usually did.

❧

At seven, they left their suite, went down the grand staircase, then followed the hall to the rear of the chateau where, on the left, was the Salon de Vénus. This was a cavernous formal drawing room with high French windows giving out onto the terrace and, beyond, beautiful formal gardens and the lake. Ann by now had become accustomed to the heavy magnificence of the chateau, and though the style had never been her favorite, she had to admit the sheer opulence of the Salon de Vénus made its decor successful by its own standards.

Five people were in the room, including Sally Mentius who, when she saw the Brandywines, came over and led them in. "Is everything all right?" she asked.

"Perfect," said Ann.

"Good. I want you to meet the others." She took them across the room to where Arnold Hirsch was standing next to his son. Ann's impression of the financier was a favorable one. As Sally introduced them, the elderly man shook Ann's hand in a courtly fashion that seemed pleasantly old-fashioned. "How do you do, Mrs. Brandywine?" he said. "Hi," muttered Martin, whom Ann was less favorably impressed by. The younger Hirsch looked ill at ease and sullen.

"And this is Lady Kitty de Ross," continued Sally, leading them to the former actress who had recovered from her morning binge sufficiently to begin working on her afternoon one.

"How do you do?" said Lady Kitty, giving Ann a coldly appraising look that, while it seemed to mentally check and approve the price tag and label of the younger woman's dress, at the same time was hardly an invitation to a budding friendship. Ann, on her part, appraised Lady Kitty's extravagantly patterned silk pantsuit, guessing the outfit to be the product of an expensive Italian couturier. Nor did she miss the four rings that studded Lady Kitty's thin fingers—in fact, they were almost impossible to miss. The solitaire marquise diamond was like a solar eruption; and the cabochon emerald on her index finger must have tipped Harry Winston's scales at a solid twelve carats. Lady Kitty obviously didn't subscribe to the school of whispered wealth.

"And this," she said, after shaking hands with Ann and Michael, "is my secretary, Hugh Barstow." She gestured to the young man standing next to her, whose smile indicated a bemused tolerance of his employer's euphemistic description of his function. He had on a mod French suit, a wild Ken Scott shirt, and a tie-dyed crimson tie which, with his long black hair, gave him the appearance of a very with-it biblical prophet. He shook Ann's hand, his brown eyes running over her figure with little attempt to hide what he was thinking. "I'm not very good at taking dictation," he said, "but I'm great at shorthand."

"I used to be a secretary too," said Ann, thinking that Dr. Mentius had certainly assembled a pride of off-beat patients.

"How nice," said Lady Kitty, watching the two of them closely as she sipped her vodka martini. "Dear Hugh wanted to be a rock singer before he took up secretarial work—like one of the Jefferson Airplanes?" She smiled with pure nastiness. "But he didn't quite manage to take off on the show business runway, did you, Hugh?"

Hugh looked at her. "A very old bird got fouled in my prop in Tangier," he said.

Lady Kitty's bleary eyes widened. "Dear Hugh," she said, "try not to be *quite* so Secaucus." She turned to Ann. "He hails from the industrial swamps of northern New Jersey. The effluvia of the pig farms has quite addled his wits, poor child."

"The pig farms may have made me punchy," said Hugh, "but the gin has turned *your* brain into tapioca."

"It's vodka," she snapped, "and that's enough out of you!" Then she smiled at a wide-eyed Sally Mentius, who looked a bit bowled over by their performance. "But he really is *very* good at shorthand."

"Oh, I'm sure," said Sally uncertainly.

There was an uncomfortable silence, broken by Arnold Hirsch clearing his throat. "Well," he said, "I think we're going to be a very jolly little group."

"Oh, I hope so," said Sally.

"I think it's going to be dreary as hell," said Lady Kitty, draining her martini. "And when do we meet the famous Dr. Mentius?"

"Right now, in fact," said Sally, who looked relieved at an excuse to change the subject. "He's waiting for all of us in the lab. Everybody bring their drinks, please, and follow me."

She led the group into the hallway, then toward the front of the chateau until they came to where a lateral corridor bisected the main one in a cruciform pattern. Here she turned to the right. At the end of this hall were two stainless steel doors antiseptically labeled "Laboratory Wing." Opening the doors, Sally stood aside as the group filed past her out of the nineteenth century into the cool, vinyl-tiled twentieth. Ann, who was in the lead, looked down the long white corridor with its illuminated Lucite ceiling. Immediately to the right were two doors marked "Pathology." She started to open them, only to find they were locked.

"Oh, not *there*," said Sally, who had just come into the corridor. "It's at the end of the hall on the left."

"Sorry," said Ann, wondering at the momentary sharpness in Sally's tone. She waited while the doctor's wife took a position at the head of the group again, then followed her as they filed down the silent corridor.

"What's the Cosmetarium?" asked Martin Hirsch as he passed one door labeled with the unusual word.

"I think you'll find the Cosmetarium one of your favorite places in the clinic," said Sally. "That's where you'll get daily massage treatments with the Dermo-Disc, which is one of Herbie's inventions. It's a little cup which sends tiny electrical charges into the skin and rejuvenates the outermost skin layers and the capillary system."

"Sounds positively gruesome!" exclaimed Lady Kitty.

"Oh no, it's a wonderful feeling. Dr. Zimmermann's in charge of the Cosmetarium, and she's really the best in her field. You'll love it. By the way, one end of the Cosmetarium is a fully equipped beauty parlor. We have two girls who are really excellent; as you can see, you won't have to leave the chateau for anything. Everything's here."

"How about a barber shop?" asked Arnold Hirsch.

Ann repressed a smile as she looked at the financier's bald pate.

"Oh, we have that too," said Sally, coming to a halt in front of two doors marked "Lab." "Well, here we are. Follow me, please."

She opened the doors and led them into a large, windowless room down the middle of which ran a slate-topped lab table cluttered with retorts, Bunsen burners, racks of test tubes, and other chemical paraphernalia. Along the walls stood tall steel cabinets with glass doors; inside them were hundreds of Pyrex bottles, steel boxes, and surgical instruments. At the end of the room was a bank of cages filled with the white rats. Three men and a woman, clad in white lab coats, were standing in front of the cages. As the group entered, they turned to look at them.

"Herbie," said Sally, "we're ready."

As Ann crinkled her nose at the unpleasant smell of the animals which was made even worse by the odor of formaldehyde, a tall, round-shouldered man with light brown hair and a sad, homely face came over to them and extended his hand. "I'm Herbert Mentius," he said. As he passed among the patients shaking hands, Ann watched him. The famous gerontologist and biochemist was nothing like what she had imagined. Far from being a brilliant genius type, Herbert Mentius seemed quiet and reserved. There was a pleasing gentleness about him that she was immediately attracted to; and his freckled hound-dog face with the sad brown eyes exuded a humane warmth which, in the cold and clinical atmosphere of the lab, was somehow reassuring. However, when he came up to her to shake her hand, she altered her first impression slightly. There was a guarded look in his eyes, almost a nervousness, which, as she thought about it, Sally Mentius also seemed to share. It was almost as if this young and attractive couple, so enormously successful in their field, were rather unsure of themselves.

"I'd like you to meet my associates," said Mentius after he had finished the round of his clients. "This is Dr. Hilda Zimmermann." He gestured to a pleasant, hefty blond woman who reminded Ann of a very intense Valkyrie. "Dr. Zimmermann is our dermatologist and is in charge of the Cosmetarium. And my two assistants, Doctors de Villeneuve and Schlessing." He indicated two young men, one dark and quite good-looking, the other contrastingly light and ugly. "I think I can say without embarrassing them that no doctor has ever had a more dedicated, intelligent, and hardworking staff than I have. I consider myself very fortunate. Now, if we can pull up some chairs, I'd like you all to take seats while I explain to you exactly what we hope to accomplish in the next two months."

De Villeneuve and Schlessing arranged some folding chairs in a semicircle at one end of the lab, and everyone took seats. Mentius leaned against the slate-topped table in front of them, somewhat like a teacher facing his class, then folded his arms and said, in his quiet voice, "Now, I think at the very beginning I should make a confession to you. You've all been brought here under false pretenses."

The remark was made so casually that Ann wondered if the man was joking. Her second thought was that perhaps this accounted for the slight nervousness she had detected in the doctor and his wife. Mentius continued to speak in slow, carefully measured terms: "The three of you have come here expecting to get the Alpha treatment, which my staff and I have been administering with a considerable degree of success for a number of years now. However, the Alpha treatment has become obsolete: or, more accurately, we hope to be able to give you something radically new and, I think you'll agree, quite extraordinary. If you choose not to take my offer, the clinic will refund all your money, including traveling expenses. However, I'm hoping I can convince you to take it. Dr. de Villeneuve, will you bring over the cage, please?"

The young doctor picked up a cage that was resting by itself at the opposite end of the lab table and carried it over to the group, passing it slowly in front of them so they could see its contents. Inside were four white rats: two quite young and frisky, the other two old, fat, and sluggish.

"A family of white rats," said Mentius. "Two parents and two of their get. Can any of you tell me which are the parents?"

Arnold Hirsch said, "I suppose the two fat ones?"

"Wrong," said Mentius. "The two fat rats, which I think you'll all agree look twice as old as the others, are actually the children."

Silence. Then Martin Hirsch said, "What's that supposed to prove?"

"I hope to be able to show you," said Mentius, as De Villeneuve carried the cage back to the table. "When I was in Harvard, I became interested in the problem of aging. As I read up on what was then known about the subject, I began to realize that the lifespan of man need not necessarily be set at seventy or eighty years. It has been almost doubled in the past two centuries, thanks to the fantastic increase in our knowledge of the human body, biochemistry, and surgical techniques; there is no reason why the lifespan can't be doubled again—or perhaps even tripled. Since the beginning of time we have thought of death as being not only inevitable, but natural. In fact, death is not natural at all. It's really an avoidable mistake."

"I'm afraid you've lost me," said Michael.

"Barring accidents, murder, suicide, or terminal diseases, what normally kills people is age. A man can easily shake off pneumonia when he's twenty. When he's eighty, it kills him—or rather, we *say* it kills him. Actually, it's not the disease, but age which has reduced his resistance to the disease that kills him. If, instead of thinking of aging as a natural process, we could think of it as a disease, and if science could isolate the cause of the disease, and find a cure for it, then there really is no reason why man could not live forever, or at least for hundreds of years. To digress a moment, I might add that given the increasing complexity of modern life, which takes longer and longer for people to assimilate, man will be forced to increase his lifespan if for no other reason than to have time to educate himself to cope with the civilization he has produced. And of course, the only feasible way for man to travel outside the solar system is to increase his lifespan long enough to survive the incredible distances involved."

"Excuse me, Doctor," interrupted Martin Hirsch, "but if man could live forever wouldn't that present one hell of a generation-gap problem?" He looked at his septuagenarian father with ill-concealed dislike. "I mean, if fathers lived forever, sons would go nuts, wouldn't they?" Arnold Hirsch's face remained impassive, but Ann thought he was anything but pleased with the remark.

"And how would anyone ever get rich?" asked Hugh Barstow. "The old people would hang on to the top jobs forever."

Lady Kitty gave him a cool glance. "You assume the young want to work. If you're at all typical, I don't think that's a valid assumption."

Hugh grinned. "Kitty baby, keeping you happy is *work*."

There was a sticky silence. Then the two young doctors in the corner burst into laughter. Dr. Zimmermann scowled at them and they quickly shut up.

Dr. Mentius, looking a little embarrassed, cleared his throat. "Obviously there would be problems. Hopefully, the generations, given unlimited time to learn to live together, could learn to co-operate instead of compete. And, of course, death control, if you'd want to call it that, would make birth control an absolute necessity, or man would squeeze himself off the planet even faster than he's doing now. Oh, it would mean a total reorganization of life as we know it. But in the long run, it should mean a radical improvement of the quality of our lives—or at least it *could* mean that. If wisdom is a coefficient of experience, which I believe it partially is, think how wise a man of three hundred could become. And shouldn't he become more compassionate, too, if the threat of the grave is removed from him? And wouldn't wars become even more senseless than they are now if life became so much more worth hanging on to? It would be possible to make earth a Utopia. And being a bit of an optimist, I'd like to think that would happen. However, all of this is far in the future."

"It certainly is," said Michael. "Unless you're trying to tell us you can make *us* live forever?"

Mentius looked at him evenly. "That's exactly what I'm telling you," he said quietly. As the group digested this remark, he signaled to Dr. Zimmermann, who turned off the lights and turned on a slide projector. At the same time, Dr. Schlessing went to the opposite end of the lab and pulled a screen down over the wall.

"There have been many theories on the causes of aging," continued Mentius, "but the most compelling one—and the one which to me is no longer theory but proven fact—is the cross-linkage theory. Dr. Zimmermann, put in the slide, please."

She inserted a slide in the projector, and a sketch of a DNA double helix appeared on the screen.

"This is a molecule of deoxyribonucleic acid, or DNA, the helical structure of which Crick and Watson discovered in the fifties—a discovery that began the revolution in modern biochemistry. DNA and its partner, ribonucleic acid, or RNA, are what we biochemists consider the basis of life. DNA is found only in the chromosomes. RNA is formed mostly outside the nucleus of the cell in what is called the cell's cytoplasm. Put very crudely, DNA carries the genetic code that gives us our physical and mental characteristics. DNA teaches RNA how to produce new cells. More exactly, RNA is the messenger from the DNA in the nucleus to the cytoplasm, telling the cell, in effect, how to replicate itself.

It is through DNA and RNA that life continues and, actually, is made possible.

"But things go wrong. Radiant energy from sunlight, X-rays, and other sources produces something called free radicals, or ions. These collide with the DNA molecules and cause tiny links, or rods, to form between the helices—like this. Dr. Zimmermann?"

She inserted a new slide which showed the double helices of the molecule connected by a number of thin rods.

"When this happens, the DNA molecule starts sending out the wrong message via the RNA to the cytoplasm of the cell. To make an awkward simile, it's a bit like radio static or television snow—interference that causes the signal to be distorted. The result of the interference is cell mutation. Now, these links can be broken up by certain enzymes—one enzyme in particular—"

"Doctor," interrupted Lady Kitty, "I know pathetically little about science which, frankly, bores me stiff. What is an enzyme? I thought it was something that appeared in laundry detergents?"

Dr. Mentius cleared his throat. "Believe me, Lady de Ross: I am not a soap salesman."

"I assumed that. But what is an enzyme?"

"An enzyme is a complex organic substance that can produce by catalytic action various chemical changes in other organic substances. Does that make it clear?"

"No, but go on. All of this is gibberish to me anyway."

"I'm sorry I'm not making myself more clear," said Mentius, rather stiffly; it was obvious the Englishwoman's flippancy grated on his nerves. "As I was saying," he continued, "certain enzymes —one enzyme in particular—can break the links between the helices. But eventually, as the body is subjected to the insults and stresses of time, disease, and bad living habits such as drinking and smoking, the number of cross-linked molecules grows, the cell mutation accumulates, and the body begins to change. The result is what we call aging.

"Now, this might not happen if the enzymes that break the links could keep up with the increase in the cross-linkage. But at about the age of twenty-five, for a reason I frankly don't understand, the chief enzyme that breaks the links—what one might fancifully call the Methuselah Enzyme, because it really determines longevity—begins to disappear from the body, throwing the equilibrium out of balance in favor of the cross-linkage. It's at this point that true aging begins. And as time goes on, it slowly accelerates until, as we all know, the body is completely metamorphosed into the state we call senility, at which point death occurs. But if the Methuselah Enzyme could be isolated, if it could be synthesized in the laboratory, if it could be reintroduced into the body by shots, then there is no reason why the cross-links could not continue to be destroyed, the cell mutation stopped, and the disease of aging prevented or cured. In short, there's no reason why man could not stay young forever."

He paused almost dramatically for such an intrinsically undramatic man. Arnold Hirsch quietly asked, "And is anyone close to discovering this Methuselah Enzyme?"

"After searching for it for ten years," said Mentius, "I'm pleased to be able to say I *have* discovered it."

His quiet statement elicited a murmur from the others.

"What is it?" said Michael Brandywine.

"I've prepared a study which you'll be given in a moment. It explains the technical side of it. But I must insist none of you discuss this with anyone outside this room. Aside from my immediate staff, no one knows about the enzyme. We've gone to great lengths to keep our research a secret, and not just to protect ourselves: I believe a discovery with the implications of Mentase must be kept under strict control."

"Mentase?" asked Ann.

"I took the liberty of naming the enzyme after myself. The two parent rats in the cage have received it, and their biological clocks have been turned backward, making them physiologically younger than their offspring. Dr. Zimmermann, will you show the film, please?" As the efficient blond dermatologist replaced the slide projector with a movie projector already set up with a small reel, Mentius explained, "We made a film record of the two white rats over an eight-week period as they were being given daily doses of rat Mentase. By skipping days, we can show the desenescing process rapidly. If any of you have seen the old film *Lost Horizon*, you may remember the scene where Margot leaves Shangri-La and is turned into a mummy in a few seconds. Well, this is the same sort of thing in reverse."

Dr. Zimmermann turned on the projector, and the film began. The first scene showed the two rats in their cage; they were old and sluggish. A calendar board on the side of the cage read "October 4." Two rubber-gloved hands appeared in the picture, picked up one of the rats, and injected a small hypo in its side.

In quick progression, the same process was repeated three times, on October seventh, tenth, and thirteenth. By October sixteenth, a noticeable change was coming over the rats: they were less sluggish and were running around in frisky circles. By the twenty-fifth, the rats had not only become energetic but were beginning to grow thinner. Mentius spoke over the whirr of the projector: "You'll notice they are losing their fat. We had put them on a special diet, of course; but as their bodies became younger biologically, they had more energy, as you can see, and naturally they were burning up more calories. Now, about Halloween, you'll notice the first truly remarkable change: their tails start to become shorter." In fact, this happened. And at the end of the film, at which time the calendar board read "November 27," the rats looked no older than six months.

As Dr. Zimmermann turned off the projector and turned on the lights, Mentius turned to the group. "I think," he said, "you'll agree the change in the rats was extraordinary? We have duplicated the same experiment with hundreds of rats; each time the results have been equally striking. Now we want to try it on humans."

Lady Kitty broke the silence. "Really, Doctor, you don't expect us to subject ourselves to this incredible experiment on the strength of that Mickey Mouse cartoon? Any third-rate quack could have dreamed up a more convincing demonstration. You might have just run the film backward, faked the calendar, and been shooting the rats full of vitamin E—or lemonade, for that matter."

Mentius remained unruffled. "You're right, I could have. But I didn't. Claude, hand our guests the progress reports, please." Dr. de Villeneuve picked up a pile of blue-covered mimeographed pamphlets and passed them around. "This is the report I mentioned," said Mentius. "It's a thoroughly documented technical explanation of the Mentase process. You may take these with you to your rooms, but I must ask you to return them next Tuesday at the latest, and to tell Dr. Zimmermann immediately if your copy is lost or stolen."

Ann opened her copy to the title page which read, "Progress Report on Project Methuselah." Leafing through the thick pamphlet, which had 233 pages, she saw a bewildering maze of graphs, charts, diagrams, and lengthy equations. She looked up at Mentius. "You don't expect any of us to understand all this mumbo jumbo?"

Mentius spread his hands helplessly. "That's the problem. Anything technically convincing won't make any sense to a layman, though possibly your husband might understand it, since I'm sure he's familiar with technical scientific literature. I certainly understand your skepticism, but I'm afraid that if you accept my offer, you're going to have to operate pretty much on blind faith."

"And what is your offer?" said Arnold Hirsch.

"To give the three of you—Lady Kitty, Mr. Hirsch, and Mr. Brandywine—the opportunity of being the first humans ever to receive the Mentase treatment. If you decide to take it, at the end of eight weeks you will look—and be physically—around thirty-five to forty years of age."

"Do you mean," said Arnold Hirsch, "you can actually reverse the aging process in us just as you did with the rats?"

Mentius nodded. "I can. At the end of the eight-week treatment, I can give you periodic booster shots of Mentase that will keep you at the age of thirty-five to forty for the rest of your natural lives."

"Does that mean forever?"

"I can't guarantee eternity because, frankly, the treatment will still be somewhat experimental. However, barring accidents and incurable disease, there is no reason I can foresee why you couldn't live at least another hundred years. Perhaps more. Perhaps, in fact, forever."

The remark was greeted by another silence. Then Lady Kitty held a cigarette up for Hugh to light. "Come now, Doctor: some of my best friends have taken your Alpha treatment, and I'll admit they looked younger when they were through. That's why I signed up. But you don't honestly expect us to believe you can turn us into immortals?"

He looked at her calmly. "Yes, I do."

"Be honest: isn't what you're really looking for guinea pigs? Rich old fools who'll jump for anyone who says he can remove a wrinkle or two? I'm rich and I'm old, but I'm no fool. And I'm certainly not happy about coming all the way to this dreary tomb of a clinic to be told that instead of getting what I came for, I'm paying ten thousand pounds for the privilege of being shot full of scientific pipe dreams. And I'm not including the three hundred pounds a week extra I'm paying for dear Hugh's secretarial talents, who's going to have to do a *lot* of shorthand at that exorbitant rate!"

"Yes, and why us?" added Arnold Hirsch. "Is there any particular reason why the three of us should be asked to take what must be a risky gamble?"

"No particular reason. As you know, I have a long waiting list of people wanting to come to the clinic. It just so happened the three of you were due to come to the clinic at the time we were ready to try out the Mentase treatment."

Ann noticed the doctor's hands, which were quite large and powerful, come together; his right hand pressed the knuckle of the index finger of his left hand, squeezed it, then passed on to the next knuckle, squeezing it and the other knuckles in succession, then returning to the index knuckle again, recommencing the odd, nervous process. As he continued doing this, he said, "I fully realize what I am asking you. I might add, I certainly don't think any of you are fools. I'll also admit you will be, to a certain extent, guinea pigs, and there is definitely an element of risk in the treatment. Although every conceivable precaution will be taken to safeguard your health, I would be lying if I told you it was a sure thing: there is always risk in anything new. On the other hand, consider what I'm offering you. The chance for at least a century more of life: life at its peak, at thirty-five years of age. Admittedly, it sounds fantastic. But I can give you the names of at least six Nobel Prize winners who will assure you the conquest of aging is not only scientifically feasible, but in fact imminent. And let's be frank: I have a very successful operation here, and a considerable scientific reputation. Would I risk it all by making a preposterous proposition to such well-connected people as yourselves unless I meant to back up my claim with performance? I tell you . . ." He leaned forward and lowered his voice for emphasis: "I can give you youth. *Real* youth, biochemical youth, not a face lift or a skin peel or a new miracle diet or a new tonic for tired blood. I can turn back your biological clock. I must ask you to trust me. You'll have to place yourselves completely in my hands. But eight weeks from now, when you look in a mirror, the face you will see will be a ghost. A ghost of the past—*your* past. You will be looking at yourself as you were when you were young. You *will* be young. Your cells will be young. You will have conquered the unconquerable: Time."

His speech had a definite effect on them: even Lady Kitty looked awed. Then the doctor straightened and nodded to his wife, who said, "Shall we all go back to the chateau for dinner?"

There was a pause, as at the end of a particularly engrossing play. Then they stood up and silently filed to the door, just as, Ann thought, one filed to the exit of a theater after the performance. And of course, it had been a performance: a carefully staged sales pitch, with everything from the film to Sally's breaking the mood at the end by suggesting dinner skillfully planned for maximum effect. Ann rather resented being manipulated. But judging from the look on Arnold Hirsch's face, at least one of them seemed to be more than halfway convinced by the performance.

❧

Dinner was held in the enormous Salle d'Hercule across the hall from the Salon de Vénus. It was named for a series of ceiling murals by the same oversexed German who had done the ceiling of the second-floor hallway; these depicted a heavily deltoided Hercules cleansing the Augean Stables. Like the other rooms of the chateau, the Salle d'Hercule sparkled with crystal and groaned with gilt. Down the terrace wall was a series of French doors, and the candles in the tall silver candelabra, which marched down the center of the long table, gleamed in the panes of the doors, through which the sunset over the lake provided an incarnadine backdrop. The candles' reflections echoed again in an enormous mirror on the opposite wall above the buffet, so that the whole room flickered with light like an immense ruby.

As the eight of them took seats at the dinner table, the punctilious footmen served the first course of an excellent meal. Sally Mentius, who was at one end of the table opposite her husband, said, "We really have an excellent chef here. But if you decide to take the treatment, I'm afraid you'll all be put on very strict diets."

"Like the white rats?" grumped Lady Kitty, inhaling on a Sobranie.

"And no smoking either," said Mentius, giving Lady Kitty a meaningful look. "Aside from everything else tobacco does to the body, it also ages it."

Looking disgusted, Lady Kitty ground out the cigarette. "Oh well, I've been meaning to stop anyway. Since you're obviously a sadistic personality, I might as well do it now. I suppose you'll be demanding we give up sex next?"

Dr. Mentius smiled. "Actually, there is a school of thought that says sex hastens the aging process."

"Oh, my God," groaned the actress.

"However, you'll be happy to hear I'm not convinced."

"Let us be thankful for small favors."

"But if you decide to take the treatment, I think I'd better prepare you for, shall we say, a certain inconvenience in your normal nocturnal schedule."

Hugh Barstow said, "Normally, she likes to give dictation practically every night of the week, Doctor."

Ann choked on her soup, as both Mentiuses looked rather embarrassed. Lady Kitty shot her "secretary" a withering look. "Am I to be spared *nothing* today?" Hugh grinned and winked at her.

"At any rate," said Mentius, trying to regain his poise, "at ten o'clock each night, the three of you would be put in a rather odd device we've developed here at the clinic called the cryogenic hyperbaric sleep capsule. This, in effect, is a hermetically sealed tube that produces an artificial atmosphere of very high oxygen pressure and very low temperature. Each of you will have one of these, and you'll sleep in them each night. I might add, they hold only one person. The point of these capsules is that the artificially high oxygen pressure cleanses impurities from the body's cells each night—and, incidentally, induces an extraordinarily deep sleep."

"I think I'd prefer sex," said Lady Kitty.

"But I'm afraid you'd have to take sleep instead—at least, after ten each night," continued Mentius. "You see, sleep therapy has been a field of study in gerontology for a number of years now. The more we learn about what sleep is and does, the more it seems that there is a direct connection between sleep and the aging process. Toxic substances that build up in the body during the day are eliminated from the body during the one or two hours of the night when we are actually experiencing 'deep sleep,' or what is known as rapid-eye-movement, or R.E.M., sleep. R.E.M. sleep constitutes only about twenty-four percent of normal sleep time, but it's the critical period during which most of our dreams occur—which is the brain's way of ridding itself of its own toxic substances, namely, tensions. The sleep capsule will extend the R.E.M. sleep each night, and in so doing extend the body's—as well as the mind's—capacity to purify itself. I think you will be quite amazed at the results." He turned to Ann. "Incidentally, Mrs. Brandywine, if the others decide to take the Mentase treatment, I would like to ask you and Mr. Barstow and Martin Hirsch to volunteer for a sleep therapy experiment."

"What kind of experiment?" asked Ann.

"It's a test to see what the effects of artificially induced sleep are on younger people. In the gymnasium, which is in the basement of the lab wing, there are three large steel tanks I designed several years ago. They're called Aquadorme tanks, and the idea is that you climb in them and your entire body gets a gentle hydromassage which, like the cryogenic capsules, induces a deep sleep. If the three of you would be willing, I'd appreciate your letting us put you in the tanks."

"How long would we be asleep?"

"About four hours. It's very refreshing, I guarantee."

"What the hell," said Hugh. "If I can't sleep for business anymore, I might as well sleep for science. I'm game."

Lady Kitty was again glaring at him. "God, you are gro-*tesque* tonight!"

"Sorry."

"Of course," continued Mentius, "everything depends on your decision about the Mentase treatment. I know I'm probably throwing you by my proposal. If I have, I'm sorry; but it was really rather unavoidable, since I neither could nor would explain all of this to you except here, in person. I realize it's a rather big decision for you to make. But I'm going to have to ask you to make it within the next twenty-four hours."

Arnold Hirsch asked, "Why so quickly?"

"Because if the three of you decide not to take the Mentase treatment, I'll have to line up other people, which would take considerable time."

"I see." There was a moment of silence. Ann looked around the spectacular room with its high ceiling, red silk walls and gilt cornices. Gods. Like Hercules, on the ceiling. Forever young. She wondered if it were possible Mentius could do what he claimed. If he could, the implications of such power were rather frightening.

"Well," said Arnold Hirsch quietly, "I can give you my answer right now. Fully realizing the risk I would be undertaking, I am willing to take the Mentase treatment."

Dr. Mentius looked pleased, although it occurred to Ann he didn't seem particularly surprised, as if he had been expecting the old man to agree. "Good. I'm delighted you've made that decision, Mr. Hirsch. For a perfectly selfish reason, I might add, because you are the oldest of the three and I'm most eager to see how the Mentase will react with you."

"I'm flattered that I hold such a curiosity value for science," said Arnold, nodding his head in a little bow. "I feel somewhat like a moon rock."

"But, Mr. Hirsch," said Ann, "don't you think it would be better to wait a few years until Dr. Mentius has perfected the treatment?"

"Ann," interrupted Michael sharply, "that's Mr. Hirsch's business, not yours."

"But why should he take this tremendous risk?" she asked, surprised at the heat in her voice. "Or Lady de Ross? Or you? If you need to try the treatment on humans, why not get convicts, like other doctors do? Lots of prisoners volunteer themselves as guinea pigs."

"But generally only lifers," said Mentius, "or prisoners with long terms. And aside from the difficulty in maintaining close laboratory control over prisoners, might I point out the dubious value of offering extended life to men in prison for their natural lives?"

"Point well made," said Arnold Hirsch, in an amused tone. Then he turned his gray eyes on Ann, who was across the table from him. "I am flattered by your concern for me, Mrs. Brandywine," he said. "Of course, I can't speak for your husband or Lady de Ross; I can only speak for myself. But in my case, it is highly unlikely I will be here by the time Dr. Mentius has perfected his treatment. I would rather take my chances now with the Mentase. If I lose, what have I lost? Not much: a few senile years at best. But if I win?" He smiled slightly. "If I understand Dr. Mentius correctly, I will have won what must be the most valuable prize of all time. As a man who has spent his entire life on Wall Street, I could hardly resist such a tempting gamble."

Ann started to rebut him, but changed her mind. Michael was right: it was none of her business what the old man decided. But what Michael decided was very much her business, and she could tell by the look on his face that he was as tempted as Mr. Hirsch.

"Well, Doctor," said Lady Kitty, "you won't have to wait for me either. I admit I don't understand a tenth of what you said, and what I did understand I'm skeptical about. But I haven't that much to lose either, and a good deal to gain. So I'll sign on."

"Excellent," said Mentius. Now all eyes turned to Michael. "And how about you, Mr. Brandywine?"

Ann put her hand on his sleeve and whispered, "Please, darling, let's talk it over."

He glanced at her; then he looked down the table to Mentius. "I'll let you know in the morning, Doctor."

Mentius looked surprised, as if he was more than half expecting Michael to go along with the prevailing acceptance. Then he nodded. "Of course. In the morning."

The dinner continued.

❧

Martin Hirsch had sniffed that unmistakable smell the moment he stepped out on the terrace after dinner: someone was smoking pot. After his eyes became accustomed to the darkness, he spotted a red glow at the end of the terrace and knew someone had just inhaled on a joint. Of course: it was Lady de Ross's boyfriend, thought Martin. She said he was an ex-rock singer. Christ, he must have a ton of pot—and hash too! Martin almost laughed out loud, thinking how easy it was going to be to circumvent his father. He walked down the terrace to where Hugh was leaning on the stone balustrade. "Excuse me," he said. "You wouldn't have another of those, would you?"

"Sure, man."

Hugh pulled a cigarette from his pocket and gave it to Martin, who lighted it eagerly and inhaled, holding the smoke in his lungs to get the maximum effect from the high. It had been a week since he had had any, and the feeling was great.

"You're the old banker's son, aren't you?" asked Hugh.

"That's right."

"What are you doing here in Retirement Village?"

"Well, it's sort of freaky." Martin explained the deal his father had made with him.

"Crazy," said Hugh.

"But he didn't count on my meeting you," replied Martin, grinning. "I'll be able to buy everything I need from you. I mean, that is, if you'll sell?"

"Oh sure, I'd sell. Except you've just taken my last joint."

Martin blinked. "You mean, you're out too?"

"That's right."

"Oh." Martin's hopes fell. "I thought you'd know a dealer around here."

"Switzerland's very tight, man. But there must be a few: they can't *all* be yodelers. Why don't we go back to the kitchen and get to know the staff? I'll bet one of them knows someone."

"Good idea."

They left the terrace and walked through the formal gardens toward the kitchen wing of the chateau. "You don't shoot horse, I hope?" asked Hugh cautiously.

"Heroin? Oh no, none of the hard stuff. Just pot and hash. And, well . . ." He hesitated.

"Bennies?"

"No. Sometimes I pop a blackbird."

Hugh whistled. "Amphetamines can be bad news, man. *Bad.*"

"I know, particularly on the way down. But I don't do it often. Just, you know, when I'm bored. What did you think of Dr. Mentius?"

"He's pretty wild. But I wouldn't be surprised if he can do what he says. Shit, nothing surprises me."

"Me too. Except if he *can* make my old man young again, I think I'd have to take off for the hills or something. The only way I keep halfway sane is thinking the old bastard can't live *too* much longer."

"Yeah. And all the world needs is another hundred years of Kitty Kitty Bang Bang, too."

"Who?"

"Lady Kitty. My, like, employer."

"Is she hard to get along with?"

"You'd better believe it. And chintzy? Man, is that woman tight!"

"My father's the same way," said Martin, remembering something. "How long have you been with her?"

"A couple of months. I had a combo called the Crying Shames. Did you ever hear of us?"

"No."

"No one else did either. Anyway, my agent had got us a booking in the Casino d'Afrique in Tangier, with *one*-way plane tickets from New York. Smart, huh? So after a week, the owner of the Casino came up to me, screamed, 'You stink!' and tore up the contract, leaving all of us with no bread and no ticket home. Nice. So there I was, roaming around the Casino, and who do I spot but Kitty Kitty Bang Bang at the roulette table eyeballing me, dig? So I look at all those rocks on her fingers and I'm beginning to see a first-class plane ticket to New York, you know? I come up behind her and pretty soon she's offering me a couple of chips to play for her—'for luck'; it's the oldest ploy in the books. So things led to things, and here I am. I guess I'll stick with her till I've saved enough money to get back to New York and either put together a new combo, or maybe try something else."

"So you've been with her a couple of months?"

"Yeah."

"Well, there was something very strange this afternoon. When Mrs. Mentius was introducing all of us to each other, she brought Lady Kitty over to my old man and introduced her to him."

"So?"

"They shook hands, and my father said, 'Glad to meet you.'"

"So?"

"He's known her for years!"

Hugh squinted through the darkness at his young companion. "Huh?"

"I'd swear he has!" insisted Martin. "My old man keeps a big yacht at Antibes, and every year he takes a lot of business partners and big clients out on it for a cruise—you know, to suck up to them or something. Anyway, Lord Henry de Ross used to be a big buddy of his before he died, and my old man's firm is trustee for his estate. And he takes Lady Kitty on these cruises every year. I'm sure of it. That's why I thought that if you'd been with her for a while, you might know why she pretended not to know him."

"Marty baby, I don't know *nothing*. Why don't you ask your old man if you're so hot to know?"

Martin didn't answer for a moment. "My old man and I don't communicate very well—which is a bit of an understatement. We don't communicate at all. He wouldn't tell me the truth. Besides, I don't care that much. I just thought maybe you might know what they were up to."

"Man, what goes on in Lady Kitty's weirdo mind is the Big

Mystery as far as I'm concerned, you know? Our only form of communication is body contact, if you know what I mean. Anyway, here's the kitchen. Put out your joint. Then let's see if we can find some pot among the pans."

They had reached the end of the long, one-story utility wing which terminated in a service drive. Now they tamped out their cigarettes on the asphalt, carefully placing the unsmoked portion in their pockets, then walked into a large garage in which was parked a pickup truck, the Daimler, and an ambulance. A door led from the garage into a sleek, modern kitchen which was empty except for a dishwasher who was at one end of the room cleaning up the remnants of the dinner, and a pretty young nurse seated at a table drinking a cup of coffee. She looked at them curiously as they came up to her.

"Excuse me," said Hugh. "Like, do you *sprechen* English?"

"Of course," said the nurse coolly. Martin noticed she was about five months pregnant. He also noticed she didn't wear a wedding ring. "Aren't you both guests at the chateau?"

"That's right."

"Then I'm sorry, but you're not supposed to be in here."

"I know." Hugh glanced around the kitchen again to make sure no one had come in. Then he took the tamped-out joint from his pocket and showed it to her. "You know what this is?"

She looked at it. "Naturally."

"We'd like to know where we could buy more. Know anybody?"

"Perhaps. It's not cheap, you know."

Martin took his wallet from his pants and pulled out two crisp fifty-dollar bills. "Plenty more besides that," he said.

The nurse eyed the money. "You'll have to pay in Swiss francs: four to the dollar."

"We will. We want an ounce of hashish, too."

"Good hash will cost you four hundred francs."

"Jesus, that's even worse than in the States!"

The nurse shrugged. "Here they are stricter."

"Okay, it doesn't matter. How about a dozen blackbirds?"

"All right, that can be done."

"When can we get it?"

"Soon. My name's Lisl Oetterli. I'm a night nurse three nights a week, and two days I work in the Cosmetarium. I'll put you in contact with someone who can get you anything you want."

"Who is it?"

The nurse smiled.

"My brother."

❧

Ann and Michael Brandywine had gone upstairs to their suite at nine thirty. Inside the living room, Michael had taken off his jacket, then pulled a leather cigar case from the inside pocket and extracted a cigar which he handed to Ann. She clipped the end as he sat down on a sofa; then she curled up beside him, lighted the cigar, took a puff, and handed it to him.

"Do you think Dr. Mentius is nuts?" she asked, waving out the match.

"Not a bit," said Michael, slowly exhaling in an attempt to blow smoke rings.

"But, darling, all this business about turning back the biological clock: you don't really believe it, do you?"

"Ten years ago, I didn't believe anyone would ever walk on the moon, so obviously I'm not a very good judge of scientific credibility. All I know is, Mentius has an excellent reputation; he's had numerous articles published in first-class scientific journals; I'm going to read that ten-ton report he gave us"—he tapped his finger on the blue-bound folder which he had set on a table by the sofa—"but even without reading it, I think it's scientifically feasible to do what he claims. Now whether he can do it successfully or not is another question."

Ann ran her hand through her long blond hair. "But the risk involved! Did you see how old Mr. Hirsch just jumped into the thing feet first, without giving it any thought at all that I could see? He must be senile! I think it sounds terribly dangerous, and I think it's pretty nervy of Mentius to drag us all the way over here under what he admits are false pretences."

"Ann, you're thinking just like a small-minded midwestern woman," said Michael, successfully blowing a smoke ring.

Ann frowned. "I don't think that's necessary."

"But it's true. You're being picky, worrying about details when Mentius has come up with one of the most extraordinary claims in history."

"I hardly call worrying about my husband's life being picky about details! And I don't like this dishonesty . . . this elaborate setup! Did you see how nervous he was in the lab, squeezing his knuckles till I thought he would crack them? He and his wife staged all this, and I don't like it."

Michael tapped his cigar ash in an ashtray. "How else could he have gone about it? Being in the drug business, I can sympathize with his problems. He'll never know if Mentase works until he's tried it on humans. And finding humans old enough and with enough time and money to allow him to conduct the experiment under properly controlled conditions is difficult."

"There are old people's homes *filled* with people who would probably have volunteered!"

"But could they pay the twenty-five thousand dollars? This place isn't cheap to run, you know."

Ann gestured helplessly. "But, darling, to hell with Mentius's problems! I'm worried about *you!* A million things could go wrong, and where does that leave you?"

He thought a moment before answering. "Well, perhaps it leaves me dead."

"Oh, great."

"I can think of worse things to die for than the idea of Mentase."

She looked at him skeptically. "Now, come on. You're not the martyr type."

She was surprised at the hostility of the look he shot her: obviously she had struck a raw spot. But his reply was cool: "All right, I'm not a martyr. I'm a very selfish man: I'm the first to admit that. On the other hand, I think Mentius is on to something so potentially useful—so truly revolutionary—that I actually don't think I'd mind giving my life for it."

"What's so useful about it?" she exclaimed. "Keeping people young? I suppose it's a nice idea, but if it really happened to you I think it might be horrible."

"That's because you're young. I'm old, so I look on it a bit differently. Have you ever been around really old people?"

"Of course. My father was a doctor: I saw lots of old people."

"You saw them as patients; you never saw them as real people. The old are never real to any of us. They're shunted away quietly into retirement villages, or sanitariums, or park benches . . . they're through. Useless. They're like garbage: our beautifully technologized society doesn't know what to do with them, so it sweeps them under the Social Security rug. Do you realize most old people have to live on something like two dollars a day? Two dollars? Now, my darling wife, you, who are young and beautiful and get expensive jewelry draped around your swanlike neck, may not be too interested in the facts of survival: but to an eighty-year-old man who has no hope of anything in the future except a precarious existence on the brink of his grave, two dollars a day is a very unpleasant reality."

Ann shifted uncomfortably. "You don't have to make me sound like some heartless ogre," she said. "Besides, I don't see what that has to do with you."

"I'm just trying to show you that, for most people, the end of life is a miserable, depressing, humiliating disease for which the only cure is death. This is supposed to be the reward of a lifetime of hard work, but I think it's a pretty rotten reward. The dread of old age is the basis for most religions, a good deal of the world's art, some of the world's science, and practically all of the world's greed: why else do people pile up wealth except to cushion their old age? Now, if Mentius, whom you dismiss as a nut, has discovered something to prevent this disease of old age, then it seems to me the man will rank with Newton as one of the titans of science—if not art, religion, and sociology as well."

Ann sighed. "Michael, I'll grant you that's probably all very true. But I think you're trying to talk yourself into this crazy experiment with a lot of fancy rhetoric, when the *real* reason you want to take it is just that you're obsessed with being old."

She knew her husband had a quick temper. For a moment, she thought she had pushed him so far it was going to erupt. Then, again, he restrained it. Quietly, he said, "If I'm obsessed with old age, it's because I have a wife who could be my granddaughter."

There was an embarrassed silence. "You see?" he continued. "Neither of us likes to mention that, do we? But the truth is that by the time you're forty, I'll probably be dead. I don't happen to believe there's anything on the other side except a big void which I'm not too anxious to jump into. Mentius is giving me a way out; and I'm pretty well decided I'd be a fool not to take it." He took a long puff on the cigar as Ann stared at him, frightened by the realization that his mind was made up and there was nothing she could do to change it. Then he added wryly, "If something happens to me, at least you'll have the consolation of being a very rich widow. I've made out a new will leaving everything to you."

"I'm not interested in that."

"Aren't you?" His tone was skeptical, which annoyed her.

"No, I'm not."

"Well, whether you are or not, you get the money. Let's hope, though, that you won't get it for a couple of centuries." There was a knock on the door. "See who that is, will you?"

Ann walked slowly to the door, upset by the implications of Michael's remark. It was not like him to throw his money up to her, and she was hurt by his doing it now. Perhaps, she thought, he's doing it because he's more frightened than he's letting on. . . .

She opened the door to admit Bill Bradshaw. "Excuse me, Mrs. Brandywine," he said. "I hate to bother you this late, but a cable just arrived for Mr. Brandywine."

"Come in, Bill," said Michael. As his assistant carried the cable to him, Ann quietly went into the bedroom and closed the double doors. Then she threw herself on the big bed and rested her head on her arm. She didn't like what was happening to her husband: she didn't like it at all. She wished they had never come to the Chateau Mirabelle, had never heard of Dr. Mentius or the Methuselah Enzyme.

But she realized she was wasting her time.

In the living room of the suite, Michael opened the cable and read it. As he waited, Bill Bradshaw idly picked up the blue-bound folder from the table and started to open it.

"Put that down." Michael's voice was surprisingly sharp.

"I beg your pardon?"

"I said: put that down."

Bill replaced the folder on the table, looking curiously at his employer.

What's the son of a bitch up to? he thought. And what the hell's in that folder?

❧

The next morning, Ann awoke to find Michael had already gone. Getting up, she washed and dressed, then went into the living room of the suite to find Sally Mentius waiting for her with Dr. Zimmermann.

"Good morning," said Sally cheerfully.

"Good morning. Is my husband having breakfast?"

"Oh, he's through with that. All three of them are in the lab having physicals. We've been waiting for you to get up so we could have the sleep capsule installed in your bedroom. . . . Hilda?" She nodded to Dr. Zimmermann, who signaled through the open door to two workmen in the hallway. They rolled in a large white enamel and stainless steel horizontal tube, mounted on a wheeled carriage, with a glass lid on its top. Ann peered through the lid as the workmen rolled the capsule past her into the bedroom.

"At least it looks comfortable," she said.

"Oh, it is," said Sally. "I've slept in them a couple of times. You feel marvelous in the morning, and they're supposed to be great for hangovers."

"I can imagine."

"I thought after breakfast I could give you a tour of the chateau. Would you like that? Now that your husband's signed up for the treatment, you're going to have a lot of time on your hands; so you'll want to see our recreational facilities. I've asked Mr. Barstow and Martin Hirsch to come too. Isn't he a strange one?"

"The Hirsch boy?"

"Yes. Sort of a hippie type, don't you think? We don't get too many hippies here, as you can imagine. And don't you *love* Mr. Barstow?" Her eyes twinkled.

"Well, I haven't talked to him much . . ."

"Talk? All you have to do is look! He's so handsome and macho—yum! Lady de Ross may be a boozehound, but she sure knows how to pick her lovers. Excuse me—'secretaries.'"

Ann laughed; then she accompanied Sally into the hall and down the stairs to the Salle d'Hercule, Sally bubbling on about the problems of raising two American children in Switzerland, about the difficulties she and Herbie had had being accepted by the locals, about the rehabilitation of the chateau, which had eaten up all the money she had and most of his. "We're total dopes when it comes to money," she confessed to Ann.

"Pardon me for being blunt," said Ann, "but I don't see how you could lose money at the prices you charge."

"We barely break even, believe me. Herbie's research costs a fortune. What would you like for breakfast?"

Ann ordered poached eggs. As she ate, Sally sat opposite her continuing to talk, so that by the time Ann had finished her coffee she felt she had heard the woman's complete life story in exhausting detail. When she finally paused for breath, she grinned with an unusual hint of embarrassment. "I like to talk, in case you hadn't noticed. And there aren't too many people here my age for me to talk to. I hope you don't mind?"

"Of course not," smiled Ann, who found she was growing to like her.

Sally hesitated. "Herbie and I are really very pleased your husband decided to try the treatment. I know you're probably worried about it . . ."

Ann nodded. "Very worried. Frankly, I tried my best to talk him out of it last night."

"That's understandable. I . . ." Again she hesitated, as if trying to decide how best to phrase something. Then she said, "I only hope you can learn to have the same confidence in Herbie I have. He really is a terribly dedicated and careful man, you know."

Ann started to ask why he hadn't been more straightforward with them. Then she changed her mind. "Let's hope so," she remarked, with a hint of dryness.

Sally smiled. "Shall we go find the others and start the grand tour?"

"I'm ready."

The grand tour took most of the morning. First, Sally showed them the Salle des Fêtes, an enormous ballroom off the entrance hall where, she said, the original owner, Léonide Leblanc, gave some "fabulous" parties. "We have dances here every week when the clinic's full," she continued. "But with just the six of you, I thought maybe we could have a discothèque party instead. And," she smiled at Hugh, "perhaps we can talk Mr. Barstow into singing for us."

"Perhaps," said Hugh unenthusiastically. Sally cleared her throat and led them across the hall to her private apartment which, unlike the rest of the chateau, was starkly modern in decor and filled with pop art, including, in the living room, a huge, sagging vinyl toilet sculpture by Claes Oldenburg.

From her apartment, they went to the basement of the lab wing. Here there was a large, well-equipped gymnasium. A muscled blond Swiss in a gym suit was executing gymnastics on a set of parallel bars when the group entered. As he came over, Sally introduced him as Ernst Stahling, the clinic's director of physical therapy. "Stahling will show you the Aquadorme tanks," she said. The therapist, who looked a well-preserved forty and seemed quiet to the point of shyness, led Ann, Hugh, and Martin through a door into a white-tiled room containing three large rectangular steel tanks, ten feet long, six feet wide, and six feet high. Each had a steel ladder attached to the side which led to a platform at the top. Stahling beckoned to them to follow him up the ladder of the nearest tank. At the top, he pointed down to the inside, which was filled with slowly circulating water. From the bottom of the tank rose eleven slender steel rods topped by foam rubber pads. "The idea," said Stahling, "is to climb down into the water, then position yourself on the padded rods. The water which is warmed to eighty degrees Fahrenheit, circulates around all parts of the body, providing a gentle massage which lulls you into a deep sleep. Would you like to try it now?"

"The test is scheduled for tomorrow morning at nine," said Sally. "If the three of you will be here then, Dr. Zimmermann will take charge of you. It really should be quite pleasant."

They climbed down from the platform and followed Sally back into the gymnasium, then to the chateau where she took them outside into the formal gardens bordering the lake. "Stahling is something of a problem to us," she confided.

"Why?" asked Ann.

"Well, he has a habit of chasing the girls on the staff. And unfortunately, he isn't very careful."

Hugh and Martin exchanged glances. "Could one of the girls he hasn't been careful with be Lisl Oetterli?" asked Martin.

"Yes," said Sally. "How did you know? He's made her pregnant, poor thing. And Lisl's not the only one. I hear there are at least three others in the village. Stahling is really *most* energetic. I suppose it must be all the exercise."

It occurred to Ann that the shy, quiet Stahling didn't seem the type for such studlike activity.

The rest of the morning was spent outside as Sally led them through the lovely gardens, woods, and plum orchards of the chateau's grounds. There were tennis courts, a heated pool, a putting green, and a boathouse with two runabouts which Sally said were theirs to use anytime they wished.

At the end of the tour, she showed them a path that led into the woods a short way past the end of the lab wing. "I have to go back to check the menus for tomorrow," she said, "but I'd recommend the three of you go see our waterfall. It's really quite beautiful, and it's a lovely walk—only about a third of a mile. Just follow that path; it'll take you right to it. There's an observation platform at the edge of the gorge which gives you a nice view."

The three agreed; and, as Sally left them, they started into the woods. When they had walked a short way on the earthen path, Ann noticed that Martin Hirsch was looking very bothered, as if he wanted to say something but wasn't sure he should.

"Martin, is something the matter?" she asked.

"Well, yes. In a way." He explained about his father and Lady Kitty knowing each other. The information confused Ann.

"You mean," she said, "that they pretended not to know each other yesterday?"

"Yes. Does that make any sense to you?"

"None at all. Are you sure they've met before?"

"Pretty sure."

"Maybe they don't like each other, and just aren't talking," said Ann.

"It's easy as hell to dislike Lady Kitty," remarked Hugh.

They walked on a way in silence, then Martin continued: "But there's something else."

"What?"

"Well, you see, I was bribed to come here by my old man. I mean, he paid me three thousand dollars to come with him, and he told me the reason was . . ." He hesitated, looking uncertainly at Hugh.

"What Marty's trying to say is, he's a pothead. Right?"

Martin looked nervous. "Well, yes . . ."

"And his old man said he wanted to keep an eye on him to try and get him off the grass."

Ann remarked, "I don't see anything unusual about that. Frankly, I think it's sort of a good idea."

Hugh grinned and pointed at Ann. "Squaresville," he said to Martin.

"I'm not 'Squaresville,'" said Ann rather testily. "And I'm not particularly against pot—just as I'm not particularly for it. It's just that I can understand Martin's father trying to break him of the habit."

"Have you ever tried pot?" said Hugh softly.

Ann looked at him. "Once. That was enough. And please don't try to convert me."

Hugh shrugged. "Can't win them all."

"But both of you are missing my point," said Martin.

"Well, what the hell is it?"

Martin took a deep breath. "It's costing Lady de Ross extra to keep you here, isn't it, Hugh?"

"So?"

"And you told me she's a tightwad, just like my old man. Now, if it weren't for his bribing me to be here, he'd never pay extra to bring me along. And no offense intended, but it seems strange to me Lady Kitty would pay extra for you."

Hugh looked surprised. "There's a bit of difference in our relationship, man. And for your information, I am *very* good at shorthand."

"Yes, but if Lady Kitty's going to be sleeping in that sleep capsule gizmo every night, and if she's going to be in the lab all day, she's really not going to have much time for dictation, is she?"

"You don't know Lady Kitty," said Hugh. "She'll find time."

They were nearing the cataract now, and the roar of the water was becoming louder. A few feet ahead of them the path broke out of the woods into a clearing, where a wooden observation platform had been built at the edge of a narrow gorge. A small river tumbled over a rock and plunged about thirty feet into the gorge, where it boiled for twenty feet before disappearing underground, becoming a feeder for Lake Windischgratz. With the pine trees surrounding the gorge, it was a beautiful picture, and since the noise of the water made conversation difficult, they said nothing more as they leaned on the wooden rail of the platform and watched the water. But Ann mulled over what Martin had said. She wasn't too impressed by her own half-joking explanation for Arnold Hirsch and Lady de Ross pretending not to know each other, and if it were true, then it was indeed strange. But she couldn't agree that Hugh Barstow was an extravagance for Lady Kitty. As she glanced at the big ex-rock singer next to her, she decided he probably was as good at shorthand as he claimed, and that Lady Kitty was probably more than willing to pay for his services. Ann realized she was coming to like him. She was glad Lady Kitty had brought him to the Chateau Mirabelle.

❧

The exhaustive physical examinations were broken off at twelve thirty to allow the three patients to return to the chateau for lunch. The diet was now in force, and lunch was a lackluster four-hundred-calorie yawn, with no wine. Lady Kitty looked unhappy, but she acquiesced in the new regime. It was the ban on smoking that was giving her the most trouble, and she complained bitterly to Mentius, begging him for something to satisfy her oral compulsion. He suggested chewing gum, which she declined.

After lunch, she wandered into the Salle d'Athène, the elaborate library of the chateau, to look for something to read until she was scheduled to return to the lab. In the center of the room was a long table piled with newspapers and magazines from Europe and America. Bill Bradshaw was standing by the table reading *The New York Times,* which, along with the *Wall Street Journal,* Mentius received a day late.

Lady Kitty appraised the good-looking young man with a practiced eye, feeling her urge for nicotine being replaced by something more primordial. "You're Michael Brandywine's assistant, aren't you?" she said, coming up beside him.

Bill looked up from the paper. "Yes."

"I'm Lady Kitty de Ross." She smiled, then picked up a copy of *Vogue* and began idly leafing through it. "I think I have a few hundred shares of Brandywine Drug stock tucked away in my portfolio. Do you think I should sell them? The stock hasn't been doing much lately except plunging through new support levels every week or so. Do you think it will start going up eventually?"

Bill chose his words with caution: Michael wouldn't like him discussing company affairs with an outsider. "Oh, I think it will go up pretty soon," he said.

Lady Kitty smiled. "Don't tell me too much."

"I won't."

She continued leafing through the magazine. "I understand you're one of those soulless robots Harvard Business School turns out with such depressing regularity?"

"We like to think we have a little soul. Not much, but a little."

"A little soul is really all one needs. Are you staying here in the chateau?"

"No, I have a room in the staff quarters down by the lake."

"Charming." She looked him over again. "Are you from the East, or are you from that vast wasteland called the West? You see, I toured the States in the thirties in *Macbeth*—I played Lady Macbeth and was sensational—so I know America slightly, which is the way I want to keep it."

"I'm from New England. Rhode Island."

"Oh yes, that's the little one." She looked at his midsection, then smiled suggestively. "Are you a little one?"

Bill turned red, tongue-tied by her remark. She laughed. "You really don't have to answer that. I take it you're not married?"

"Divorced."

"How nice. I think divorce builds character, don't you?"

"I never thought of it that way." Then he added, "But it can be awfully expensive."

"Ah, always the man of business! I can see we two should get along famously. Perhaps you could give me some business advice: stock tips and things like that?"

"Mr. Brandywine doesn't like me to . . ."

She held up her hand. "I wouldn't dream of prying into his affairs. No, I meant general advice. The broad economic spectrum. Perhaps you'd like to come up to my suite and have a cocktail with me? Orange juice for me, of course: the doctor is being most strict about the sauce. But I could dream up something interesting for you."

He hesitated. "I think I'd better not."

"That's a shame."

"Why?"

She casually twisted the marquise diamond ring. "Well, I think an attractive young man on the rise, so to speak, can sometimes profit by making contacts with those older and more established than he. It allows him to broaden his horizons, don't you think?"

Bill's eyes were on the diamond. Then he looked up at Lady Kitty. "I guess my horizons will just have to stay narrow."

Her smile vanished. "Harvard obviously didn't teach you how to recognize an attractive proposition." Slamming the *Vogue* shut, she turned and stalked out of the library, leaving Bill smiling to himself.

The next morning, Ann, Hugh, and Martin gathered in the gymnasium for the sleep test. Stahling took the two men into one locker room while Dr. Zimmermann took Ann into another. "Please take off your clothes," said the pleasant if slightly Wagnerian blonde. "And put on this bathrobe." She indicated a terrycloth robe on a hook.

Ann began to undress. "What will you do during the tests?" she asked.

"*We* do nothing. The computer does everything for us. We'll attach two monitors to your forehead, which will record your brain waves while you're asleep. This information then is fed to our computer, which analyzes the results. The computer has made life much easier for us."

"I can imagine," said Ann, putting on the bathrobe. Dr. Zimmermann removed her nurse's uniform and put on a tank suit. Then she led Ann out to the white-tiled room containing the Aquadorme tanks. Hugh Barstow had already climbed to the platform of one of them. Now he took off his bathrobe, threw it to the floor, then, stark naked, held his nose and cannonballed into the tank, yelling "Geronimo!" and shooting up a wall of water as he hit. "Hey, it's groovy!" he called.

"I'd recommend *climbing* into the water," said Dr. Zimmermann to Ann, with a hint of disapproval at Hugh's performance. She led her up to the platform of the nearest tank, took her bathrobe, and held it as a screen as Ann climbed down a steel ladder into the tank. The water reached to her shoulders, and its warmth was marvelously relaxing. For a moment, she floated on her back. Then, with little difficulty, she positioned herself on the foam rubber pads, which were so cleverly located that she could hardly feel them support her in the water. Only her head was out of the water, being tilted slightly upward by the head pads, and the sensation was like drifting in air.

Dr. Zimmermann, who had climbed into the tank after her, waded through the water to Ann's side and pulled two wires from a pipe next to her head. "These are the monitors," she explained as she pressed the small recording devices onto Ann's temples with adhesive tape. "Is the tape too tight?"

"Oh no," said Ann.

"All right. I'll turn on the hydromassage now. Just close your eyes. In a few minutes, you'll be asleep." She waded back to the edge of the tank and climbed out. A moment later Ann heard a click followed by a low hum. Then she felt the water begin to surge softly over and under and around her, caressing her naked body with a languorous warmth that was more than faintly erotic. In a surprisingly short time, she found herself drifting into a relaxed sleep. She put up no resistance, and her body sank into a bottomless void of pleasure.

❧

When she awoke, she was surprised to find she was lying on the bed in her suite. Her first sensation was a dull headache somewhere on the left side of her skull. Her second sensation was one of extreme fatigue. With some difficulty, she sat up and looked at her body. Someone had put her clothes back on. She rubbed her forehead weakly, then shifted herself to the edge of the bed and climbed off. To her amazement, her legs crumpled and she fell to the floor.

As she pulled herself up, she wondered at the weakness in her legs. If this was the result of four hours of hydromassage, then Mentius's Aquadorme tanks were anything but "refreshing." Slowly, she stood up, using the bed to help her to her feet. Then she made her way to the bathroom. Inside, she leaned on the washbasin and looked at her reflection. Her face was haggard, and there were two faint red marks on her forehead that she assumed had been made by the adhesive tapes. Splashing her face with water, then taking two aspirin for her headache, she went back into the bedroom. She was beginning to feel better, though she was still weak. She sat down on the bed again for a few minutes to allow her strength to build. As she waited, her stomach began to rumble, and she realized she was ravenous.

She got up, feeling stronger, and went through the living room of the suite to the corridor, which she crossed, knocking on the door to Hugh Barstow's room. After a moment, he opened the door. He looked equally tired and had the same red marks on his forehead that she did.

"Do you feel as awful as I do?" she asked.

"Yeah. That's the last time I sleep for science. Christ, I feel like I've been run over by the E train. How about some lunch? You hungry?"

"Starved."

They went downstairs to find the Salle d'Hercule empty, as was the rest of the first floor of the chateau. "Look," said Hugh, pointing to a large silver bowl on the buffet which was filled with plums, bananas, and berries. They hurried to the bowl and started eating. As Ann consumed plum after plum, she realized she was making a pig of herself, but she was too hungry to care. When finally her stomach had stopped grinding, she licked her fingers and went out on the terrace which, despite the fact it was a brilliant day, was completely shaded. "That's strange," she said to Hugh as he joined her.

"What?"

"Well, the sun sets over there," she pointed across the lake, "and now it's over *there*"—she pointed in the opposite direction, toward the chateau—"which means it must be morning. Except I thought they were going to keep us in those things four hours?"

Hugh glanced at his wristwatch. "It's ten thirty in the morning," he said, surprised.

"Do you suppose we only slept an hour?" she said. "I couldn't have gotten that hungry in that short a time, though."

"What's the date?" He was looking at his watch again.

"Friday, the ninth of June."

"Guess again."

He held out his arm. Ann looked at his watch, which had a small calendar window on one side of the dial.

"Lady Kitty gave me this watch, and it's never wrong. See the date?"

Ann nodded. The calendar read Monday, the twelfth of June. "Hugh," she said softly, "what do you think they did to us those three days?" Her voice sounded frightened.

Hugh looked at her. "That's what we're going to find out," he replied. "Come on. Let's go find the great Dr. Mentius."

They hurried back inside the chateau.

PART TWO

MARTIN Hirsch was totally confused.

Lisl Oetterli had come into his room and wakened him, telling him that she had changed his appointment with her brother.

"Why?" Martin had said, wondering, as Ann had, at his general sense of fatigue and feeling of intense hunger.

"Because the Mentius Mafia kept you asleep for three days," she said.

"The who?"

"The Mentius Mafia. That's what the staff calls the three doctors who work with Dr. Mentius, because they're so secretive. Anyway, they kept you out for three days, and I told Kurt you wouldn't be able to pick up the order till this morning. He's waiting for you now. It'll take you at least twenty minutes to get there, so you'd better start now."

"But wait a second: why did they keep us asleep that long?"

Lisl shrugged, "How would I know? Please hurry. Kurt hates to be kept waiting."

She left the room and Martin climbed out of bed, his legs feeling weak from the three days of disuse. He checked his wallet to make sure he had the money. Then, when he had walked around the room a couple of times to get his legs operative again, he hurried out of the chateau and started through the woods toward the northwest corner of the two-hundred-acre park, where, at a dead apple tree near the Lausanne-Windischgratz highway, he had arranged to meet Lisl's brother to pick up the drugs. As he hurried as fast as he could, he tried to imagine why Dr. Mentius would have kept them unconscious for so long a time. But by the time he reached the meeting place and spotted Kurt Oetterli sitting on the stump of the apple tree, he still didn't have the faintest hint of an explanation for the biochemist's odd behavior.

Kurt was a big man, about thirty, whose face might have been handsome if it weren't so deeply pitted with acne scars. He was wearing a leather motorcycle jacket, tight pants, and boots; on the ground by his feet was a white-and-red-striped crash helmet. He obviously cultivated the motorcycle-gang tough-guy look. But there was a hint of cruelty in his face that came naturally without cultivation, and as Martin sank onto a large rock, he readily believed what Lisl had told him: that her brother had direct connections with the Mafia in Marseilles.

Kurt watched Martin trying to catch his breath. "You're out of shape," he said in a soft, accented voice.

"No, I'm just pooped . . . from some test . . ." puffed Martin.

"Yes, my sister told me about the sleep test. 'And on the third day, the three volunteers arose from the dead.' Dr. Mentius lied to the three of you, didn't he?"

Martin nodded. "You might say."

"Any idea why?"

"No."

"What's going on in the chateau? My sister tells me some peculiar stories."

"About what?"

"Oh, about the Mentius Mafia. And a very super-secret project they've been working on for three or four years."

Martin had caught his breath. "Do you have the stuff?"

Kurt reached inside his jacket and pulled out a small brown-paper package, carefully tied with string. "When someone keeps secrets from me, I get curious. Why are there only six guests in the chateau? Why is the guest wing closed?"

Martin was eyeing the package hungrily. "Is that it?" he asked.

Kurt nodded. "The complete order. Including the blackbirds."

Martin pulled his wallet from his pocket and hastily removed some bills. "Here—six hundred Swiss francs."

Kurt shook his head. "The price has gone up."

"The hell with that! We made a deal with your sister!"

"The price has gone up," reiterated Kurt, leaning forward. "I want the six hundred francs; plus I want to know what the doctor is giving your father and the other two."

Martin hesitated, then shrugged. "What the hell. What do I care if you know?"

"That's the spirit."

"He's giving them something he calls the Methuselah Enzyme. It . . ." Martin stopped. His eyes had caught the gleam of steel flashing underneath Kurt's jacket as he leaned forward. It was the butt of a revolver in an armpit holster. Martin glanced nervously at Kurt's eyes. Then he continued: "It's supposed to be a miracle enzyme that Mentius makes some pretty wild claims for."

"Like?"

"He says it can keep you young forever."

Kurt stared at him a moment. Then he laughed. "And that's what your father's paying twenty-five thousand dollars for?"

"Yes."

"Mentius is smarter than I thought. That's real sucker money."

"Maybe it'll work."

Kurt stood up. "Sometimes I think I'm in the wrong business. The real money's in the youth racket." He took the cash from Martin, then handed him the packet. Martin eagerly started untying the string.

"Don't bother," said Kurt. "It's all there. I don't cheat my paying customers. When will you want more?"

Martin stuck the package under his coat. "In ten days."

"Lisl will arrange the time. *Ciao.*"

"*Ciao.*"

Kurt headed through the bushes to the road, where he had parked his motorcycle.

When Martin returned to the chateau, he met Ann and Hugh in the entrance hall outside the door to Mentius's office.

"Where've you been?" said Hugh.

Martin glanced at Ann, then said, "I went to meet Kurt. I was a little late for the appointment."

"Yeah. You know about the three days, then?"

"I know. I told you something freaky was going on here."

Ann said, "We've sent word into the lab wing that we want to talk to Dr. Mentius. I think it would be best if you stayed with us so we can present a united front."

Martin surreptitiously pressed the package under his coat. He was anxious to get it to his room and hungry for the hashish, but he realized Ann was right, so he stayed. In a few minutes Dr. Mentius came into the hall from the direction of the lab wing. He was wearing his white lab coat and was glancing at some papers on a clipboard. When he came up to the group, he smiled at Ann. "Mrs. Brandywine? My secretary said you wanted to see me."

"Yes, we do," said Ann. "The three of us are a bit annoyed."

Mentius looked at the others. "Then I assume you found out what day it is?" he said. "I can understand why you're upset. Come into my apartment and I'll explain the whole thing to you."

He opened the door that led to his private quarters, and the three of them filed into the large, modern living room. Ann glanced at the Oldenburg toilet sculpture which hung rather eerily at one end of the room, partially reflected by the metallic paper Sally had covered the walls with. The room was furnished with white sofas, Barcelona chairs, and stainless steel and glass tables, the effect being strikingly different from the rest of the chateau. As they sat down, Mentius looked into the adjoining kitchen where his two children were noisily fighting.

"Boys," he ordered, "go to your room and stop yelling."

"Jeremy stole my comic book!" wailed a young voice from the kitchen.

"Jeremy, give him back his comic book—and *stop fighting!*" He closed the door and joined the others, shaking his head wearily. "Sometimes they're a bit of a trial," he said, sitting down in a stainless steel and leather chair. "As a matter of fact, they're a bit of a trial *all* the time. Now, the sleep test. I apologize for the trick we played on you, but there is a reason for it. And naturally I checked with Mr. Brandywine, Mr. Hirsch, and Lady de Ross before we did it, and they gave me their permission."

"Hold it," interrupted Hugh. "Kitty-baby has no business giving any 'permission' about what can be done to me. She doesn't own me, you know."

Mentius looked uncomfortable. "I realize that, Mr. Barstow. But still I thought it best to ask her."

"Why didn't you ask *us?*" said Ann.

"I didn't ask you for the same reason I had to trick you. When people know they are going to be unconscious for any unusual length of time, such as three days, they put up either a conscious or an unconscious resistance to it—which is only natural, after all. But the problem to us is that resistance distorts the brain waves, which in turn distorts the very purpose of the test. It's the old question of the chicken and the egg. So in order to induce a long, peaceful sleep in you, we couldn't very well tell you that we were putting you out for three days. I sincerely hope I haven't inconvenienced you, and if I have, I apologize. There's not a great deal for you to do here, and I assumed you wouldn't mind after I told you what we'd done."

"But I *do* mind, Doctor," said Ann. "Aside from everything else, when I woke up I felt perfectly awful. I still have a headache . . ."

"That's probably from the xenon gas. We gave you a mixture of eighty percent xenon to twenty percent oxygen to protract the deep sleep. Xenon is almost the perfect anesthetic, but sometimes it leaves people with a headache. It should go away soon. The three of you probably also felt a sense of fatigue when you woke up, which is natural after such an unusually long sleep. Again, that will soon pass. Actually, the rest was very good for you."

The three of them looked at each other uncertainly. Then Ann said, "Dr. Mentius, I suppose we have to accept your explanation, but I'm not very happy about it. I don't like being put out of commission for three days, like some dog being chloroformed in the pound. I might possibly have volunteered if you'd asked me. But I like to know what's happening to me, and I certainly don't like being fooled. So please, the next time, if there is one, *ask.*"

She noticed Mentius's right hand had begun squeezing the knuckles of his left hand, in the same manner she had seen the night they first met him. "I'm sorry you feel this way, Mrs. Brandywine. Your husband assured me you wouldn't mind."

"That still doesn't give you the right to use me as a guinea pig."

"That goes for me too," said Hugh.

"And me," added Martin. "As far as my father is concerned, it wouldn't surprise me if he gave you permission to drown me, much less gas me."

"I don't think that's a justified remark," said Mentius, who looked rather shocked. "From what your father's told me, I think he's quite fond of you."

Martin laughed. "When you get to know him a little better, you'll find there's a big difference between what my father says and what he does."

Jeremy Mentius ran into the living room from the kitchen, crying. He threw his arms around his father.

"Daddy, Jeffrey hit me!" he wailed.

"Why?"

"Because I hit *him!*"

Mentius sighed. "I told you to go to your room! Where's your mother?"

"I don't know. But Jeffrey shouldn't hit me."

Mentius got up, taking his young son's hand. "Excuse me a moment," he said to the others. "I'd better get these two in bed for a nap."

"I hope it's not a three-day one," said Hugh dryly.

Mentius turned slightly red, then led his bawling son back into the kitchen.

"What do you think?" Martin said, keeping his voice low. "Did you believe him?"

Ann stood up. "Oh, I *believe* him," she said. "It's just that I think his methods aren't very admirable. But it's really my husband I'm mad at."

"I can't say I blame you," said Hugh. "I think all three of them were pretty damned casual about the three of us."

They started back to the hall. Martin, who was pressing his package close to his ribs to prevent it from slipping out from under his coat, nudged Hugh and said softly, "You want to come to my room and check the package?"

Hugh glanced at the bulge under his jacket, then nodded. "Good idea."

He held the door for Ann, then followed her out into the soaring entrance hall.

"Well," he said, shrugging, "I guess we're all three days older."

"I guess," said Martin, adding gloomily, "but I wonder if we're three days wiser?"

Ann said nothing, but hurried up the grand staircase to her suite to wait for her husband to return from the laboratory.

❧

Bill Bradshaw looked at the statement and couldn't believe his eyes.

It had arrived that morning in the mail from New York, and he had opened it, forgetting that Michael had given him strict instructions not to open any mail from his stockbroker that had "Personal" typed on the envelope, as this did. Now it was too late. In for a penny in for a pound, he had thought as he opened the statement and read it. It recorded the transfer of one hundred thousand shares of Michael's Brandywine Drug Company Class A common stock to something Bill had never heard of: the Société Gérontologique, 17 Place St. François, Lausanne, Switzerland. A copy of a letter from the Internal Revenue Service was enclosed, which noted and cleared the stock transfer.

Bill knew that Michael Brandywine had been having money troubles for almost three years, troubles that had gotten progressively worse and that had forced him to liquidate most of his real estate holdings. He had lost almost three million in the Alaska North Slope oil syndicate, which, even to a man conservatively worth fifteen million, was a blow. Then there had been the trouble at Brandywine Drugs. Placidine, the company's most profitable product, had, because of lackadaisical advertising, lost ground to Excedrin, giving up over seven percent of the headache-remedy market to the more aggressive product. This had put Placidine in the red after years of operating in the black.

Even worse, the company had been hit with an eight-month strike in two of its biggest plants, which had forced it to suspend dividends for two years in a row, badly depressing the stock on the market. The total effect on Michael's personal finances had been crippling.

Bill admired the way his employer kept all this gloomy news from his young wife. But why should such an important transaction as shifting so much of his stock to an unheard-of company be kept hidden from his assistant, to whom he paid twenty-two thousand a year to know all? It made no sense. What was the Société Gérontologique, and what was the point of keeping it a secret? Of course, the name implied something involving aging, which in turn smelled of Dr. Mentius.

Which brought Bill to the other question that had been plaguing him ever since his arrival at the Chateau Mirabelle. Just what was the treatment Michael was taking? Whatever it was, he was sure it involved something more than what he presumably was undergoing, because both Michael and his pretty wife were being so tight-lipped about it. Bill had asked discreet questions among the clinic's personnel and found out from Stahling, the physical therapist, that Mentius had been working on a secret project for a number of years, but that no one except his closest associates had any idea what it was. Could it be something the Société Gérontologique had been set up to manufacture?

The weird three-day disappearance of Mrs. Brandywine—which her husband had vaguely explained as a "sleep therapy test"—only compounded the mystery as far as Bill was concerned. For five years he had slaved for Michael Brandywine, earning far less than he could have made in a normal corporate position as a business school graduate, but sacrificing present salary for future opportunities and a firsthand inside look at how the big cats like Michael operated. The mysterious maneuvering going on at the chateau smelled to Bill of big money, and Bill's finely tuned antennae were seldom wrong.

But since, obviously, Michael didn't want him to know, he would have to go to another source of information; and Lady Kitty de Ross's unsubtle approach to him in the library the week before now seemed to Bill to present an opportunity he might profit by. Naturally, it involved the possibility of actually having to take the old whore to bed to find out what he wanted. But while that could get complicated—particularly if Michael found out about it—Bill thought he could handle it. And although it might be rather repulsive, Bill Bradshaw wasn't an overly fastidious man when it was a matter of getting what he wanted. Fastidiousness was definitely a luxury for a man whose father had been a bus driver in Providence, whose mother was a schoolteacher, and whose wife was collecting $800 a month alimony for what apparently was going to be the rest of time.

Thus, when Michael Brandywine returned to his suite from the lab at five that afternoon, Bill handed the resealed envelope to him and watched as he opened it, relieved that he hadn't noticed the careful paste job he had done on the envelope flap. Michael glanced at the statement without comment. Then he told his assistant he was feeling tired and was going to take a nap, and that he could have the rest of the day off. Thanking him, Bill left the suite, hesitated a moment, then crossed the large corridor and knocked on Lady Kitty's door.

When she opened it, she gave the young businessman a curious look. "Well," she said slowly. "Change your mind?"

He smiled. "Maybe my horizons need broadening after all."

"Good. I'm in an extravagantly horizon-broadening mood. Come in." She held the door for him as he entered the living room of her suite, which was an exact duplicate of the Brandywine suite opposite it. "Frankly," said Lady Kitty, closing the door, "I've been bored silly writing invitations for a birthday party I'm throwing in a few weeks. It will be a costume ball, actually, and it should be an absolute Saturnalia. I'm asking *everybody* . . . I hope you'll come?"

"I'd love to."

"Good. May I fix you a drink?"

"Yes, thank you."

"A martini? Mother's milk is so good for the soul."

"That would be fine." While she made the drink, he looked around the room which, again like the Brandywines', was luxuriously furnished with good reproductions and better antiques. The only difference was that the tables, chests, and the Louis Quinze desk were covered with dozens of silverframed photographs of Lady Kitty, most of them taken in the thirties and forties, representing her in various stage roles.

"How do you like my rogues' gallery?" she asked, surreptitiously checking her pink Chanel suit in a mirror as she stirred the gin. "Being an advanced narcissist, I always take a few pictures with me whenever I travel."

"They're very interesting," said Bill.

"You make them sound like a museum exhibition."

"I didn't mean to. You were a beautiful woman."

She looked at him coldly. "I still am. Lemon?"

"Please. And I didn't mean to imply you're not beautiful now. In fact, I like mature women."

"God, that ghastly euphemism! 'Mature' always sounds like an old grape . . . Oh well, the price of age and experience. Here." She handed him the martini. "I only wish I could join you. This wretched ban on booze is most tiresome, but there you have it: doctor's orders must be obeyed, particularly at the price he's charging. I'm sure my liver is in an advanced state of shock with all the orange juice I've been feeding it. Do sit down. What made you change your mind?"

She sat in a fauteuil, gesturing to him to take a chair opposite, which he did.

"Let's say I got lonely."

"Dear boy, I know how you feel. And you couldn't have come to a better place for warmth and companionship. This clinic is enough to depress anyone; but since we're all travelers together on this dreary voyage, we must all do what we can to cheer each other up, don't you think?" She smiled.

"That's the way I feel," he said, sipping the drink.

"How is it?"

"Delicious."

"I learned to mix drinks doing drawing room comedies. Thirty years ago that was practically all one did in plays, except in the second act when one always got raped on the sofa . . . discreetly, of course. If the thing was a hit, when we'd get bored we'd mix real drinks on stage." She laughed. "I can remember once I was doing a revival of *Private Lives*—I was *much* better than Gertie

Lawrence: she saw my performance and was positively puce with envy—and we were using real mother's milk and I got absolutely squiffed on stage. The director was furious with me, and tried to send on my understudy for the second act—that little bitch! Well, he couldn't have done anything to sober me up faster. I was like a judge in minutes! I went on and sailed through the play. They loved me, but then they always did. I was the best thing that ever hit the West End."

Bill grinned. "I guess you were your own press agent?"

"Of course. I loathe false modesty. If you're good, trumpet it to the skies—and I was good. We had style in those days; not like today, where all one has to do is expose one's crotch on stage to become a star. Look what's happened to the West End and Broadway. A bunch of armpit-scratchers posing as actors. God, I wouldn't have them in my house, much less actually *pay* to see them scratch on stage. Tedium, tedium, tedium. I despise the whole scene. Haven't been in a theater for years, and I love plays—absolutely adore them! Have since I was a child. But they can't even do Shakespeare decently! If Hamlet isn't a homosexual sleeping with Rosencrantz and Guildenstern and Horatio and God knows who else—probably Yorick!—he's a social protester, sort of a medieval Danish Yippie, which is idiotic. Ah well, I shan't bore you with my rantings about the state of the drama. Suffice it to say, what the theater desperately needs is *me*. So. And how is Mr. Brandywine? Has his little wife come out of that cataleptic fit they put her into?"

"Yes. What was it they did to her?"

"Oh, some sort of idiotic test Mentius wanted to do. You know scientists: they're never happy unless they're plugging an electrode into your navel."

"Mr. Brandywine said it was some sort of sleep therapy?"

"That was it, sleep therapy. Personally, I know a much *better* kind of sleep therapy . . ." Again, she smiled.

Bill shifted uncomfortably. "Has Dr. Mentius been giving the three of you sleep therapy? I mean, you and Mr. Hirsch and Mr. Brandywine?"

"You haven't seen our sleep capsules? But they're absolutely fascinating! Come bring your drink . . . I'll show you mine. It's right in the bedroom."

Getting up, she took his hand and almost tugged him out of his chair.

"Each night I crawl in the thing, push the little button that's inside, close the lid, and *voilà!* In moments I'm dead to the world. The high-pressure oxygen cleans out your cells, or some such nonsense, but I must admit when the alarm wakes me up in the morning I feel fantastically fit. The only problem is, the damned thing's not big enough for two . . . Here we are."

She led him through the double doors into the large bedroom where, beside the big French bed, the sleep capsule stood, its white enamel sides and glass lid glaringly sterile compared with the lavishness of the room. She opened the glass lid. "See? There's the little control panel. You push buttons and the temperature goes down, except you don't feel it because you're asleep. Then in the morning, it defrosts itself automatically and wakes you up. Dr. Mentius designed it. Such a clever man."

"Then this was what Mrs. Brandywine has been in?"

She frowned. "No, that was something else," she said shortly. "Do you believe in mixed bathing?"

"I beg your pardon?"

"Mixed bathing."

"You mean like in Japan?"

"I don't mean *public* mixed bathing, dear boy. There's no fun in that. I mean private mixed bathing. You've never done it?"

Bill took a deep breath. "I can't say I have."

"But you haven't lived! How depressing life must be in Rhode Island . . . Would you like to try it?"

"You mean now?"

"Of course now. There's my bathroom; it's huge and done in the most deliciously whorish taste—you'll love it. It has a capacious tub which easily holds two, and I really must bathe before dinner. Why don't you join me?"

Bill tried to take this in stride. "You certainly don't beat around the bush, do you?"

She smiled. "It all depends on whose bush I'm beating around. *Do* come. I feel I like you immensely, and there's no quicker way for two people to get to know each other than crawling absolutely nude into a tub together. One lets one's hair down and acts completely natural—marvelous! It's all the rage in London . . . I'll draw the bath. You can undress here if you want. And bring your drink with you."

She went to the bathroom door, then turned and looked back at Bill, who was standing beside the sleep capsule.

"Well?" she said. "You said you wanted to broaden your horizons."

He hesitated. Then he set the martini on the lid of the capsule and started taking off his coat.

❧

Ann had been asleep in the bedroom of her suite when Michael returned from the lab, and it was Bill Bradshaw's voice which awakened her. She sat up and stretched. Then, as she heard Bill leaving the suite, she got up and went to the small Empire vanity to brush her hair. In a moment, Michael came in. She watched his reflection in the mirror. "How are you, darling?" she said coolly. "I've missed you the past three days."

Michael closed the doors, not failing to catch the edge in her tone. "I understand from Dr. Mentius you're not very happy about what he did."

"Did you expect me to be?" she said, continuing to brush. "Getting slipped a three-day mickey isn't exactly my idea of fun. Frankly, I'm amazed you let him do it."

He came up behind her, putting his hands on her shoulders and leaning his face down beside hers. "I probably shouldn't have," he said, watching her face in the mirror. "But he gave me such a long song and dance about how important it was for science, and I didn't see how a long sleep could exactly hurt you."

"I'm sure that's what the wicked witch told Snow White after she gave her the poisoned apple."

Michael smiled and kissed her, rubbing his hands up and down her arms. "I apologize."

She pushed his hands off and turned to face him. "Michael, Mentius apologized too; but don't you think it's a little late? I mean, it's like somebody knocking you down and stealing your purse, then saying, 'Golly, I'm sorry.' "

"Don't you think you're making a mountain out of a molehill?"

"Maybe. And maybe you're making a molehill out of a mountain."

He ran his hand over his chin, then shrugged. "I guess I'm only making things worse, so I'll shut up."

"But don't you see why I'd be a little annoyed?"

He said nothing, but instead opened a drawer of the vanity and pulled out an oblong package wrapped in red paper. He handed it to her. "For you," he said quietly.

She removed the gift wrapping, revealing a black velvet box stamped with the mark of a Lausanne jeweler. Inside was a Piaget watch with a blue face surrounded by diamonds. She looked up at him.

"Your waking-up present, Snow White. Put it on."

She obeyed.

"Do you like it?"

How beautifully pat, she thought. He knew I'd be angry, so he had this all ready to shut me up . . . just like the necklace and earrings?

"Michael, it's beautiful, but . . ."

"Now wasn't that worth sleeping three days for?"

Or was it to cheer me up? Oh, God, I don't know. . . . She sighed and gave up. "All right. So I survived the sleep test. So I'm one of science's heroes."

He laughed and put his arms around her, kissing her neck. "You really like it?"

"Oh, Michael, it's gorgeous. You knew I'd love it."

After a moment, he began making love to her. She wanted it. After three days of artificially induced sleep, she wanted love hungrily. He brought her to her feet, continuing to kiss her; then they went to the bed and lay down.

"Michael," she whispered as his hands began unbuttoning her blouse, "do you love me?"

"Um," he said distractedly, kissing her neck.

"Say it."

"I love you."
She smiled and relaxed.

❧

When they had finished, she lay in his arms, contented.
"Catch me up, darling," she said.
"On what?"
"On what you've been doing the last three days I've been zonked, of course."
"That's simple. We've been in the lab by day, and in that icebox sleep capsule by night. Very exhilarating."
"What do you do in the lab?"
"Well, let's see. First, we get our daily shot of Mentase."
"Where?"
"In the seat. Left cheek one day, right cheek the next."
"Does it hurt?"
"I try not to sit down too often."
"Then what happens?"
"Then we go through two and a half hours of tests. Each day we get a complete physical, because they want to make sure the Mentase isn't causing some sort of reaction anywhere. Those two young Swiss doctors have to keep what looks to me like about a hundred charts on each of us."
"It sounds dull."
"It is; but they're thorough and they're careful, which is nice to know. When they're through, we break for lunch."
"What happens after lunch?"
"We take an hour-long nap. Then we do an hour of exercise."
"Good Lord, you'll certainly be in shape!"
"Yes, that part of it's good for me. I've really never felt better in my life. Let's see: that brings us up to three o'clock. Then they take us into the Cosmetarium where we get a steam bath, a massage, a facial . . ."
"For men?"
"For men. Then Dr. Zimmermann goes over our entire bodies with the Dermo-Disc—that's the little cup that shoots electric charges into you and is supposed to rejuvenate the skin tissue.

Then we get mud packs while Lisl Oetterli gives the three of us scalp treatments and sets Lady Kitty's hair."

"What does she shampoo on old Mr. Hirsch's head? He's bald as a billiard."

"He may not be when she gets done with him. By the way, if you want I'll make an appointment with Lisl for you. Lady Kitty says she's excellent."

"Good. Ask her if she can take me on Tuesdays and Fridays."

"I will."

Ann hesitated. "Do you think it's worth the money? I mean, do you think all this rigmarole will actually work?"

"It's too early to tell," he said. "We'll just have to wait and see."

They didn't say anything for a while. Then Ann said, "Michael, can you think of any reason why Lady Kitty and Mr. Hirsch would pretend not to know each other?"

"Who told you they did?"

"Martin Hirsch. He said he's certain they've known each other before, but they pretended not to know each other when they got here. Do you have any idea why?"

He didn't say anything for a moment; then he snickered.

"I have a very good idea."

"What?"

"But don't tell the kid."

"I won't. But what's all the secrecy?"

He turned on his side and propped his head in his hand.

"Well, the three of us are getting to know each other pretty well, being thrown together so much of the time."

"I can imagine."

"And old Mr. Hirsch seems to trust me. At any rate, he told me that he and Lady Kitty had a little fling a couple of years back on his yacht. He wasn't sure if Martin knew that Lady Kitty was one of his clients, so they more or less agreed to pretend not to know each other, just to be on the safe side."

"That seems rather elaborate, don't you think? I mean, just to protect Martin's sensitivities? After all, he's hardly a baby."

"I know, but Arnold Hirsch is a bit old-fashioned. And I think he can't stand the idea of his son thinking he's a dirty old man."

Ann smiled. "In a way, that's sort of nice, don't you think? With most parents trying to be so chummy with their children, it's nice to meet one father who's still trying to be holier-than-thou—you know, the vengeful father-figure."

He didn't answer for a moment. Then he said casually, "Oh, Arnold Hirsch is that. He's that, in spades."

As Ann snuggled her naked body closer to his, she wondered what he meant.

❧

"I see you're not a 'little one.' Bravo!"

Lady Kitty was sitting in the enormous marble tub in her enormous marble bathroom. Bill Bradshaw had just come in. He was naked, and she was admiring his trim physique and generously proportioned member. "Come right in, the water's fine."

Bill set his martini on the chaise percée next to the tub, then stepped into the sudsy water. Lady Kitty flipped a handful of suds at him and laughed.

"Relax. You look as if I'm about to bite you—not that I wouldn't. Now: you sit at that end facing me, and we'll sort of intertwine our legs, which can be devastatingly erotic. Do you like my bath oil? Doesn't it smell divine? It's made especially for me by a parfumier in Paris. One of those tiny little shops with those huge huge prices, but I always say one should never stint about baths. I've always thought the greatest contribution of Rome to civilization wasn't the Pax Romana or law or Caesar or any of that drivel—but baths. Baths made Rome great. Don't you agree?"

Bill was lowering himself into the water. He found he was getting a kick out of the situation, and out of Lady Kitty. There was a stagey theatricality about her that was funny in a campy way, almost as if she had never gotten out of those thirties drawing room comedies, but was still living the spirit and style of them and still, definitely, on stage. But it would be foolish to underestimate her, he thought. Beneath the staginess was a shrewd intelligence. Besides, surprisingly, she was rather sexy. She had piled her hair on top of her head and tied it with a pink ribbon. The skin of her arms and breasts was firm and as pink as the ribbon, kept in shape by years of expensive massage; the idea of making love to her, he decided, was rather exciting. It would definitely be a pleasure, not a duty.

As the water swirled around his stomach, he leaned back against the marble tub and relaxed, carefully extending his legs toward Lady Kitty. Suddenly, he felt her foot press against his genitals. He bolted upright, a look of shock on his face. She guffawed. "*Got* you!"

"Watch that, if you don't mind."

"Dear boy, I wouldn't hurt you for the world—not for the world. What lovely strong shoulders you have! And what delicious black hair on your chest! Hairy chests have always been an absolute thing with me—so virile and apelike. The only thing wrong with dear Hugh's body is that his chest is smooth as a baby's, which is rather dull."

"What about Hugh? Won't he be mad if he finds out I'm your new tub partner?"

"Of course not. Hugh does what he's told. He's an employee of mine, nothing more. He has no rights or privileges as long as he's on my payroll. Besides, I'm bored with him."

"Then why did you bring him along?"

She shrugged. "To amuse me during this tedious Mentase treatment."

Bill looked at her. "What's Mentase?"

He noticed a guarded look come into her eyes. "Oh, it's one of those asinine scientific words that sound impressive but really mean nothing. Now: what would you say if I asked you to take that cake of soap and come down to my end of the tub and rub-a-dub-dub it ever so gently over my superb tits? I adore being rubbed, absolutely adore it. Do you think I could coax you into doing that? Then I'll soap you, if you'd like. You'll love it."

Bill got out of the water and knelt in the middle of the tub, straddling Lady Kitty. Taking the cake of soap, he began rubbing it tenderly over her shoulders and breasts. She closed her eyes and sighed with pleasure.

"Divine. Absolutely divine. And you're so good at it! I can't believe you haven't done it before."

"They gave a course in tit-rubbing at the business school," he said, his eyes on something on a small table next to the chaise percée. Beneath a pile of *Vogues* and *Elles* was the same blue-covered folder he had seen in the Brandywine suite, the folder which Michael Brandywine had ordered him not to look at. As he felt Lady Kitty's hand pressing his genitals, he decided he wanted to read the folder.

"Why don't you slip down on top of me?" whispered Lady Kitty, who was getting aroused. "Just slide your body right down on mine."

"But we'll drown!"

"Idiot! I don't mean to *submerge* . . ."

"Do you want to do it here?"

"Yes, yes: here! Right in the tub!"

"Then why don't I let the water out?"

"God, you are the *least* romantic man! All right, let the water out. Then come lie on me. I want to be crushed in your manly arms—absolutely crushed!"

Repressing a strong desire to snicker, Bill pulled the plug, then lowered himself on top of Lady Kitty, who was writhing with sudsy ecstasy.

"You really dig sex, don't you?" he said.

"I adore it! Absolutely adore it! I've adored it ever since I was a little girl."

When the water had drained from the tub, she took his erection and inserted it in her. Their slick bodies merged.

Not bad, thought Bill. Not bad at all.

❧

When they had dried off, they went into the bedroom, where Lady Kitty put on a white peignoir. "You're good," she said. "Very good."

"So are you," said Bill truthfully.

"I think one should be creative about sex," she continued, sitting on the side of the immense bed. "People tend to make it so dull . . . in and out, in and out. Tiresome. Sex should be as exhilarating as a good dinner, and like a good dinner, half the pleasure is in the way the food is presented. Oh, don't put your clothes on yet."

Bill had reached for his underwear.

"Why?"

"Dear boy, I like to look at you. You're a beautiful man. I definitely don't like to look at your clothes. You dress with all the flair of Mr. Kosygin."

"Thanks. But don't you have to go to dinner soon?"

"Not for a while. Where do you eat?"

"With the staff."

"A Harvard man eating with the staff? Shocking. I'm surprised you'd stand for it."

"I don't mind."

"Why do you work for Michael?"

"The experience."

She eyed him shrewdly. "Learn the secrets of life at the top?"

He shrugged. "Why not. I already know the secrets of life at the bottom."

"I suppose you have a point. Why don't you come over and sit next to me instead of standing in the middle of the room like a clod?"

"Well, if you don't mind, I have to go to the john."

She laughed. "Why should I mind? We all share *that* secret of life at the bottom."

He returned to the bathroom and closed the door. Then, taking an amused glance at the tub, he pulled the blue-covered folder from the pile of magazines, sat down on the chaise percée, and began reading the "Report on Project Methuselah."

He didn't need to read far before he realized he'd found what he wanted.

❧

Three weeks passed uneventfully.

Ann filled her days with reading, sunbathing, swimming, and playing tennis with either Hugh Barstow, who was terrible, or Sally Mentius, who was excellent. Ann's increasing friendship with the doctor's chatty wife had offset her initial resentment of

Mentius's tactics, and it was largely through Sally that Ann came to grant that Mentius was, as his wife claimed, a careful man. He was almost too careful, in a way, for it was primarily the rigorous controls he and his associates maintained on the three patients that kept them in the lab from nine to five each day, excluding Sundays, and though she appreciated the need for them, Ann couldn't help but begin to resent the grueling schedule that kept her husband away from her so much of the time. It was aggravated by the fact that when he did return from the laboratory at five each afternoon, he spent the next hour to hour and a half with Bill Bradshaw, going over the day's business. Then, of course, each night at ten he climbed into the sleep capsule, closed the glass lid, and quite literally turned himself off till the next morning. As Dr. Mentius had predicted, their sex life was seriously curtailed by this schedule. And what infrequent moments of tenderness Ann was able to salvage from the small amount of time she was allowed with her husband were made somehow mechanical and unsatisfying by the very irregularity and hurried quality of their lovemaking. Because she saw so little of Michael, she began to worry that their relationship, which had always been somewhat tenuous because of his secretive nature, was deteriorating: she was less and less aware of what he was thinking and feeling. But after a while, something beside the infrequency of their contact began to alter their relationship; and it was something so, to her, truly miraculous, that at first she discounted what she saw as a trick of her imagination.

For by the third week of the Mentase treatment, it was becoming increasingly apparent that it was working.

Arnold Hirsch had lost ten pounds, and his banker's paunch had diminished to a slight bulge. Of course, the loss of weight could be attributed to the strict diet he and the others had been put on. But no diet could cause the change in his face. The sagging skin around his chin was tightening, and the skin itself was taking on a youthful ruddiness and losing its deep lines. While he had previously carried himself well for a man in his mid-seventies, there had been a slight stoop to his shoulders. This too had vanished, and he was walking erectly and with the springy step of a healthy man in his mid-fifties.

Lady Kitty's face, which had borne the harsh evidence of years of martinis, cigarettes, and indiscriminate sex, was softening in an equally remarkable manner. The pendulous bags under her once-bleary eyes were disappearing, and the eyes themselves had become bright and clear. When she had arrived at the chateau, her hair had had the cemented look of endless colorings that even the best hairdressers could not avoid. Now her hair, which had been reset in a new, more youthful style, looked softer and more natural, and glowed with a sunny golden color. No beautician, Ann knew, could have wrought such a complete transformation. And certainly the ex-actress's neck—notoriously the harshest indicator of a woman's age—was losing its gaunt look and assuming a middle-aged softness that was enormously flattering.

But it was with Michael that Ann detected the most miraculous change. On the evening of the third Thursday of the Mentase treatment, she was putting cuff links into his shirt as they dressed for dinner, when she noticed his hands. Though Michael had always been youthfully trim, his hands had had the gnarled look of an old man. The veins had been prominent, the knuckles slightly enlarged from incipient arthritis, and the skin flecked with liver spots. Now the knuckles were reduced in size, as were the veins, giving his hands the softer look of youth. But most extraordinary, the liver spots had entirely vanished.

"Is Mentius putting some sort of makeup on your hands?" she asked wonderingly.

"No. Why?"

"But, darling, your liver spots are all gone."

He inspected the back of his hands. "I know. I noticed it the other day. It's the Mentase."

Ann's voice took on an awed tone. "Then it really is working, isn't it? It's really making you younger."

"It seems to be. Mentius says in two more weeks we'll break through the sound barrier, which is what he calls the biological age of fifty. He says that's when over fifty percent of the cross-linkage will have been broken down."

"The links between the DNA molecules?"

"Yes. And then the really striking differences will begin to show. I'd say the treatment's turning out to be well worth the twenty-five thousand dollars, wouldn't you?"

She could hardly disagree. And that night, as she lay alone in her bed watching the white sleep capsule, which held her husband like a deep freeze holding a sirloin, Ann's mind swirled with the implications of Mentius's apparent success. There were the cosmic implications that he and Michael had discussed: the changes in the structure of society that would be inevitable if any appreciable portion of the population could maintain permanent youth and cheat death. With the population explosion becoming an increasingly grave problem and with sociologists predicting worldwide disaster in another few decades if some form of control weren't imposed on the earth's progenitive impulses, Ann could see how Mentase could fantastically aggravate the problem. But that didn't seem as immediate to her as the effect on herself and her marriage if, as seemed probable, her husband managed to halve his age. Michael had said they didn't like to discuss the difference in their ages, and he was right; it was something she tried to ignore. But of course it couldn't be; it made a difference, and she knew it. Unconsciously, she submitted to his wishes much more than a wife would submit to a man her own age. Michael was, she supposed, a father-figure as well as a husband, and the result was that she remained, to a degree, more of a child than a wife. The incident of the Piaget watch was an example. It was typical of Michael to buy her off, to shut her up by giving her a present, almost as if she were a child.

But what if he became closer to her own age? Would their relationship change? And how? Could a man's personality remain the same if his body "desenesced," to use Mentius's awkward neologism? Wasn't personality, to a degree at least, a reflection of one's physical condition? Wasn't an invalid's outlook on life conditioned by his sickness, and wouldn't the outlook change if the sickness were cured? Certainly, the old had a different view of life than the young: that was becoming more apparent with every day's headlines. The old were inherently more conservative, if for no other reason than that their life was behind them instead of before them. But what if the old suddenly were given a future of almost limitless life?

She couldn't believe Michael's personality wouldn't change. And what would that mean for her?

As she stared sleeplessly at the white capsule, through whose glass lid the faint blue nightlight glowed eerily, her future began to look as uncertain as once, such a short time before, it had looked secure.

Besides swimming and playing tennis, Ann had been going to the clinic's gymnasium every morning at nine thirty for an hour of exercise. The following day, Friday, she put on her leotards and went to the lab wing, stopping on the way to the gym at the Cosmetarium. Sally Mentius was planning a discothèque party that night in the Salle des Fêtes, and Ann wanted to make a hair appointment with Lisl Oetterli. But when she came into the Cosmetarium, one end of which was a fully equipped beauty parlor with two chairs, she found a new Italian girl had replaced Lisl.

"My name is Rosa," said the girl, who obviously spoke little English, but was trying. "Lisl is gone for a month."

"Oh? Is something wrong?" asked Ann.

"You didn't hear? She had a . . ." She stopped, gesturing helplessly. "What's the word? Ah, *sì:* she had a meescarriage; that's it. And the doctor gave her a month's vacation to rest. I'm taking her place."

Ann made her appointment with Rosa, then went on to the gymnasium where Stahling was working out on the parallel bars. Though Ann had been in the gym a number of times now, she still had not managed to get on a friendly basis with the physical therapist. It wasn't that he was unfriendly so much as that he was painfully shy, particularly, she thought, around women. Now she said good morning to him and began a series of limbering-up exercises at a bar he had installed for her on one wall. Remembering what Sally had told them about Stahling, Ann said casually, "I hear Lisl had a miscarriage?"

She was interested in the reaction of the supposed father, but it was hardly what she expected. Leaping off the parallel bars, he looked at her sullenly. "Excuse me, Mrs. Brandywine, but why did you say that to me?"

Ann looked uncomfortable. "Well, I just heard about it from the new girl upstairs, and . . . I was just making small talk . . ."

He shook his head. "That's not the truth, is it? Isn't the truth that Mrs. Mentius told you I had made Lisl pregnant?"

"Well, yes, she sort of implied it," Ann said, wishing she hadn't brought up the subject.

"It's a damned lie," he snapped. "That Lisl's a slut, and Mrs. Mentius had no business involving me in that filthy mess."

"What mess?"

"You don't think she really had a miscarriage?"

"What was it, then?"

He hesitated. "Mrs. Brandywine, I admire Dr. Mentius a great deal. He's been good to me, and I think he's a brilliant man. But what he's doing with these girls is disgusting."

"Do you mean *Mentius* is the father?" said Ann, genuinely surprised.

"No no, not that. He arranged to have them made pregnant."

Ann looked confused. "Arranged?"

"Arranged. Oh, it's been kept a big secret, but you see, my roommate, Kurt, is Lisl's brother, so I know what really happened. Lisl's one of them, and there are several others in Windischgratz —sluts like her. They've all been made pregnant, and now they've all been aborted by Mentius, who paid them to have it done."

"*Paid* them?" asked Ann, shocked.

"Yes. They did the whole thing for money. I'm far from being a prude, but I think it's disgusting. And Mrs. Mentius telling people I'm the father makes me damned mad."

"I don't blame you," said Ann. "But who *is* the father?"

"Lisl claims she was artificially inseminated."

"And then aborted?"

"Yes."

"But that doesn't make any sense at all!"

He shrugged. "I know. But that's what Lisl says happened. Mentius told her it had something to do with some tests he wanted to make on fetuses. I don't know. At any rate, while I don't particularly like Lisl, I believe her. Now the doctor's given her a month off to get her out of the chateau so none of you will start asking embarrassing questions. But since Mrs. Mentius is spreading lies about me, I don't see why I shouldn't defend myself, do you?"

Ann agreed, thinking that if what he said were true, Sally's behavior was anything but admirable. Nor was her husband's; and as Ann recalled her resentment at the way Mentius had tricked them into taking the sleep therapy test, she couldn't help but wonder why he was indulging in more subterfuge. Later that morning, when she joined Hugh Barstow at the tennis courts, the story became even more muddled.

"We have a new mystery," she said to Hugh as they took their rackets from the slip cases.

"What now?"

She told him what Stahling had said. Hugh's reaction was even stranger than the physical therapist's had been. To her surprise, he burst out laughing.

"What's so funny?" she asked.

"Sally Mentius," said Hugh. "If she and the good doctor are trying to cover up some funny business by making Stahling the bad guy, they sure as hell picked the wrong horse."

"Why?"

"Well, you see, Marty and I know this Kurt Oetterli. We, um . . ." He hesitated. "Well, let's say we have a business relationship with him, you know?"

"I know," said Ann, who several times had smelled the marijuana smoke seeping under the door that connected her bedroom with Martin Hirsch's. "It's those little brown packages you get from him."

Hugh squirmed. "Anyway, we've found out some things about this Kurt, and he is one sick baby."

"How sick?"

"Well, it depends on how you rate sickness these days, which I'll admit is pretty tricky. But let's say he's sick *enough*. At any rate, he and Stahling are a little more than roommates."

Ann blinked with surprise. "Oh. But Stahling doesn't *look* that way."

"They usually don't. Which is probably what fooled Sally Mentius. But Lisl told us. She hates Stahling."

"And he hates her."

"Yeah, it's cozy. Anyway, like I said, Mum Mentius sure picked a beauty to be the phantom father, if you know what I mean. Do you want the first serve?"

"But wait a minute, Hugh," said Ann. "Whatever Stahling's sex life is, don't you think we should find out the truth about Lisl? If Stahling's right about what Mentius did to her, then I'd like to know why he did it."

Hugh looked uninterested. "What do you care what Mentius does with the local chicks? Maybe he gets his kicks knocking them up with test tubes, then aborting them. Who knows? Nothing would surprise me. Come on, let's play tennis. I'm going to learn how to play this goddamn game if it kills me, which it probably will."

She started to argue further, then changed her mind. But as she aced Hugh twice in a row with well-placed services, she couldn't help wondering what Mentius was up to.

❧

That night after dinner they all went to the ballroom of the chateau where Sally Mentius had set up a hi-fi. In a rather feeble attempt to create a psychedelic mood, she had also hung strings of lightbulbs around the ornate walls of the Salle des Fêtes, then had them connected to a timer which winked and blinked them like a theater marquee. A waiter stood by, ready to pass glasses of lemonade which, as Lady Kitty sourly put it, "is hardly going to make the party swing." But it was an attempt. Hugh had volunteered to play disc jockey for the party, and as they entered the room, an electric rock number blared from the speakers so loudly that Dr. Mentius, who was more at home with Mozart and Buxtehude, winced. Arnold Hirsch, however, brightened considerably. To Ann's surprise, he came up to her and asked for a dance. "I know what you're thinking," he said. "The old fogey probably doesn't know anything newer than the gavotte. But I may surprise you." And, in fact, he did. Leading Ann out onto the huge empty dance floor with its intricate marquetry design, he broke into an energetic bugaloo. Ann laughed with delight and shouted over the music as she joined him, "Where did you learn that?"

"I've been practicing in my room!" he shouted back. "Part of my rejuvenation process."

Michael asked Lady Kitty to dance, and they joined Ann and Arnold, Lady Kitty breaking into a totally uninhibited dance she claimed to have made up herself, which resembled an apoplectic version of T'ai Chi. Martin Hirsch, looking bored and irritable, was sitting on the sidelines with Dr. Mentius and Sally. Though Sally tried to get him to dance with her, he sullenly declined. And after fifteen minutes, he excused himself and left the room. His father noticed this and frowned, but he said nothing to Ann, continuing his bugalooing with undiminished energy until his younger partner began to wish he'd wear out so she could sit down.

Hugh had just put on a particularly fortissimo rock number when there was a crash of glass, and an elbow smashed through a pane of one of the ornate glass doors that ringed the room. As the dancers swung around, the door burst open and Stahling literally fell into the room, sprawling on the gleaming parquet. Dr. de Villeneuve came in after him, grabbing his arm as he shouted angrily at him in German. Stahling shouted back, kicking viciously at his shins and struggling to free himself.

Mentius hurried over as Hugh lifted the needle from the record, stopping the music.

"Let him go, Claude," said Mentius. His assistant obeyed, and Stahling got to his feet. Ann saw that he was drunk; in fact, from the way he was swaying back and forth, royally drunk. He stared at Mentius. "You bastard," he said, slurring his speech. "Telling those lies about me."

Dr. Mentius looked at him with evident confusion. "What lies?"

Stahling pointed angrily at Sally Mentius, who was sitting at a nearby table watching with a frightened look on her face. "Ask her," he said. "Ask your wife what lies. She knows."

Mentius turned. "Sally, what's he talking about?"

Sally hurriedly got up from the table and came over to her husband, saying quietly, "Herbie, let's go to your office . . ."

"What's wrong?" said Stahling. "Afraid your rich patients will hear? Well, they *should* hear!" He pointed woozily at Ann. "*You* know, don't you, Mrs. Brandywine? What I told you was the truth, wasn't it? Or don't you believe me?"

Ann hesitated. "I'm not sure . . ."

"What *is* this?" said Mentius to his wife, with annoyance.

Sally looked miserable. "Herbie, it's just that I was uneasy about Lisl and the others, and I . . ." She glanced guiltily at Stahling.

"And she decided to make up a story about *me* being the father of the babies," finished Stahling. "Which was a hell of a thing to do!"

"I know," said Sally, "and I'm truly ashamed and sorry about it. I shouldn't have done it."

"But Mrs. Mentius," said a quiet voice from the door, "your husband is the one who should apologize, not you. For what he's done to my sister."

They turned to see a man in a motorcycle jacket standing inside the smashed door, his hands in his pockets, a slight smile on his pocked face. "Or aren't you admitting what you did, Doctor? Why don't you tell your patients? I'm sure they'd be fascinated with the whole procedure. Tell them what goes on in Pathology."

Mentius looked coolly at Kurt Oetterli. "I'm not ashamed of what I did, if that's what you're implying. And your sister was well paid for it."

"Perhaps. I'm not sure you can put a price on that." He looked around the room. "You have a very nice place here, Doctor. Very nice, and very private. Cut off from the outside world so your rich patients won't have anything bothering them." He looked back to Dr. Mentius. "But don't get the idea you can use the outside world without the outside world using you." He turned to Stahling. "Come on, Ernst. You've made a big enough ass of yourself. Let's get out of here."

"Not before I quit," slurred Stahling, glaring at Mentius.

"You're not going to quit," said Kurt. "And don't get so uptight about the lie Mrs. Mentius spread. Maybe you should be flattered." He smiled. "After all, nobody who knows you would believe it."

Stahling ignored him. "I'm quitting," he repeated with wounded dignity. "As of now. Resigning." With drunken haughtiness, he sniffed at Mentius, then weaved toward the door. When he reached Kurt, he turned and looked back at his former employer. "I would never work for a killer," he said, belching loudly. Kurt took his arm, muttered at him in German, and led him out. Mentius said to De Villeneuve in a low voice, "See that they get out all right. Tell Oetterli we'll give Stahling two months' severance pay."

"Yes, Doctor," said De Villeneuve, starting toward the door.

"But he was drunk, Herbie," said Sally. "He'll change his mind about quitting in the morning."

Mentius looked at her, then said to De Villeneuve, "Tell Oetterli what I said."

De Villeneuve nodded and hurried out of the room as Dr. Mentius turned to his patients. "I apologize for this," he said. "I'm afraid Stahling went a little off the deep end. We'll talk about it later. Mr. Barstow, why don't you put on some more music?"

Hugh hesitantly put on a new record and, as the music blared, the couples started dancing again. But the life had gone out of the party. And within ten minutes, they had all excused themselves and gone to bed.

❧

Ann waited until midnight, far past the time when Michael would be sound asleep in his capsule; then she got out of bed, slipped on a skirt and sweater, and went out of the bedroom through the living room of the suite into the large corridor. The chateau was silent. Crossing the corridor, she knocked lightly on Hugh Barstow's door. After a moment, he opened it. She whispered, "Is Lady Kitty still awake?"

He shook his head. "She's in her deep freeze for the night. A bomb couldn't wake her."

"May I come in?"

"Sure."

She went into his room, which was connected to Lady Kitty's bedroom by a large solid door, the same way Martin Hirsch's room across the hall was connected to Ann's bedroom. As Hugh noticed her looking at the door, he said, "She keeps it locked, so don't worry. Even if she weren't in her deep freeze, she wouldn't come in. She hasn't been in more than three times since we got here."

"Why?"

Hugh shrugged. "Who knows? Well, that's not exactly true: *I* know. But anyhow, you're not interested in my love life, or lack of it. What's up?" He turned off a portable radio he had been listening to and sat down, motioning to Ann to take a chair. He was still dressed.

"What did you think of Stahling's performance tonight?" said Ann, sitting down.

"I thought it was pretty weird."

"It's more than that. Obviously, both Stahling and Kurt believe the same version of the story, and whatever that is, it must be unpleasant enough for Sally Mentius to have felt obliged to make up a lie about it."

Hugh rubbed the side of his nose thoughtfully. "What do you think is in Pathology?"

"I'd certainly like to see."

"Yeah, me too. But they keep it locked, remember?"

"Couldn't we pick the lock?"

He shook his head. "That's no good." He thought a moment, then got up and went over to the window to look out. "Come here." She joined him. He pointed down at the roof of the lab wing, which was some five feet below his windowsill. "We could climb out this window and get on the roof. Then, you see that air-conditioning vent?"

He pointed to a large steel vent in the middle of the roof. Though it was a cloudy night, there was enough intermittent moonlight for Ann to see it.

"If I could get a rope, I could climb down that vent and crawl through the air-conditioning ducts till I got to Pathology. Then I could take a look around and if there was anything worth seeing, I could let myself into the room and unlock the doors. But I'd need your help. You game?"

She hesitated. "What if we got caught?"

He shrugged. "What can they do to us? Kick us out? Frankly, I wouldn't mind. This place is getting to me."

Ann thought a moment, then nodded. "All right. Where can you get a rope and flashlight?"

"Wait here," he said, going to the door. "Turn out the light."

She obeyed, watching him as he opened the door slightly and looked out into the corridor.

"I'll be back in a little while," he whispered. Then he let himself out into the hall and closed the door.

Ann waited over fifteen minutes in the dark, wondering if what she was about to do wasn't foolish. However, her curiosity about what was in Pathology overruled her caution, and when Hugh finally returned with a coil of thick rope, a flashlight, and a short aluminum ladder, she had decided to be a wholehearted accessory.

"Where did you get them?" she asked.

"Stole them from the garage."

Quietly, they placed the aluminum ladder on the roof, leaning the top against their windowsill. Hugh climbed out, with Ann following him. They easily made it to the roof. Then Hugh tied one end of the rope around his waist and looped the other around a short pipe near the vent.

"Now, as I go into the vent," he whispered, "you hold the other end of the rope. The pipe will take most of the strain. All you have to do is ease the rope out around the pipe as I go down. Understand?"

"Yes."

"When I get into Pathology, I'll give the rope one jerk. If there's anything worth seeing, I'll give two more jerks. That means you're to climb back in the window and come down to the lab wing. I'll let you in, if nobody's around. If there's somebody down there, or there's nothing particularly interesting, I'll give the rope three jerks, which means I'm climbing back up the vent. All you'll have to do is make sure the rope doesn't slip around the pipe."

"All right. Good luck."

"Yeah, I'll need it. Hope they haven't got the air-conditioning on. I'll freeze my ass."

Hugh climbed into the vent and let himself down as Ann held the rope. Though twice he seemed to get stuck, after twenty minutes she felt a sharp tug, indicating he had made it to Pathology. She waited for five more minutes, feeling a chill as the night wind began to blow in softly from the lake.

Then there were two jerks on the rope.

She hurried to the aluminum ladder and climbed back into Hugh's room. Letting herself out into the dark corridor, she hurried downstairs to the lab wing. A few night lights were on, but otherwise the chateau seemed deserted. She pushed through the stainless steel doors into the long white corridor of the lab wing. Hugh was standing in the open Pathology doors, motioning to her.

"Did you find anything?" she whispered as he hustled her inside and closed the doors. The room was pitch-black.

"I found out why Sally Mentius was so nervous she tried to blame it all on Stahling," he said, turning on the flashlight. He aimed the beam at a steel tank which rested in one side of a large double sink, then he led Ann over to it. "Take a look at this," he said. She peered in at the top of the tank. Inside, the steel walls narrowed slightly to form a chute, which led to a set of rotating knife blades.

"What is it?" she asked. "A meat grinder?"

"Bull's-eye."

He pointed the light at the counter next to the sink. On it stood five large glass jars. In three of them, floating in what looked like alcohol, were dead human embryos in approximately the fifth month of development.

Ann leaned against the empty sink, bent over it, and vomited.

In the morning, she came into the Salle d'Hercule where Dr. Mentius, Sally, Michael, Arnold Hirsch, and Lady Kitty were eating breakfast. She said nothing as she took her seat next to Michael, ignoring the polite greetings of the men. Her husband looked at her white face.

"Is something the matter?" he asked.

"Yes, there is," she said. "Dr. Mentius, would you answer a question for me, please?"

"Of course, Mrs. Brandywine."

"Do you believe an unborn baby is a human being?"

She watched his face intently.

"It's certainly not a conscious human being," he said carefully. "It lives, but until it has consciousness, it is only a potential human."

"Then I take it you feel no guilt when you murder the embryos in Pathology?"

Michael clanked his forkful of scrambled eggs onto his plate. "Ann, what in hell are you talking about?"

"Simply that Stahling was right. Dr. Mentius is a killer. Hugh and I broke into Pathology last night and found three dead embryos and a sickening machine that he apparently grinds them up in. Your great Dr. Mentius is nothing but a butcher."

Michael was furious. "You meddling bitch, you had no right to go in there!"

She was stunned. "No *right?* What about him? Does he have the right to grind up babies?"

"There's a perfectly valid reason for what he's doing—"

"Then you *knew* about this? You knew even before Stahling came in last night?"

"Of course I knew. I've known all along. So has Lady Kitty and Arnold. For Christ sake, don't make such a big thing out of it. The babies were aborted at the end of the fifth month. You're always yelping about how they should make abortion legal in New York—why should you make a scene about abortion in Switzerland, particularly when it's helping your own husband? Or don't you give a damn about your husband anymore, since you've taken to breaking and entering in the middle of the night with your precious Hugh?"

Ann stared at him.

"Michael, have you *seen* what he does in there?"

"Please, Mrs. Brandywine," interrupted Mentius. "I understand your shock, which is exactly the reason we have gone to great lengths to keep this a secret from you. But I think if you'll let me explain why we have to do it, you'll understand our position more sympathetically."

"I could never be sympathetic to butchery," she said, "and no amount of fast talk from you can convince me it's anything else!"

"You see?" Sally Mentius said to her husband. "I knew this would happen! That's why I tried to blame it all on Stahling . . ."

"That was a foolish idea, Sally," Mentius said tightly. "And I'd appreciate it if you'd let me know what you're doing from now on." He turned to Ann. "Mrs. Brandywine, I don't intend to 'fast-talk' my way out of anything. But you have to understand I am working with the biochemical building blocks of existence—deoxyribonucleic acid and ribonucleic acid. The human body is extraordinarily complex, and I am affecting its fundamental balance. Mentase is one of millions of enzymes in the body, only a fraction of which science has identified. There's a remote possibility that by reintroducing Mentase artificially into the body, its biochemistry may be put out of balance. We are taking every possible precaution to guard against this, which is one reason we have to keep the patients in the lab so much of the time. So far, fortunately, nothing seems to be going wrong. However, there's one thing my staff and I have seen happen in a few of the rats which were given Mentase, and which we are taking special steps to guard against. This is an imbalance in the ribonucleic acid in the brain cells, which can cause a loss of memory. That's why I needed the embryos."

Hugh, who had just come into the dining room, let out a low whistle. "Man, what's Lady Kitty's memory got to do with those bottle babies?"

"There are two theories of what memory actually is: the synaptic theory and the RNA theory. I won't bore you with the former, which deals with the nervous system, because I don't believe it. The second theory I do believe. It postulates that memory is stored by a chemical rearrangement of the structures of the ribonucleic acid molecules present in the brain cells. In other words, our memories, which constitute all our knowledge and ultimately our intellects, are stored in the RNA in our brains. If the supply of RNA is some way diminished, our memory is diminished also.

"When the rats began to lose their memory, we injected synthesized RNA into them. It did no good. But when we injected RNA extracted from the brains of baby rats into them, their memories were slowly restored. Now, to guard against the possibility of a memory loss in our human patients, I have had to have a supply of RNA on hand to give them in case the first signs of memory loss occurred. But I wouldn't dare give them animal RNA for the obvious reason that there would be a terrible risk in injecting, say, a rat's memory bank into a human—though I'll admit that some humans behave as if they had been receiving rat RNA. Nor could I use synthesized RNA, which is not only practically impossible to obtain in any appreciable quantities but had been ineffective with the rats. So I was forced to use RNA from human brains, and preferably from humans who had not yet formed memories of their own. The answer, obviously, was embryos—practically the only answer, since we couldn't use living, conscious humans. But because the procedure is somewhat ghoulish and would arouse outcries from sensitive people like yourself, I was forced to operate in secret. I considered approaching my friend, Dr. Bernardi, who runs the maternity clinic in Lausanne and who has a fairly regular supply of stillborn infants. But I was not only unsure of his reaction to my request, I was also extremely loath to tell him the reason behind it, for fear of his bringing in the local authorities and fouling us up in bureaucratic red tape. So I decided to hire five local girls, recruited by Lisl, and impregnate them artificially. Then, after five months, I aborted the embryos which, since there was no known father, the mothers had practically no emotional or sentimental attachment to. It was expensive, but the girls were willing."

He paused a moment. "To any doctor, of course, life is sacred. But there is a hierarchy of life. After all, a virus is alive. Cheese mold is alive. RNA, for that matter, is alive. Unless one is a Hindu or an antivivisectionist, which I'm not, one must agree that the lower life forms must on occasion be sacrificed for the higher forms. So the fact that the embryos live doesn't—at least in my eyes—make my destroying them murder, particularly when they are being used to benefit conscious human beings. I've aborted five and destroyed two, which has given us enough RNA for an immediate emergency. The other three embryos we're planning to destroy today. I don't like doing it anymore than you like my doing it. But I'll defend it. And while I take full responsibility, I honestly feel no guilt in what I've done."

There was a moment of silence. Then Ann quietly got up from the table.

"Where are you going?" said Michael.

"To my room to pack," she answered. Then, to Mentius: "Everything you said may make beautiful sense to a scientist, Doctor. But I've seen the knives in that machine. I'm afraid I couldn't spend another night in a human abattoir. I'm going back to New York."

Michael angrily called after her, but she walked out of the room without answering.

❧

Minutes later, Michael stormed into their suite to find Ann packing. He came up to the bed and started taking her things out of the suitcase. Angrily she tried to stop him. "Michael, I'm leaving!"

"No, you're not. You behaved like a squeamish ass downstairs."

"Squeamish? Because I object to having babies turned into sausage? God, what would it take to make *you* squeamish?"

"Herbert Mentius is a fine and brilliant man and you're acting as if he's some sort of ghoul."

"Maybe, but he's become obsessed with making the Mentase treatment work. And obsessed people find it easy to rationalize what they do. Look what he did to us in those Aquadorme tanks! Oh, he explained it all and it was all perfectly harmless—except the fact remains he robbed us of three days of our lives."

"You're exaggerating."

"That's *exactly* what he did. Now he's grinding up babies to help older people keep their memory, and his marvelous ability to rationalize makes it all sound as bland as taking aspirin. Even he admits he was afraid to tell the doctors in Lausanne what he's up to, which doesn't sound to me like the most ethical thing going. It obviously doesn't bother you, but it bothers the hell out of me—call me squeamish if you like. So I'm going home. You don't need me here. Good Lord, I hardly ever see you, what with that damned sleep-capsule thing."

She gestured angrily at the sleep capsule at the foot of the bed. Michael looked at it, then laughed. "So *that's* what it is."

"That's what *what* is?"

"That's what's making you mad. You don't like my sleeping in the capsule, isn't that it?"

"I'm not *fond* of you being in that tin tube every night, no. But that's not why I'm yelling . . ."

"Come here."

She stopped her packing. "Michael, you can't sweet-talk me into staying. If you'd seen that thing in the lab . . ."

"I know, but come here anyway."

Reluctantly, she obeyed. He took her in his arms and kissed her. "Please stay," he whispered. "I know it's hard on you—it's hard on both of us. I'm as eager to get out of here as you are . . ."

In spite of herself she began to relax in the warmth of his arms. "Oh Michael, I want to go home! This place gives me the creeps."

"I know. But the treatment is working, and we'll be home soon. Tell me you'll stay. Please. I really want you to."

She looked at him closely, trying to read his mind. Did he really need her after all? Or was this just an act? Was he maneuvering her, as he had maneuvered her with the diamond watch? Now was it sex?

A knock on the door diverted their attention. "Excuse me," said Dr. Mentius, who was standing in the bedroom doorway with Arnold Hirsch and Lady Kitty behind him. "May I talk to you a moment?"

Ann and Michael went into the living room of the suite where Mentius said, "Mrs. Brandywine, I understand your reaction, and I honestly don't blame you. But I'm sure your husband wants you to stay—we all do, for that matter. While I'm aware the treatment is a strain on all our nerves, I hope we can keep together till the end. And despite a certain amount of unorthodoxy in my methods, I think you'll agree that already the Mentase has made some remarkable changes in your husband."

"I don't deny that."

"So I wanted you to know that we won't use the three other embryos, and there will be no further production of RNA. This way, I hope there will be no reason you can't stay with us. I give you my word there will be nothing else done that will offend your sensitivity, which I respect."

Ann said nothing for a moment, trying to gauge his sincerity. Then Lady Kitty spoke up. "I think *we* should have something to say about that!"

Mentius turned to her. "Lady Kitty," he said rather forcefully, "it's desirable that this group stay together, and that means that Mrs. Brandywine stays."

"It's more important to me that I don't lose my memory! If there's a real danger, I want all the protection I can get."

"It's not a danger, just a possibility," Mentius said. "And we have enough RNA to handle an emergency."

"But what's 'enough'? If I start to go blank, won't you need a great deal of the stuff?"

"That depends . . ."

"Please don't equivocate with *me*, Doctor. After all, what gets first priority around here? I, who may lose my memory, or the midwestern sensitivities of Mrs. Brandywine? She's not paying ten thousand pounds for the treatment, and it's not her memory that's being jeopardized. I'm paying the money and taking the risk, and I want protection."

For a moment, no one said a word. Ann noticed that both Mentius and Michael had turned to Arnold Hirsch, who had been listening without interrupting.

"Well?" said Lady Kitty.

"Perhaps I might be allowed to cast my vote," said Arnold, "since I'm taking the risk also. First, I think Dr. Mentius should tell us how great he considers the possibility of a memory loss to be."

"I can only tell you what happened with the rats," answered Mentius. "We gave fifty rats the Mentase treatment. Out of those fifty, three of them experienced temporary memory loss."

"Then that's six percent," said Arnold. "Allowing for variables, I think we can safely say there is a ten percent possibility that one of us may have difficulty. Since there are only three of us, I think the odds are greatly in our favor; and I definitely think, as the doctor has said, that Mrs. Brandywine ought to stay."

"Why?" asked Ann.

"Because, frankly, the treatment is an exhausting and frightening experience for all of us. I want my son near me, and I'm sure your husband wants and needs you."

"But you didn't bring Martin here to keep you company. You bribed him to come here so you could try to get him off drugs."

Arnold's eyes widened slightly, but otherwise his face remained impassive. Ann felt a grudging admiration for the way he could keep his emotions under near-perfect control. "What you say is only half true, Mrs. Brandywine, I *did* want to be with my son. Unfortunately, since my son dislikes me, I knew the only way I could get him to come was, as you say, to bribe him."

Ann felt momentarily embarrassed. Then Michael put his arm around her waist. "As I told you, it's important you stay," he said. "All of us need support. If you feel so strongly about the embryos, then as far as I'm concerned I'd rather take the chance on my memory than lose you."

"Well then," said Arnold, "that's two votes for Mrs. Brandywine staying. I'm afraid you're in the minority, Lady Kitty."

The ex-actress turned her large eyes on Ann. Her face, which looked as if it had already shed ten years, was icy.

"All right, I'll go along with the majority. But if something happens to one of us, Mrs. Brandywine, I will hold you personally responsible." She turned to Mentius. "Shall we go down to the lab?"

The doctor nodded, and they filed out of the suite.

❧

She sat alone for a while, thinking about what she had just heard. Then she went downstairs to the Salle d'Hercule where Hugh was still at the table, drinking his coffee. Everyone else was gone, and the footmen had cleared the plates.

"I'm surprised you didn't come up to see the show," she said, taking a seat next to him.

"I've got a headache," was his listless reply. "The last thing I need is a lot of excitement. Are you leaving?"

She shook her head. "No. They sort of ganged up on me and talked me out of it." She picked up a spoon and toyed with it. "Hugh, do you see much of Martin Hirsch?"

"No."

"He hardly ever comes downstairs for meals. Where does he eat?"

"When you're popping blackbirds, you don't have any appetite."

"Blackbirds?"

"Amphetamines. They give you a freaky high, and a worse low afterward. Between the blackbirds and the hash, Marty-baby doesn't need food."

"I see. You don't suppose he sees much of his father?"

"Are you kidding? They haven't said two words to each other since we got here."

"But Arnold must know he's smoking. I've smelled the marijuana fumes coming under the door between my bedroom and his; and Arnold's suite is on the other side of Martin's room. So why doesn't he smell it too?"

"Maybe he does."

"Then why doesn't he do something about it?" she exclaimed. "Does it make any sense to pay your son three thousand dollars to come here so you can keep an eye on him, be with him, and then, a, do absolutely nothing while he sits in his room using drugs all day, and b, never say a word to him the few times you do see him?"

"It doesn't make any sense at all," said Hugh. "So?"

She glanced around the mammoth red dining room to make sure none of the footmen was present. "Hugh, remember when we first got here, you and Martin and I walked to the waterfall? And Martin was wondering why his father had brought him, and Lady Kitty had brought you?"

"I remember."

"I'm beginning to wonder the same thing. I mean, just now, it seemed so important to all of them not only that I not leave, but that none of us leave. But why is it so important? Take you, for instance. How much do you see of Lady Kitty?"

"Not much, thank God."

"You said last night she kept the door between your rooms locked, and you said you knew why."

He nodded, rubbing his hand over his forehead. "Yeah, it's a simple enough reason. She's banging your husband's assistant—what's his name?"

Ann looked surprised. "Bill?"

"That's him. I've heard him in her bedroom quite a few times. Christ, once they even got in the tub together and took a bath! That's one of Kitty Kitty Bang Bang's favorite indoor sports, and it sounded like he dug it too."

Ann smiled. "What a sly one Bill is! He's so serious most of the time—you know, all business."

"Guess again. Anyway, to answer your question, Lady Kitty doesn't miss me, and I sure as hell don't miss her. So why am I here? You tell me. Except I still don't have enough money to go home."

Ann ran her index fingernail slowly back and forth under her chin. "Lady Kitty certainly likes variety, doesn't she?"

"Given half a chance, she'd take on the whole human race."

"Michael told me she and Arnold Hirsch had slept together at one time. That's why they pretended not to know each other."

Hugh shrugged. "Could be. Anyway, what brilliant conclusion have you come to?"

She sighed. "I'm not sure. Maybe they really do need us here for moral support. I suppose it is frightening for them." She smiled at Hugh. "All right: I'll try to quit playing detective. How about a set of tennis?"

He shook his head. "No thanks. I'm going back to bed."

"Is the headache that bad?"

"Worse," he said, getting to his feet. She noticed he looked unusually pale.

"Would you like some Placidine?" she suggested.

He forced a smile. "I hate to tell you, Ann, but your husband's miracle headache pill stinks." He started for the door. "See you around the funny farm."

❧

That evening at nine thirty, Bill Bradshaw knocked lightly on Lady Kitty's door, looking nervously behind him at the door to his employer's suite. Knowing Michael Brandywine's uncertain temper, Bill had gone to great lengths to keep his meetings with Lady Kitty a secret, and so far he thought he had been successful.

But every time he came to her suite he was risking meeting either Michael or his wife in the hall. And though he had suggested to Lady Kitty they choose some other place, she had refused on the grounds that the price she was paying for her suite entitled her to use it. So he took the chance. It was worth it, he figured, if he was successful with her, and so far he had no reason for pessimism. She had not seemed adverse to his carefully made suggestion that he "guide her" in a few investments. She had, in fact, seemed mildly interested. And though he had to operate with supreme tact—and, in the process, keep Lady Kitty in a good humor, which was no mean trick—he allowed himself to believe that things were really going very well.

However, when she opened the door, her look was distinctly chilly.

"Oh, it's you," she said. "Come in." She held the door as he came into her living room. "Do you want a drink?" she asked as she returned to the chair she had been reading in. "If you do, you know where it is." Picking up the skirt of her pale green peignoir, she sat down and opened a copy of *The Love Machine*. Then she picked up a half-eaten apple from the table beside her and took an angry bite.

"Are apples on your diet?" said Bill, pouring himself a Scotch.

"They are now."

"How's the book?"

"I'd rather *do* it than read about it." She put the book down. "How is that repulsive toad of a woman across the hall?"

"You mean Mrs. Brandywine?"

"Do you know any other toads around here? Of course I mean Mrs. Brandywine. Simpering little bitch!"

"What's she done?"

She gestured impatiently. "You wouldn't understand. It's just that she's such a little Pollyanna—God! She makes me sick." She glanced at Bill. "Does she play around?"

"I don't think so."

"What about with Hugh? I've seen them together a lot, and her husband's beginning to get suspicious."

Bill shook his head. "I wouldn't bet on it. She's pretty much a straight arrow."

"I *loathe* straight arrows."

Bill sat down next to her. "Come on, tell me. Get it out of your system."

She shrugged. "Oh, it happened this morning. A tedious brouhaha with Mentius. She made trouble for all of us over some stupid moral principle."

"How did she do that?"

"Don't try and pump me, dear boy. I tell you what I want you to know, nothing more."

Bill looked into his highball glass. Lady Kitty's anger at his employer's wife was perhaps a propitious sign after all. Should he make the move now? It was risky, but why not? It was always going to be risky, and a better opportunity might not present itself for a long time. If it was going to work, he couldn't afford to wait much longer.

He looked up at her. "What if I told you I know a lot more than you think?"

"And just what do you mean by that incomparably fatuous remark?"

"Just that I know what Mentase is."

She looked genuinely surprised. "How did you find out?"

"For one thing, I've watched you and the others getting younger faster than can be explained by any regular rejuvenation treatment. And I read the report that was in your john."

Now she looked angry. It was a calculated risk to tell her the truth, but he felt it necessary.

"I don't like spies."

"Not even if they're on your side?"

Her plucked eyebrows raised. "And how are you on my side?"

He leaned forward in the chair. "Michael Brandywine is up to something," he said. "He's transferred a lot of his Brandywine Drug stock into a company someone has set up here in Lausanne. He's keeping the whole thing under wraps—even I'm not supposed to know about it."

"Then how did you find out?"

"I read a report from his broker. It was a mistake, I wasn't supposed to see it. But I didn't tell him."

She looked interested. "Go on."

"Now, it doesn't take any brains to figure that if Mentase can do what it's supposed to do—and judging from the way the three of you look, it can—it's going to be one of the most valuable products in history."

"True."

"And I can't believe it's just a coincidence that Michael Brandywine is here, taking the treatment, and at the same time transferring stock to a company called the Société Gérontologique."

"That's the name of the company in Lausanne?"

"Yes. Are you interested?"

"Definitely. Fascinated, in fact. I think you're really on to something."

"So do I," said Bill, feeling exhilarated by her encouragement. "I figure Brandywine is trying to sew up the marketing rights to Mentase, which must be worth billions. And the idea came to me that someone else ought to have a crack at them."

"For instance?"

He hesitated, watching her eyes which, in turn, were watching his. "Well, you."

"I see." She mulled this over. "Yes, why not? Except I'm not in the drug business."

"But you have capital!" said Bill eagerly. "And I have know-how! I know almost as much about the drug business as Michael Brandywine—Christ knows, I ought to, the way I've worked for him all these years. If I had your money behind me, I could make a deal with Mentius and set up our own company."

"Ours?"

"Ours. You could be chairman. I could be president, or whatever. Hell, the titles aren't important. If I had enough money to bid for the rights to Mentase, once we had them there isn't an underwriting house in the world that wouldn't fight for the chance to finance us. Christ, they'd be falling all over themselves. We could set up the production facilities, create a first-class promotion campaign, and then sit back and watch the money roll in."

He paused. Lady Kitty seemed to be absorbing what he had said. She got up and walked thoughtfully around the room, rubbing her finger over the tops of several of her photos' silver frames. Then she looked at him.

"I've underestimated you, Bill. Oh, not in bed—you've quite lived up to expectations there. But I had no idea you could be so ingenious."

He smiled hopefully. "You *do* see it, then?"

"Oh, most definitely. Of course, it all depends on whether the rights are still available. Brandywine may have already made a deal with Mentius."

"Then we'd be in no worse shape than we are now, would we?"

"But, dear boy, I'm not in bad shape."

"Well, I meant as far as the rights are concerned. And I have the feeling he's still negotiating with Mentius. If he had the rights sewn up, what point would there be in all this secrecy?"

"Well, there might be *some* point," she said thoughtfully. "How much do you think the rights would cost?"

"I have no idea. But unless Mentius is a fool, I'd think it would take at least several million up front. Then of course he'd get the royalties."

"Several million?" She leaned against the desk, eyeing him. "That's a lot of money."

"Mentase will make more."

"I suppose you're right. Yes. So, I take it you want to sound him out?"

"I'd like to. But I couldn't do it unless you'd back me up with cash."

"But dear boy, I'd be a fool not to, wouldn't I?"

"I think so." He grinned. "But it's your money, and without you I'm nowhere. So I'm prejudiced."

She laughed and came up behind his chair. "I know, but you've used your brains, and I admire that. Cleverness is a rare commodity, and it deserves a reward." She rubbed her beautifully manicured hands through his thick black hair.

It worked! he thought. Goddamn, it worked!

"When you're in my shoes, you've got to use your brains."

Suddenly she leaned over him, dug her long nails into his right cheek, and scratched them fiercely down his face. As the pain shot through him, he jumped out of the chair, clapping his hand to his searing cheek. He stared at her. "What the hell are you doing?"

She was standing behind the chair, eyeing him contemptuously. "That's your reward for using me, you little pimp."

He was staring at the blood on his palm. Quickly, he pulled a handkerchief from his pocket and held it to his face.

"I don't understand—"

"I won't tell Michael about your tacky attempt at treachery because I don't want him to know I've been sleeping with you. If you're smart, you'll keep quiet too. Now get out of here. And don't come back peddling your dreary charms."

"But why? What's wrong? It's a good idea. You said so yourself!"

"It's so good, don't you think it's already been thought of?"

"By whom?"

"By me, for one. For your information, I happen to be the third largest stockholder in the Société Gérontologique, 17 Place St. François, Lausanne. Now get out. You've got a long way to go before you're ready to play with the big boys and girls. A *very* long way."

She watched him as he made his way uncertainly toward the door. As he passed the mirror, he looked at his reflection. "I think you've scarred me."

"It will give your face character. A quality it sadly lacks."

He put the handkerchief back to his cheek. "You really are a filthy bitch."

She smiled. "Dear boy, that's probably the truest thing you've ever said."

❧

Ann hadn't seen Sally Mentius for several days. The reason, she thought, was that Sally was ashamed for the lie she had told about Stahling. Then one sunny afternoon as Ann was sitting on the terrace of the chateau rereading *The Charterhouse of Parma,* Sally came up to her.

"Would you like to take a boat ride?" she asked.

"I'd like to very much."

"Good. I'll give you a tour of the lake."

Ann put her book aside and joined Sally as they started through the formal garden toward the boathouse.

"Do you like Stendhal?" asked Sally.

"He's one of my favorite authors."

"Mine too." She said nothing for a few steps, as if searching for a new subject. Finally she said, "I understand Hugh Barstow's not feeling well. Headaches."

"Yes, he had one at breakfast the other day."

"I told him he should let Herbie take a look at him. There must be something wrong when they keep up for so long."

Another silence. Ann had the feeling Sally was making small talk to avoid saying what was really on her mind. They reached the pier and went into the boathouse, where a handsome Chris-Craft runabout was tied up. Sally threw off the lines, and the two women climbed in the boat, giving a push to float it out of the slip. Then Sally started the motor, circled the boat around, and began to follow the wooded shoreline in a leisurely circumnavigation of the lake.

"I wanted to tell you," she finally said, "that I felt very bad about what I did to Stahling."

"Did he quit?"

"Yes, and it was really my fault. I feel dreadful about it. And about lying to you. I don't *like* lying."

She said the last rather grimly, and Ann felt she meant it.

"Well, it's all over now," said Ann. "Maybe I shouldn't have made such a fuss about it, I don't know."

"There are some things that I suppose are necessary whenever something new like Mentase is discovered," continued Sally. "I was as disgusted as you were about the fetuses, but Herbie told me he thought it was necessary so I went along with it. At any rate, I didn't want you to dislike me. I hope you'll accept my apology."

"Of course," said Ann, glad to be friends again.

"You see," Sally went on, "I love Herbie very much. He's terribly bright and terribly dedicated. But in some ways he's weak. No, that's really not the word . . ."

"Obsessed?" suggested Ann.

"Yes, I suppose that's what it is. He is obsessed with this whole treatment and Mentase. I can understand it: He's worked so long on it—it's been over ten years. And he's had to overcome so many obstacles: not just the scientific problems, but money problems, colleagues' skepticism. . . . God, it's really been a struggle at times. Anyway, now that it seems to be actually working, and he seems to be so close to a real victory . . . well, you can imagine his state of mind. And needless to say, he's trying his damndest to make sure nothing goes wrong. He's even . . ." She hesitated as she guided the boat around a small, pine tree-covered islet. "Well, he's even been devious about some things. I don't like the word, but there it is."

"You mean about the fetuses?"

"Yes, and putting the three of you out for three days without telling you. Let's face it, he was devious. I don't think he should be, but he seems to feel it's necessary." She added sourly, "Arnold Hirsch certainly thinks it is."

Ann looked surprised. "Arnold? What does it matter what he thinks?"

"Well, it doesn't, actually."

Ann felt she was suddenly lying again, despite her announced dislike for it.

"The other day," said Ann, "when everyone was trying to talk me out of leaving the chateau, I remember that your husband seemed to, well, almost defer to Arnold Hirsch. Why would that be?"

Sally was staring straight ahead.

"I have no idea," she said. Ann thought she was still lying. Then, suddenly, she turned and looked directly into Ann's eyes.

"But I'll tell you one thing," she said quietly. "I hate Arnold Hirsch."

This time, Ann knew she was telling the truth.

❧

That night Ann was awakened from a troubled sleep by a sound in her room. Michael was, as usual, asleep in the capsule. A figure was scurrying past the windows. She could hear its heavy breathing. She froze.

Now the figure was invisible in the darkness. She carefully reached for the bedlight switch. Then the figure loomed over her bed. She screamed and rolled over, turning the lamp on and, simultaneously, knocking it to the floor. The figure plunged a knife into the mattress beside her. Sobbing with fright, she fell off the bed onto the floor and looked back.

It was Martin Hirsch. He was sitting on the side of the bed, giggling. He was wearing a filthy sweatshirt, khaki pants, and sneakers, and he looked as if he hadn't shaved for a week. In his hand was the knife, which he pointed at Ann.

"Scared you, didn't I?" he said.

She whispered, "How did you get in?"

He pointed to the double doors that led from the Brandywine bedroom to his room. They were open. He touched the knife. "I sprang the lock. It's easy, particularly with a few blackbirds to boost the imagination."

He threw himself at her from the bed, plunging the knife toward her neck, freezing as its point touched her throat.

"Martin, stop it—"

He laughed and stood up. "Come on! Kicks! It's all kicks. Uppies are the greatest kick of all. You live, man, really live! Live dangerously! You see how thin that little old line between life and death is. Thin as this knife blade, you know? Do you want some ups? I'll give you a pill, if you want. I've got plenty in my room."

She shook her head. He shrugged. "You don't know what you're missing."

He spotted the sleep capsule and hurried over to it, peering through the glass lid at Michael. "There he is," he said softly. "Michael Brandywine, big tycoon, like my old man. Titan of Wall Street, all that jazz. He looks like a corpse in his glass coffin. Don't you hate tycoons?"

"I don't know," said Ann weakly, playing along, hoping he would come off his high.

"I do. I hate all tycoons. All big deals. All perfect people. Did you know my father is perfect? Pluperfect. *The* successful man. The pillar of the community. Just like your husband, I'll bet." He slowly drew the point of the knife across the glass lid.

"What are you doing?" said Ann.

"Playing. Playing cutthroat. The perfect death for the perfect man. Cut the throat and within thirty seconds the brain is dead.

But those thirty seconds . . . is the brain still alive? I read once where Somerset Maugham was on Devil's Island, and the executioner told him one of the men he was going to guillotine had said if his head was still alive when it fell into the basket, he would wink at him. And Maugham said the executioner told him the head winked."

Ann shuddered. "Martin, stop playing ghoul. And please put that knife away before you hurt me or yourself."

He was now cutting a large X in the glass. "Oh, I wouldn't hurt anyone," he said, "except maybe my father. Yes, I'd hurt my father if I had the nerve. The old Oedipus bit, you know. Kill the father, sleep with the mother. Except I killed the mother." He giggled. "Do you suppose that means I want to sleep with my father?"

He looked up at her. "It really was my fault, you know. The accident, I mean."

"What accident?"

"The one that killed my mother. My father hushed it up, naturally. He couldn't let it get in the papers that the son of the Arnold Hirsch, one of the richest, most respected men in the country, that *his* son was driving a car stoned on pot and that he lost control and smashed the car into a tree. And that his mother was sitting next to him, and that she was *decapitated?*" He looked as though he were reliving the experience. "And that her head fell into his *lap?* His own mother's head? I mean, it was something out of Grand Guignol! Except . . ." And now he turned directly to Ann. "Except the head didn't wink, you know? It just looked surprised."

He stood for a moment, staring at her. Then he started roaming aimlessly around the room, flipping the knife into the air and catching it by its handle. "That's why my father hates me, of course," he continued in a calmer tone. "I killed his beloved Marion through the worst of all possible crimes, by his standards: irresponsibility. Pot. A stupid weed killed his wife. So I'm no good. All the young are no good, according to him. We are all funky, creepy, lazy, worthless, dirty, grubby, disgusting freaks who *kill* . . ." He stopped and lowered his voice. "But he killed her too. Killed her by his perfection. For the last fifteen years they had never slept together once, and Mother wanted to. . . . She told me! She wasn't that old. But he was. Or he didn't care. Or it was too dirty for him, too animal, too . . . grubby. So they were both sleeping like in these cryogenic capsules, you know? Cool, perfect, clean . . . untouched. He killed her too."

He stopped, suddenly seeming to wind down. He looked at Ann, then closed his eyes and shook his head as if trying to clear his mind.

She said, "Do you mean your father's impotent?"

He nodded. "A flat tire."

"Then . . ." She stopped, thinking what Michael had told her about Lady Kitty. Cautiously, she came closer to Martin, who had sagged into a chair. "Martin," she said softly, "you told me your father had known Lady Kitty before he met her here."

"That's right."

"Would it be possible that he and Lady Kitty had been sleeping together?"

"How could that be? I'm telling you, he's impotent. What gave you that idea?"

"My husband. He said that's what your father had told him."

Now Martin was sitting up. "And you believed that?"

"Of course I believed it."

"Then you're stupid. You mean you haven't figured out what's going on here yet? They're lying to us! All of them, including your husband. Do you know your husband and my father meet?"

She sat on the edge of the bed. "You mean in the lab?"

"No, other places. I mean, I'm sure they talk in the lab, too, but your husband comes to my old man's suite. I've overheard them talking together a couple of times."

"Talking about what?"

He raised his knife in a gesture of mock conspiracy. "When tycoons meet, they plot! They plot the death of youth! Kicky, isn't it?"

"Martin, be serious. What are they plotting?"

He lowered the knife. "I *am* being serious. He and my father and Lady de Ross have formed a company that's going to manufacture Mentase. It's called the Société Gérontologique, except it's not going to be just another drug company."

"Wait a minute. You mean they've formed this company since they came here to the chateau?"

"No! You don't understand anything, do you? They did it a long time ago."

"But how could they? They didn't know each other?"

He shook his head wearily. "But I'm telling you, they *did*. My father has known Lady de Ross for years, and he's known your husband too—how long, I don't know. This whole thing about first meeting each other when they got here was an act."

"Martin, what is it you've heard them saying?"

"I've heard my father and your husband talking on the phone—like, to big international lawyers, dig? They've got two of them coming to Lausanne in a couple of weeks—that's where this Société has its office. And the lawyers are going to start going to all the capitals of the world and make distribution deals for Mentase."

"What distribution deals?"

He shook his head impatiently. "You can't sell Mentase on the open market—don't you see that? Do you think every Joe Blow Schlepp is going to be able to run down to his friendly corner drugstore and pick up a bottle of immortality? Of course not. It's going to be sold to a limited number of people on a very selective basis. Those that qualify get it, those that don't, zap."

"What do you mean, those that 'qualify' get the Mentase?"

"All I know is, that's the phrase my father used on the phone. But knowing my old man, I assure you he's not going to be giving it out to Yippies. My father is really a Fascist, you know."

"Oh, come on, Martin. That's such an overworked word."

"All right, he doesn't have an armband and jackboots. But I can guess who's going to 'qualify' for the Mentase treatment. Bankers. Fat cats. Conservatives. It's going to be the Establishment's answer to pot. Christ, while my generation is spaced out on grass, *his* will be shooting Mentase and outliving us! For the first time in history the whole cycle of generations will be reversed. The parents will bury their children—and not from childhood diseases. From old age!"

The idea was so stunning that for a moment Ann almost believed it. But it was too monstrous. Too baroque. Or was it?

"You think I'm making this all up, don't you? You think I'm just some freaky head."

"I don't know," she said uncertainly.

He started back toward his room. "Ask my old man," he said. "Go ask him. Maybe he'll tell you the truth. I doubt it, but ask him." He started to close the door, then he leaned around, stuck the knife up in the air and, in his mock-conspiratorial put-on pose, said, "The death of youth! The perpetual youth of age! Spooksville, *nyet?*"

Grinning devilishly, he slowly closed the door.

❧

Ann's mind was too full of what Martin had said to sleep. If what he told her was true, and not drug-induced fantasy, then the elaborate charade that had been going on since they arrived at the chateau made some sense. The Société Gérontologique was potentially a frightening thing, and anyone involved with it would be careful to keep its existence—and certainly its purpose—quiet. But could it be possible her husband was involved with it? Her own husband? It seemed incredible, but Mentase had seemed incredible at first, and now she was seeing its power become more evident every day in the desenescing faces of Michael, Lady Kitty, and Arnold Hirsch. Should she confront Michael and force him to tell her the truth? But she had done that already, and he had squirmed out of it. No, the more she thought about it the more she decided Martin was right. She should go to Arnold Hirsch. He was the key: quiet, courtly, unobtrusive Arnold, who had surprised her so much with his bugalooing at the discothèque party.

She would go to Arnold Hirsch. But she would be careful. There was obviously a conspiracy of silence—a Mentase conspiracy, as she thought of it. If they were all playing for such high stakes, they wouldn't tolerate anyone—even her—asking too many questions.

❧

In the morning, Ann met Sally Mentius in the entrance hall of the chateau. "A letter for you," said Sally. "It's from Larchmont."

"That's my brother," replied Ann, taking the letter.

"And here's an invitation." She handed Ann a heavy envelope with a coronet embossed on the flap. "It's from Lady Kitty," continued Sally, adding dryly, "Her family crest is two men couchant on an actress rampant."

Ann smiled as she removed an invitation from the envelope. It read: "The pleasure of Mr. and Mrs. Michael Brandywine's company is requested at a bal masqué in honor of Lady Katherine de Ross. Eight thirty o'clock. Saturday, the eighth of July. The Chateau Mirabelle. Windischgratz. RSVP." Ann looked up. "Why's Lady Kitty giving a party?"

"It's for her birthday. Or rather, her *un*-birthday, as she called it. It's to celebrate passing fifty the other way."

"How weird."

"It is, but I suppose she has a point, I mean, it *is* something to celebrate, isn't it? And she's having a tremendous blast: well over two hundred people are coming, all her International Set pals. It should be a real show. Herbie's not very happy about it, though."

"Why?"

"Well, it comes halfway through the treatment, which is bad. And he doesn't like a lot of people running all over the place. But she insisted, so he gave in. She's having the whole thing catered, so at least I'll be able to give the staff the weekend off, which they should like." She lowered her voice. "Did you hear about Hugh Barstow?"

"No."

"He has a brain tumor."

Ann looked shocked. "Oh, no!"

Sally nodded. "His headaches kept getting worse and finally he went to Herbie, who took an EEG—you know, an electroencephalogram—and there it was—a tumor."

"Does he think it's malignant?" asked Ann, thinking about easy-going Hugh who didn't seem as though he had a problem—certainly not a health problem—in the world.

"He hopes not. He's taking it out this afternoon, at two. Of course, if it is malignant . . . Well, it could be very iffy for Hugh. But if it isn't, Herbie says he can be up and around in a few days."

"God, poor Hugh! Where is he?"

"In the infirmary, in the lab wing. They're operating in the surgical suite at the very end of the wing."

"May I go to see him?"

"Not till after the operation."

"Could I send him something? Some flowers, at least?"

"I was going to have the gardener fix something nice from all of us. Nothing funereal, but cheerful. What do you think?"

"Definitely. A brain tumor!" She hesitated. "Is Lady Kitty upset?"

Sally sniffed somewhat disdainfully. "Wait till lunch and see for yourself."

❧

Lady Kitty didn't mention Hugh once during lunch. Instead, she babbled on to Michael about the decorations for the party and the guest list, taking every opportunity to drop as many European titles as she could manage and making it obvious that she intended it to be *the* party of the year. Mentius was not at the table—Sally explained that he never ate before an operation—nor was Arnold Hirsch who, Sally said, had gone to his suite with some package that had arrived for him that morning from Paris. Deciding now was as good a time as any to approach him, Ann excused herself and went upstairs to the front of the chateau, where an enormous picture gallery ran the length of the facade. At the end of the gallery was the door to Arnold's suite. She knocked and waited. After a moment, he opened the door. To her surprise, his normally bald pate was covered with a rich head of sandy-colored hair, replete with long, youthful sideburns. She blinked at the hair, which brought a smile to his face. "You like it? It's another miracle of Mentase."

"You mean that's grown in since the last time I saw you?"

"No, I'm afraid even Mentase doesn't work that fast. It's a hairpiece I ordered from Paris. It was delivered this morning, and I've been indulging myself by preening in front of the mirror like a superannuated peacock. Did you wish to see me?"

"Yes, for a moment, if I could."

"Certainly, come in." He ushered her into the living room of his suite, which was even larger and more luxurious than Ann's. There were rich Gobelin tapestries on two of the walls depicting, like most of the murals and friezes in the chateau, a mythological orgy of plump nymphs and muscled satyrs. The ceiling here, like the corridor's, was also a pride of nudes, this time floating in a mist of ocean spray as they attended the birth of a voluptuous Venus.

"Quite something, isn't it?" he said, pointing to the ceiling as he led her to a sofa. "I'm told this was the actual apartment of Léonide Leblanc, the woman who built the chateau. They called her Mlle. Maximum, presumably from her attitude toward sex. Judging from the ceilings, she couldn't get enough of it, at least pictorially. You *do* like my hairpiece?"

"It's very flattering," said Ann, thinking that he could almost pass for a man in his forties, what with the rejuvenation in his face and the false hair.

"I've been bald for thirty-five years. But look . . ." He carefully removed the hairpiece and leaned his head down toward Ann, pointing to his scalp which was sprouting a thin crop of sandy fuzz. "That's the real thing."

She inspected it curiously. "Is *that* due to Mentase?"

"Yes." He replaced the hairpiece. "And the interesting thing is, it's not coming in gray, which one would expect, but rather in the color my hair was when I was a young man. But I'll wear the toupee until it's all out. May I offer you a drink? I've been observing Mentius's prohibition, but I keep a bottle on hand just in case."

"No thanks, nothing for me."

"I imagine you've been as pleased as we have at the success of the treatment?" he continued. "Your husband is looking terrific. It's a genuine miracle, isn't it?"

She nodded.

"You know, I can actually feel my blood becoming richer. It's a magical feeling, particularly when you think that you're the first person in history to experience an actual reversal of the biological clock. I can understand what Mr. Armstrong must have felt like when he first stepped on the moon. But there—I'm beginning to sound like a Geritol commercial, aren't I? Ah, I see you're looking at my good luck charm! Let me show it to you."

Ann's eyes had wandered to a bombé chest against the wall. On its pink marble top rested a glass and steel box about twenty inches high and ten inches square, inside of which stood a graceful figurine of a Chinese woman. Ann followed him to the chest and examined the statue. "Do you like it?" he said.

"It's exquisite."

"I have over a thousand pieces of Chinese art in my collection, but this is by far my favorite. I take it with me wherever I go. My wife gave it to me ten years ago, and I like to think it's sort of a good luck charm. The figure is a T'ang Dynasty portrait of the Empress Wu Chao, a quite remarkable woman who ruled China for a good part of the seventh century. The statue isn't the most valuable piece I own, in a monetary sense, but I almost think I'd rather lose the rest of my collection than this. Isn't the carving beautiful?"

"It's one of the loveliest things I've ever seen."

She noticed he was watching her closely, as if trying to judge the real purpose of her visit. "I sometimes wish I had devoted my life to art," he said, accompanying her back to the sofa. "Not that I have any talent, because I don't, but to be with the beauty of the past—the Voices of Silence, as Malraux poetically calls it—is to me one of the supreme pleasures of life. What an honor to surround oneself with the finest achievements of the human race! I think I would have made an excellent museum curator, if I hadn't been what my son rather unflatteringly calls a 'money-grubber.' I believe he paid you an unexpected visit last night?"

She looked surprised. "How did you know?"

Arnold hooked his thumbs in the vest pockets of his tailored English suit. "Martin thinks I'm unaware that he's done nothing since we came here except sit in his room smoking pot and whatever else he's on currently. But I do know, naturally. I smell the stuff through the door."

"Then why don't you do something about it?"

"What's there to do? I've tried to keep the drugs away from him, but it's practically impossible. As you know, I even bribed him to come here with me this summer, hoping by keeping an eye on him I might possibly be able to stop him somehow . . ."

"But you haven't kept an eye on him! You never see him."

He sat down opposite her. "How can I? He's almost always high. Short of breaking into his room and pulling the pipe out of his mouth, what can I do? Last night I heard him roaming around in his room, and then he started picking at something. I didn't realize till now he was breaking the lock to your room, or I'd have tried to stop him. But I assume from the fact that you're here that he did go into your suite. I hope he didn't cause too much of an uproar?"

"Well, he was high on amphetamines."

Arnold shook his head. "Good God, why he takes that poison—!"

"He was a little wild at first, and he scared the wits out of me with a knife."

"Did he threaten you with it?"

"Yes, but I think it was as if he was playing a sort of game."

Arnold nodded. "He does that periodically. I've discussed it with a psychiatrist, and he thinks it may be an attempt to rid his subconscious of the guilt he feels for his mother's death by acting out a charade of violence. Whether that's the case or not, I have no idea." He frowned a moment. "I suppose there's only one thing left for me to do. And that's to try and *force* him to give up the drugs, before he hurts someone even more than he already has."

"How can you force him?"

"I'm not sure, but there must be some way. I know it's supposed to be almost futile, but there seems to be nothing else left to try." He looked at her rather guardedly. "I suppose he talked about me?"

"A little, yes."

"I'm one of his pet topics of conversation. Did he blame me for his mother's death?"

"Yes. And other things."

"Don't look uncomfortable: I know what he thinks. He's told me often enough. Did he say we'd had no sexual relations for—I think it's supposed to be fifteen years?"

"Yes."

"Of course, the young like to explain everything in terms of sex, which is a hangover from the oversimplifications of Freud. But I won't deny what Martin says. A man doesn't enjoy discussing his sex life—or lack of it—with near strangers, but since Martin has already told you, I might as well be honest about it. In my late fifties, I became impotent. It would be foolish to pretend this didn't cause a strain in our marriage. My wife was perfectly healthy, and she missed a normal sex life. As often happens, she turned her affections on her son and began to smother him. The result was anything but good for Martin, though I don't think it perverted him. If anything, he strikes me as sort of a neuter. He doesn't seem to be interested in anything but his drugs. I've been told the French students have a slogan, 'The young make love, the old make obscene gestures.' But from what I've observed of the young, the reverse seems closer to the truth. It certainly is in Martin's case, and I haven't made any obscene gestures lately that I can remember." He smiled. "In fact, I may even be making love again."

"The Mentase?"

"The Mentase. It's not only growing hair, it's growing horns." He paused and cleared his throat, a bit embarrassed by his revelations. "Well, I really didn't mean to be quite so blunt. At any rate, as far as Martin is concerned, I think I can guarantee he won't invade your suite again."

She hesitated.

So far, Arnold Hirsch had been courteous, amiable and, seemingly, honest to a fault. She wondered if it might not seem ludicrous, under the circumstances, to accuse him of masterminding the monstrous conspiracy his son had attributed to him. On the other hand, she had to know. And if her question insulted him, then so be it. Quietly, she asked, "Actually, Mr. Hirsch . . ."

"Arnold, please."

"All right, Arnold. And please call me Ann."

"I intend to."

"Actually, it wasn't Martin I came to see you about."

He raised his bushy, half-sandy, half-gray eyebrows. "Oh? Then what was it?"

"My husband."

"What about your husband?"

"I understand he's been coming here to talk to you."

Now Arnold seemed to turn off, as if a warning light had flashed and he had dropped a curtain over his mind. "What are you getting at?"

"The Société Gérontologique."

He remained silent for almost half a minute, watching her, apparently thinking over the proper response. Then he burst into laughter.

"I didn't realize I was making a joke," she said.

"Oh no, the joke's on me. My God, one of the best-kept secrets on Wall Street, and you find out. Marvelous!"

"Then you and Michael *did* know each other before you came to the chateau?"

"Oh yes. Your husband came to my office six months ago with a rather unusual proposition. He said that a certain doctor had just come to him trying to get him to finance a most remarkable discovery, one that could be fantastically profitable."

"You mean, Mentius had come to Michael six months ago?"

"Exactly. He needed money to complete his research on Mentase, and he thought Brandywine Drugs, being one of the largest drug companies in the world, might be interested. Your husband, in turn, thought I would be interested, and I was." He paused to check his watch. "This is rather a long story—certainly long enough to merit ordering a bottle of Mentius's excellent champagne." He picked up the phone and dialed the service wing. "It's not every day a lonely old man like me has a chance to spend some time with a lovely young thing like you, and it should be suitably celebrated. And don't tell me I'm not supposed to drink. I know it. Hello, this is Arnold Hirsch. Send up a bottle of Taittinger Blanc de Blancs, please, with two glasses. Thank you." He hung up and smiled at Ann. "Champagne, alas, is my great weakness. Now, where were we?"

"Mentius had come to Michael in New York, and he went to you."

"Well, your husband arranged for me to meet the doctor. He impressed me enormously, but it turned out the finances of the clinic were in a shambles. Though it was a success as far as the International Set was concerned, he spent much more than he took in from rich old fools like me. There was a huge capital investment in the chateau itself, with its laboratory; this had eaten up all of his own and his wife's inherited money. But the Mentase research was what was killing him financially; of course, it was almost a passion with him, which was why he was looking for more money. Although he had what struck me as startling evidence that it worked, he could get no foundation to back him, mainly because there's snobbery in science, just as in everything else, and apparently gerontology is looked down upon as being not quite respectable: a rich man's toy at best, at worst a breeding ground for charlatans. People laughed at his claim and said he was a quack. It was the old story of supposedly intelligent men not recognizing genius when they stumbled on it.

"However, I didn't laugh at him. He wanted three million to develop Mentase, in return for which he was willing to give up exclusive manufacturing and marketing rights to whoever financed him. Your husband, who had some financial reverses of his own, was unable to put up more than a million. He explained to me that he couldn't get any more than that out of Brandywine Drugs' research funds without bringing down the wrath of his other stockholders, and he felt, as I did, that until Mentase was ready to market, it should be kept as much under wraps as possible. That is why we decided to keep it a secret even from our families. No offense intended to you, my dear, but wives have a tendency to gossip. And once word of something as startling as Mentase is out, it spreads like a California brushfire in October."

"I *never* gossip," snapped Ann, who didn't like the implication of his remark.

"That's what your husband said. However, I insisted; so you can blame all this on me. Anyway, Michael wanted me to come into the venture, putting up the remainder of the front money."

"And you agreed?"

"Not right away. I haggled with them, to drive a hard bargain; pretended I wasn't all that interested, and in fact I wasn't at first. But as I thought about Mentase, and the implications of it, I became more and more interested. You see, I am seventy-three years old—chronologically, that is. According to Mentius, I'm now in my middle fifties biologically. I enjoy life. I've always been terrified at the thought of becoming senile, as is everybody. For some years now I've had advanced arteriosclerosis, and last year I had a minor stroke. Happily, I recovered from it, but my doctor who, thank God, tells the truth, said it was just a matter of time before I'd have another stroke which would either put me in a wheelchair or the grave. Consequently, my future at the time was anything but rosy. So I told your husband and Dr. Mentius that I would finance them if they would give me the Mentase." He rubbed his chin. "Of course, Mentius said it was far too risky—the usual quite reasonable objections of a careful scientist. But I insisted. The only possible chance for me would be that the Mentase would, while it rejuvenated my body, rejuvenate my arteries as well and give me a new lease on life. So though I conceded the risks, if I were to profit at all from Mentase, considering the short amount of time it seemed was allotted to me, I had no choice but to plunge in.

"In short, Mentius finally agreed and contracts were signed. I was to arrive at the Chateau Mirabelle six months later for the Mentase treatment; Mentius categorically refused to begin earlier, saying he couldn't possibly be ready before then. Later, your husband told me he had decided to take the treatment too. He said he was convinced it would work, and he was as eager to regain his youth as I was. It was then we decided to play out our little game with you and the others, at least until we could tell whether the treatment was working or not. Now, there seems little point in your not knowing about the Société, though it's important it doesn't spread beyond our little group."

"Exactly what *is* the Société?"

"The holding company I've set up here in Switzerland to produce Mentase when the time comes."

"Why Switzerland?"

"For tax purposes. And beyond that, Mentase will be a product for the entire human race, not just Americans. It seemed more logical to produce it in a neutral, cosmopolitan country like Switzerland. Also the industrial climate here is much more favorable than at home, and the Swiss banking laws enable us to operate much more freely. I am the major stockholder in the company. Your husband has transferred a good deal of his holdings into it, making him the second stockholder. Dr. Mentius has five percent of the shares. And the other stockholder is our colleague here at the chateau, Lady de Ross."

"How did she get into the act?" asked Ann.

Arnold smiled. "Lady de Ross proves that the best-laid plans often get fouled up by what I might call the best-laid women—excuse my vulgarity, but let's be blunt: Lady de Ross is a bit of a nymphomaniac."

"You don't have to apologize to me; I'm hardly one of her fans."

"But her late husband, Lord de Ross, was a friend of mine, and my firm handles his estate, which is enormous. So it behooves me to be nice to her—actually, she rather amuses me—and every year I invite her for a cruise on my yacht. Four months ago she was aboard on a cruise I made around Sardinia. Her cabin was next to mine, and she overheard a radio-phone conversation I had with Dr. Mentius. No matter what you think of her, it would be a mistake to underestimate her. She's a shrewd woman. Without batting an eye, she marched into my cabin and said that if I didn't arrange for her to have the Mentase treatment too, she would tell everything she knew to the press. Naturally, being a former actress and a vain woman, she was as eager to recapture her youth as I was. Well, there was nothing to do but include her in the scheme. I even went so far as to allow her to invest a considerable sum in the Société, which she did. And there you have it—the whole rather complicated story, which proves what they say about Wall Street: it's a dark and mysterious place. And here's our champagne. Bravo! Just in time for me to propose a toast to you, me, Michael, Lady Kitty, and the success of our esteemed Dr. Mentius."

A footman had brought in the bottle of Taittinger, which he proceeded to open and serve. When he had left, Arnold raised his glass to Ann. "To all of us."

"To Mentase," corrected Ann.

"Yes, to Mentase," echoed Arnold softly. "And to its quite extraordinary future."

They drank. Then Ann set her glass down. "A future which includes, according to Martin, some rather unusual sociological features?"

Now he looked surprised. "What do you mean?"

"Martin said he'd overheard some phone conversations you'd had with lawyers about setting up 'distribution deals' for Mentase in various countries."

"Yes, I have. Though I didn't know he was interested enough to eavesdrop."

"Martin seemed to feel the distribution deals would be a way of limiting who got the Mentase."

Arnold looked puzzled. "I beg your pardon?"

"He thinks you want to use Mentase as a weapon against the young."

"You mean by giving Mentase only to, say, those young people who seemed 'safe'?"

"Something like that."

Arnold laughed as he finished his champagne. "What an extraordinary mind my son has! And you believed this?"

"I . . ." She hesitated. "No, I didn't exactly believe it . . ."

"But you thought you'd bring it up to see my reaction? Is that it?"

"I suppose so."

He stood up to refill her glass. "Well, my reaction is that it is an ingenious idea, worthy of our noble Vice-President, at the very least, and that I'm rather surprised my son's drug-drenched mind could conceive of anything that challenging. But I'm a financier, not a politician or a social philosopher. My interest in Mentase, aside from what it can do for me physically, is only in how much money it can make. So I'm afraid I'll have to disappoint you."

He smiled pleasantly at Ann, and she decided to say nothing more, for the time being.

❦

"Arnold tells me your wife has found out?" said Lady Kitty later that afternoon. She was naked, stretched on her stomach on a massage table situated at the opposite end of the Cosmetarium from the beauty parlor. A large machine hummed softly; it was the Dermo-Disc. Attached to it was a long steel arm, jointed like a dental machine, at the end of which was a disc which Dr. Zimmermann was holding against Lady Kitty's left buttock. Her plump cheeks were dotted with hypodermic scars, each representing one day's Mentase shot, and her flesh dimpled by a Rubensesque excess poundage that she had, over the years, controlled but not conquered, jiggled slightly from the electric current pouring out of the disc. A white curtain surrounded the massage table on four sides, providing privacy. Next to her, in a similarly curtained oasis, Michael Brandywine was waiting his turn with the Dermo-Disc. He too was naked and stretched on his stomach. The Cosmetarium was otherwise empty.

"Yes, he told me too," replied Michael. "Frankly, I'm just as glad. She was beginning to be a pest with all her questions."

Lady Kitty stretched luxuriantly as the tiny electric charges stung softly into her flesh. She enjoyed the daily Dermo-Disc treatment. Not only was it effective—and how she gloried in the new fresh skin that was slowly recarpeting her body—but it was a definitely sensual experience being bombarded by the tiny shocks, and Lady Kitty was all for sensual experience.

Dr. Zimmermann placed the disc on the small of her back. Lady Kitty almost purred. "Do you think dear Ann will be angry with you for keeping so many secrets from her?" she continued.

"Probably," replied Michael. He too was luxuriating. He was tired, and stretching on the massage table was relaxing. He felt drowsy and good.

"What will you tell her?"

"The truth. That Arnold insisted we keep it a secret." He wished Lady Kitty would shut up so he could go to sleep. The hum of the Dermo-Disc acted like a sedative, and he would rather listen to that than Lady Kitty. Not that he disliked her. In fact, he found her becoming rather attractive. But right now he would rather sleep.

"She seems to be a rather feisty girl," said Lady Kitty.

"Who?"

"Your wife, dear boy. Ann. She seems to get her back up rather easily."

"Yes she does. But she can be handled."

"She's attractive. I like the way she dresses. So sort of quaint boutique-ish."

"The quaint boutique is Bergdorf's. I pay the bills."

She laughed lightly. "Of course. Bergdorf's." The little bitch dresses like a rag doll, she thought.

She said nothing more for a few minutes, and Michael was almost asleep. Then he heard her voice pitch itself a few tones lower and insinuate itself through the white canvas curtain separating their tables.

"If you're free when we get done here, why don't you drop up to my room for a cocktail? Orange juice, of course."

Michael's eyes opened. The implication was painfully obvious, and for a moment the vision of the actress, whom he had watched for three weeks grow increasingly appealing, flashed in his mind and awakened a spark of fleshly interest. It quickly died. He was having too much trouble with Ann to get entangled in a mess directly across the hall from his suite. It was too important to keep Ann placated until the end of the treatment.

"Thanks, but I have some calls I have to make," he said.

"With young Mr. Bradshaw?"

"Yes."

"But it was precisely young Mr. Bradshaw I wanted to talk to you about, dear boy."

Michael frowned. "What about him?"

"Come to my suite and I'll tell you," she said softly.

Michael pondered the yeas and nays of this. Then, rather impatiently, "All right."

"I think you'll find it worthwhile."

She said no more, and he closed his eyes again, pleased that she was letting him alone at last, but curious what she was after. That is, besides himself.

At six, the nurse led Ann into the infirmary in the lab wing where, in a small white room, Hugh Barstow lay in a hospital bed.

"Are you sure it's all right?" whispered Ann to the nurse.

"Oh yes, madame. Monsieur Barstow has been awake for a half hour now. But only five minutes. Then he has to be bathed."

"By you?"

The pretty French girl smiled. "Yes, madame."

Ann tiptoed into the windowless room which was dimly illuminated by a small lamp by the door. Despite what the nurse said, Hugh looked asleep. The sheets were up to his chin, and his eyes were closed. She noticed, to her surprise, that there were no bandages on his head.

"Hugh?" she whispered.

He opened his eyes.

"Hi."

"They said I could see you for a few minutes."

"Pull up a chair." His voice was weak, but he sounded in good spirits, considering that he had been out of surgery a mere four hours. She took a white chair and placed it next to the bed, then sat down.

"Thanks for the flowers," he said. She noticed a huge bouquet of fresh flowers on the bed table. "I'm glad someone was worried about me."

"We all were," she lied, thinking of Lady Kitty's total lack of concern over her lover's fate.

"Sure. I'll bet Lady Kitty cried all the way to the bathtub."

Ann tried to keep a straight face. "Dr. Mentius told us he got the tumor out and that it was benign. So you're going to be all right."

"Yeah, I take back everything I ever said about him. He saved my life, you know? I was really scared. I mean, I almost couldn't see, the pain was so bad."

"But it's all gone now?"

"Not quite, but it's nothing like it was. And the relief of knowing it's all over . . ."

"I can imagine." She looked again at his scalp. "Where did they cut into you?"

"In the side. See?" He turned his head slowly and raised his nearly shoulder-length hair. Ann saw a small square bandage on the left side of his skull.

"Doesn't look like much, does it?"

"No. I'm surprised they didn't shave your head."

He turned his head back. "That's out of date. Mentius has all the latest gimmicks, including something called stereotaxic surgery."

"What's that?"

"The way he explained it to me, it's like a tiny electric needle they put through your skull into the brain. They've got computers that know exactly where to guide it."

"How would the computers know that?"

"They program the exact location of the tumor. You know, from X rays."

"Oh, I see," she lied.

"And they put this aluminum cage on my head, shaped like a cube, which they attached with rubber-tipped screws to keep it in place."

"What's that for?"

"The electric needle's attached to the cage, see? And the cage keeps the needle in the same relative position to the head, or otherwise the head might move and screw everything up. Then Mentius and the computer guide the needle down through a little hole in the skull to the tumor, and zap: it's out."

"Sounds simple."

"It only takes about ten years to learn how."

"Anyway, I'm glad you're through with it. When will you be out?"

"I guess in a couple of days."

She hesitated. "I've been doing a little snooping while you were sick."

"Find any more bottle babies?"

"I found out Arnold Hirsch is a sly old man—or ex-old man. He and the rest of them have been putting on quite a routine for our benefit."

"Like what?"

She explained what Arnold told her. When she finished, he said nothing for a moment. Then, "They really like to play games, don't they?"

"The name of the game could be Generation Gap," she said, "if what Martin thinks is true."

"What does Martin think?"

"That this Société is some sort of Fascist plot to control the young by outliving them."

"That's pretty wild."

"I know. That's what his father said. But I wonder . . ."

She was interrupted by the young nurse coming in to announce that the five minutes were up. Ann replaced the chair, then leaned over Hugh and kissed his forehead. "That's to get well on," she said.

"Feel better already," he grinned. "Want to climb in here with me and try my shorthand?"

"I'll leave that for your nurse," she whispered. Then she noticed something on his forehead. "Hugh, what are those two red marks on your skin?"

"That's where the screws held the aluminum cage in place. Mentius said they screw them so tight against the skin they leave a mark for a day or two."

She stared at the marks. "That's odd."

"Why?"

"They look like the marks you and I both had when we got out of the Aquadorme tanks—remember? The marks that were supposed to be from the adhesive tape they used to keep the brainwave monitors in place."

"So?"

She was frowning. "Hugh."

"What?"

"Remember when Martin Hirsch met us outside Mentius's office and the three of us went in to see Mentius—just after we had gotten out of the tanks?"

"I remember."

"Well, I just thought of something, and I'm pretty sure I'm right about it. I don't think Martin had any red marks on his forehead."

"Madame, please," said the nurse. "I must give Monsieur Barstow his bath."

"So he didn't have any marks," said Hugh. "I can't remember. But what would it mean if he didn't?"

"I don't know," she said. "But I'm going to ask Dr. Mentius."

The nurse led her out of the room.

❧

Herbert Mentius was exhausted.

The operation on Hugh Barstow had been exacting, but it was the Mentase treatment itself that was draining his energies and putting a strain on his nerves. He was afraid, afraid of the dozens of things that could go wrong with his three patients, for he was acutely aware of the risks he was taking. He had agonized over the decision to start the treatment before his research was completed. But Arnold Hirsch had insisted, and Mentius had desperately needed the financing he offered him. So he had sacrificed caution for expediency. But the price he paid was a conscience that plagued him with guilt, and fears that brought him insomnia. The result was an exhaustion which was eating away at the coolness of nerve he knew he must preserve to make the treatment a success. One slip—one more Stahling, for instance—and the delicate house of cards he had been forced to erect would fall apart.

So when Sally Mentius went to the door of their apartment at quarter past six that afternoon and brought Ann Brandywine into their living room, he wished he had some excuse to avoid meeting her. He could see she was angry, as angry as she had been when she discovered the embryos. And he knew he would have to lie to her again. He wished he didn't have to. He disliked the pretense, the elaborate quadrille they were all forced to continue dancing, but it was necessary. It probably would have been necessary even without Arnold Hirsch's insistence, but Arnold made it mandatory.

"Ann wanted to see you, Herbie," said Sally. Mentius stood up and forced a smile.

"Of course. Would you like a drink? Sally was about to fix us our solo cocktail for the day."

"No thank you. And Sally, I wish you'd listen to this."

Sally and her husband exchanged looks, then the three of them took seats. Ann said, "Dr. Mentius, what did you do to Hugh and me while we were supposedly asleep those three days in the Aquadorme tanks."

He felt his nerves tightening, but he kept his face a mask. "I thought I explained that to you? We conducted a series of tests . . ."

"I don't think that's the truth, Doctor." Her voice was soft but angry. "Of course, I've been lied to so many times these past weeks I suppose I'm more suspicious than usual. But there were marks on our foreheads when we got out of the tanks that are just like the marks Hugh has on his forehead now, which you told him were caused by the stereotaxic cage. And I don't remember Martin Hirsch having any marks on his forehead when *he* got out of the Aquadorme tank, so the marks can't have been caused by the monitor tape; which leaves the conclusion that they were caused by the stereotaxic cages. Which means you must have used them on Hugh and me while we were in the tanks. I'd like to know why."

Dr. Mentius shook his head. "That's a fairly dazzling logical sequence, Mrs. Brandywine. But you don't come out with a logical answer."

"Doctor," she said, watching his right hand squeeze the knuckles of his left, "you're not half as good a liar as Arnold Hirsch." She turned to Sally. "Do you know what your husband did to me?"

Sally glanced at Mentius. "He did exactly what he told you," she said.

"Sally, I think you're lying to me again. You said you hated the lying, but I think you're doing it again."

Sally said nothing.

"Why won't you be honest with me? Why can't you tell me the truth? Is it so horrible that I can't know it?"

Mentius said wearily, "I *have* told you the truth, Mrs. Brandywine."

"All right," she said, "but I'm warning you I'm going to find out what happened. And if I find you did do something without my permission—or if there's any other attempt made to do something to me—I'll have my brother, who's an excellent lawyer, slap a malpractice suit against you that will make medical history." She started out of the room, pausing as she passed Sally. "I'm sorry, Sally, but maybe you can talk some sense into him."

She left the apartment. After she had gone, Sally looked at her husband. "Herbie?" He closed his eyes. "You know as well as I there was no other way."

PART THREE

LADY Kitty de Ross was expecting Michael Brandywine in her suite at five thirty, but he was late. The ex-actress profited from the extra time by rechecking herself in the full-length mirror in her ornate bathroom. She had put on the simple black cocktail dress that had cost her five hundred guineas at Balenciaga but which, by the elegance of its cut, would have been a bargain at twice the price. Black cocktail dresses came and went in the never-ending merry-go-round of fashion fads, but Lady Kitty found that this dress, which she thought of as her "attack armor," had the greatest effect on men of any of her outfits, and whenever she was most anxious to score she pulled it out and put it on. A single rope of Burmese pearls and the huge marquise diamond Lord de Ross had given her more years ago than she liked to remember were the only jewels she wore. She looked uncluttered. And, she decided with satisfaction, she looked gorgeous.

She went into the living room of her suite and checked her bar tray. A tall pitcher of fresh orange juice had been brought up by a footman, along with an ice bucket, several bottles of soda water, and a dish of freshly picked mint. Lady Kitty had been experimenting with the limited possibilities of nonalcoholic cocktails, and she had found that a combination of half orange juice and half soda water, when laced with fresh mint, made a drink which, while it didn't put one in orbit, was certainly refreshing. She would make Michael Brandywine one of her Kitty Whiskers, as she had dubbed the drink. Then she would turn on the charm. Lady Kitty knew how to be charming. In fact, she was a professional at it.

Michael knocked on her door at quarter till six. There was a muffled quality to his knock that amused Lady Kitty as she went to let him in. He would be nervous about that revolting little wife of his, naturally; afraid she would see his coming into wicked Lady Kitty's den of evils. Good. Let her see him. Wicked Lady Kitty would enjoy nothing more than taking on the "sweet" Mrs. Brandywine in an all-out war.

"Dear boy, you're late," she said as she opened the door. Michael hurried inside with almost comic haste. "Was it your wife who kept you?"

"Who else?" he said. "She went down to see Mentius about something. I waited for her to get back."

"Do you think she's smelling more white rats?"

"Yes I do. But she didn't say a word to me when she returned. In a way, I almost wish she'd blown her stack. She makes me nervous when she's quiet."

Lady Kitty smiled. "Beware the woman who doesn't talk! Would you like a Kitty Whisker? It's the best thing this side of a martini, though I'll admit that's not saying much."

"All right." He glanced at the dozens of photographs that covered the furniture. Lady Kitty watched him as she made the drinks. Nice-looking, she thought. Handsome, even, in a sort of lean executive way, and of course improving all the time as he gets younger. And with a certain brusque American dash, which is attractive as long as it doesn't become boorish.

"Here you go," she said, bringing him the drink. "Orange juice, soda, and a sprig of mint. All it needs is gin."

"But it needs that badly," he said, taking a sip.

"I couldn't agree more. Sit down."

They both sat. "What about Bill Bradshaw?" he asked.

"Yes, dear Mr. Bradshaw. I've been wondering for several days whether I should tell you. Did you notice his cheek?"

"The scratches? Yes. He said he ran into a cat in heat."

Lady Kitty looked startled, then she laughed. "Marvelous! The cat in heat was a Kitty-cat."

Now it was Michael's turn to look startled. "You mean, you and Bill . . ."

"Me and Bill. A tender but short-lived romance that I'm afraid will inspire few poets. I naturally hesitated telling you, since we are, after all, business partners. But dear Mrs. Brandywine has found out, and so I decided to make a clean breast of the whole thing. *Mea culpa.* Dear boy, you're looking cross. I hope you're not angry with me?"

"I'm angry with Bill. I'm not paying him to make love to my friends."

"Well, I must admit I didn't exactly discourage him. My Achilles' heel are young Achilles who quite often, to make an atrocious pun, turn out to be heels. Mr. Bradshaw is a vivid case in point. You see, he tried to make a business deal with me at your expense."

"What kind of deal?"

"He read a broker's report which was not meant for his beady eyes. Rather cleverly, he deduced that your transferring stock into the Société was not merely an exercise in international finance, but was involved with Mentase."

"How did he find out about Mentase?"

"Ah, my fault. He read Mentius's report, which I had rather stupidly left in my bathroom."

"What was he doing in your bathroom?"

"You're getting a bit personal. The point is, he tried to get me to finance him in an attempt to sew up the rights to Mentase for himself, not realizing that this had already been done by the three of us. I informed him in no uncertain terms that he had missed the boat—or, more precisely, the gravy train."

"The little bastard," said Michael. "For five years I trusted him, then he pulls something like this."

"You didn't suspect he was hungry?"

"I knew he was ambitious, but I thought he was honest."

She laughed. "From what I've heard, business schools don't waste too much time on business ethics. There is a magic moment when the flea starts dreaming about becoming the dog. Though it's none of my business, I would strongly recommend you get rid of him."

"Mr. Bradshaw has just joined the unemployed. By the way, I appreciate your telling me."

"But we're all in the same boat, aren't we? What is bad for you is bad for me, and vice versa."

"I suppose that's true."

She picked an invisible piece of lint from her black skirt. "Which brings me to another thing I've been thinking about."

"Which is?"

"Arnold Hirsch."

Michael eyed her closely. She's a shrewd old bitch, he thought. Very shrewd.

"What about him?"

"Well, let me put it this way. I've known Arnold for years. My late husband, dear Lord de Ross, knew him intimately. Arnold is a man of high intelligence and a bit of a financial wizard. He also has an absolutely gorgeous yacht."

"I know all this."

"But you don't know Arnold personally as well as I do. He's changed recently—since his wife died, in fact. He was devoted to her in his chilly way, and her death came as a great shock to him. He withdrew into himself. While he was always something of a sphinx, he became almost obsessively clandestine. And, of course, he became a bit of a fanatic, didn't he? About his son, I mean, and the so-called youth movement."

Michael nodded. "I know."

"I don't trust fanatics, particularly when my money is invested with them. They are amusing to watch on television, but to deal with? Well, they're unstable. Give me a good, solid, level-headed cynic any day over someone who believes in a cause."

"What are you getting at?"

"Actually, you've invested even more money with Arnold than I have. We both have a quite substantial stake in his stability, and in the stability of the Société Gérontologique. But since he is the principal stockholder, we're both fairly well at his mercy, aren't we?"

He looked at her thoughtfully. "I'm beginning to see a light at the end of the tunnel."

She smiled. "The simple point I wanted to make was that acting separately, we have little way to, shall I say, restrain Arnold from possible excesses? Whereas together, we should be able to control him. Not that I'm counting on the need to arise. But the prudent investor tries to foresee all eventualities."

Michael said nothing for a moment. She's got a point, he thought. She's definitely got a point.

"Since this seems to be Candor Hour," he said, "I'll admit that I don't entirely trust Arnold either. But on the other hand, I don't particularly trust you."

She laughed. "Bravo. Nor do I trust you. But there's a simple way to remedy that, isn't there?"

"Which is?"

"Well," she said, taking a sip of her Kitty Whisker, "we'll just have to get to know each other better, won't we?"

His eyes traveled slowly up her long, shapely legs. "I think I've just come out of the tunnel," he said.

"Dear boy, you're about to go in it."

❧

Ann had said nothing to her husband.

The network of conspiracy was apparently growing wider. Arnold Hirsch, Lady Kitty, Michael, and now Dr. Mentius and even Sally. Sally, at least, had tried some sort of honest communication with her, which was more than Michael had done. But Ann knew that if she wanted to find out the truth, whether it meant confirming or exploding her suspicions, she would be wasting her time trying to make the others talk, including her husband. If Mentius wouldn't, none would. She had no choice but to attack from the flank.

The following morning, she ordered the chateau's limousine to pick her up at nine and take her to the town of Windischgratz on the opposite side of the lake from the clinic. When they arrived in the main square of the town, she told Dieter, the chauffeur, to let her off at a coffee shop she had spotted and to pick her up in an hour and a half, after she had done some window-shopping. As the enormous Daimler pulled away she entered the coffee shop, asked if there was a phone she could use and, when one was pointed out to her, asked the operator for the number of Ernst Stahling. When they were connected, she identified herself and asked if it would be possible for her to see him for a few minutes.

"Yes, of course, Mrs. Brandywine. I remember you, naturally. Where are you now?"

She told him and he agreed to meet her at the coffee shop in ten minutes. When he arrived, he joined Ann in a corner booth.

"It's good to see you again," she said.

"Yes. I'm afraid the last time we met under less pleasant circumstances. In fact, the next morning I had the hangover of my life."

"I think you were justified in saying what you did. It turned out you were right, you know."

He looked rather despondent. "Oh, I know I was right, but a lot of good that does me now. Mentius gave me severance pay and good letters of recommendation, but there aren't many jobs that pay as well as the one I had at the clinic, particularly for someone my age."

"Your age? But you're very young."

"No one over forty is young when he's looking for a job." A waitress came over and they ordered two Cappuccinos. Stahling offered Ann a napkin. "But I shouldn't bother you with my problems. What did you wish to see me about?"

"What really happened to the three of us when we were put in those tanks? And I know all about the sleep therapy business. I want to know what *really* happened."

Stahling shook his head. "You're asking the wrong person. I don't know."

"Why? You were in charge of the Aquadorme tanks."

"But after the three of you went to sleep, the Mentius Mafia told me they were taking charge of you."

"The who?"

"The Mentius Mafia: that's the nickname the staff has given Zimmermann, Schlessing, and De Villeneuve. They gave me the sleep therapy story, which I didn't particularly believe either, and they said they had to take you upstairs to the infirmary where they could chart your pulse, breathing, and so forth."

"But I thought that's what the monitors were supposed to be doing," she interrupted.

"That's what I said to them. But Zimmermann said they had to give you xenon gas to keep you asleep for the three-day period, and they could only give that upstairs. So they took you out of the tanks, and that was the last I saw of you."

"Did they take Martin Hirsch out of his tank too?"

"The young boy? Yes, they took him too."

Ann thought a moment. "Why do they call them the Mentius Mafia?"

"Because they stay so close together and are so secretive."

"About what?"

"The project they've been working on with Mentius for about four years now. No one has any idea what it is, though we assume it has something to do with aging, since that's Mentius's field. They're all dedicated as monks. None of them hardly ever speaks to the rest of us."

"Then to find out what happened to us in the infirmary, I'd have to ask one of them?"

"You'd be wasting your time. They don't talk."

"They must talk to *someone*?"

"Not about the project. They all have rooms together on the first floor of the staff quarters down by the lake. They eat together. I almost said they sleep together, which they don't. But they might as well."

"They have no families?"

"No. None of them is married. I think De Villeneuve's parents are alive in Zermatt, but as far as I know the rest of them have no connections at all."

"No love life."

Stahling waited while the Cappuccinos were served. Then he tasted the thick cream floating on top of the black coffee.

"Dr. Zimmermann has no interest in sex at all, as far as I can tell. She's a machine. Schlessing seems to be sort of a neuter as well. There's a girl in town he goes out with occasionally, but most of the time he's either working in the lab or, when he's off, listening to his record collection. He has a passion for Bach. The room I sometimes stayed in when I didn't come home for the night was right above his, and more than once I had to bang on the floor to get him to turn down the volume."

"That leaves De Villeneuve. What about him?"

"He's the youngest. He couldn't be more than twenty-five, I'd say."

"He's nice-looking."

Stahling smiled rather slyly. "I noticed. He's been known to play around with some of the girls on the staff. Discreetly. There's a lot of discreet playing around on the staff."

"I can imagine. Tell me more about Dr. de Villeneuve."

"There's not much to tell. He's intelligent, dedicated; totally in awe of Mentius, as they all are. He likes to take hikes and swim. He reads a great deal of technical literature, but hardly anything else. As far as I know he has no interest in politics, art, films . . ."

"He sounds rather dull."

Stahling shrugged. "He's a scientist."

"Not all scientists are dull."

"This one is. Are you thinking of getting him to tell you what happened?"

"I'm thinking of trying. What would you say is the best approach?"

"May I be blunt?"

"Please."

He looked her over. "There's really only one thing he might be interested in."

Ann turned slightly red. "You certainly were blunt."

He shrugged. "What do *you* think happened to you?"

"I don't know. I only have the vaguest notions, really. But I know they did do something—something they don't want me to know about." She raised the cup of coffee to her lips. "I intend to find out what it was."

"If you need help, don't hesitate to call me."

"Thank you. I will."

"You see, my friend Kurt Oetterli feels rather strongly about what Mentius did to Lisl, his sister. So both he and I have a debt to pay back to the doctor, and we'd both like to pay the debt."

"I'll remember that."

❧

When she returned to the chateau, Ann took a walk down to the staff quarters by the lake. It was a two-story wooden structure, undistinguished architecturally, which contained twenty separate rooms to house the staff and which reminded Ann of a cheap college dormitory. It was hidden from the chateau by the surrounding trees, and the only thing that could be said in its favor was its magnificent view of the lake. It was almost noon, and the building seemed deserted. She went into the drab and rather depressing entrance hall which bisected the building. A bulletin board displayed thumbtacked notices; beside it was a pigeonhole letter box. She checked the names Scotch-taped beneath each hole and spotted "Dr. de Villeneuve, 1-A." A sketch of the floor plan on the bulletin board showed her that 1-A was the front corner room on the far side of the ground floor from the chateau.

She was about to leave when she saw Bill Bradshaw coming down the stairs, carrying two suitcases.

"Bill," she said, "where are you going?"

"I guess your husband didn't tell you?" he answered, setting the suitcases down beside her. "I've been fired."

"Why?"

"Let's say I committed a business indiscretion. Actually, I don't blame him for booting me, I guess. I'd have done the same thing in his place. Anyway, I'm out."

"I'm sorry," she said truthfully. She liked Bill. "What are your plans?"

"I'm not sure. I may bum around Europe for a month or so, then go home. I've got a few bucks saved in the old sock. I'm glad I had a chance to say good-bye to you, though. I've enjoyed knowing you."

"And I've enjoyed knowing you." Feeling rather awkward, she shook his hand and wished him good luck. Then as he picked up his bags, she said, "By the way, do you know Dr. de Villeneuve?"

"I know which one he is."

"When does he usually come down here from the lab?"

"That bunch generally doesn't show up till dinner. They eat at their own table."

"Then what do they do?"

He looked at her curiously. "Go to bed, I guess. I really don't know. No, wait. De Villeneuve takes a swim in the lake when it's warm enough."

"Where?"

"Out in front. There's a pier about fifty feet past the end of the building. There's my taxi . . ." A cab had pulled up behind the building and honked. Bill started toward the rear door of the entrance hall. "Good-bye, Mrs. Brandywine."

"Good-bye, Bill. And good luck."

She watched him climb in the cab. Then she started back to the chateau.

That night, she waited till Michael was asleep in his capsule. Then she put on a white bathing suit, some beach clogs, and a turtleneck sweater, and left the suite. Making her way downstairs, she left the chateau by the terrace doors and walked down to the lake. It was a calm night, but a rather chilly one, and she was glad she brought her sweater. She followed the shoreline till she reached the staff quarters. A few lights were on, including the corner room which was De Villeneuve's. She made her way to the pier beyond the staff quarters, then walked to the end of it and sat down, dipping her toes in the cool water. She had left her watch in her room, but she guessed it must be close to eleven o'clock.

She waited.

Fifteen minutes later, she saw the light in De Villeneuve's room go out. She waited another twenty minutes, beginning to feel the chill of the night seep into her bones.

Finally she gave up and returned to her room. I'll try again tomorrow night, she thought. And then the night after that. It's the only way.

She wondered how far she would have to go to get him to talk.

❧

But the weather became her enemy.

The next day a slow-moving front settled over the area and it drizzled for three days. When the front finally passed through, an unseasonal cold snap moved in behind it, making any thought of midnight swimming ludicrous. Ann was frustrated by the delay, but she had no alternative but to wait.

Life continued as usual in the chateau. When she saw Michael, he casually commented that Arnold had told him about the scene in his room. "I'm glad he told you about the Société," he said. "I really didn't like all this secrecy." Ann said nothing, and though she didn't quite believe what Michael had said—she knew from experience that he was automatically secretive—she was still impressed by his natural and pleasant attitude. And as the rainy days dragged by, she began to wonder if perhaps her suspicions weren't unfounded. Yes, they had been secretive about the conditions of their arrival at the Chateau Mirabelle and the existence of the Société Gérontologique, but as she thought about it, she had to admit perhaps they had had some justification. Certainly not keeping the Société a secret was to invite trouble. And as far as some gloomy plot against Hugh, Martin, and herself—well, the more she thought about it, the less she could believe that her husband would actually allow Mentius to do anything serious to her without her knowledge or permission. Nor did Herbert or Sally Mentius seem capable of doing anything seriously unethical. As for the red marks, she had asked Martin Hirsch if he remembered seeing them on his forehead after the Aquadorme incident, and he'd said he had no idea whether they had been there or not, he'd been too beat and hipped on the prospect of getting some drugs; and she couldn't be *positive* the marks on Hugh's forehead after his operation were the same as those she'd seen after the Aquadorme treatment—the ones they'd explained were from adhesive tape holding the sleep monitors in place. So she still had no proof for her suspicions. Moreover, if there had been something done to her that she didn't know about, there was nothing in her physical condition to indicate it, except for a vague listlessness that went with the languid pace of life at the chateau. She began to feel sheepish about her suspicions, and she wondered if perhaps she weren't making a fool of herself trying to lure Dr. de Villeneuve out of his room to quiz him about something that had happened almost a month before—if it had happened at all.

Then, on the fourth night of the cold snap, she was lying in bed reading an Agatha Christie thriller when she heard a light tap on the door leading to Martin Hirsch's room. The lock had long since been replaced, and the workman had, at Arnold Hirsch's suggestion, put a bolt on Ann's side of the door to discourage any further "invasions" by his son. Now Ann went to the door, slipped the bolt, and opened the door a crack.

"Mrs. Brandywine?" whispered Martin. "May I see you a moment? No knives, honest."

She let him in. He looked pale and haggard, but he seemed rational, at least as rational as when she had asked him about the red marks, which was the only other communication she had had with him for some time. He glanced at the sleep capsule. "Is your husband zapped for the night?"

She nodded and led him into the living room, turning on a light.

"My father's put guards on me," he said as Ann offered him a chair. "He's hired six private detectives from Lausanne, and they're watching me round the clock."

"Why?"

"To keep me from getting drugs. At least that's the excuse he gave me. Except I don't believe it."

"Why?"

"He doesn't really give a damn whether I'm a head or not. He'd be just as happy if I took a couple of sugar cubes and walked off the roof."

"Martin, you may be wrong about him," she said. "At least from the way he talked about you to me, he seemed to care."

He looked at her with surprise. "How can you say that after finding out the lies they've been feeding us?"

"I know about the lies. And while I don't like what they did, it doesn't necessarily follow that your father doesn't care about you, or my husband about me."

Martin shook his head. "You really don't get it, do you? I suppose you don't believe they're going to use Mentase against young people either?"

"But Martin, how could they do it? It seems impossible to do something like that on a worldwide scale."

"Okay, I figured you wouldn't buy that. All right, then you tell me why you think the guards are here."

"I don't know, but it seems reasonable to have them here to keep you from getting hash."

"Don't you think there's an easier way, if that's what they want?"

"They?"

"My old man and your husband and Mentius and Lady Kitty. They're all in this, whatever it is, together. They all know Hugh and I have been buying from Kurt Oetterli; now if they *really* were only interested in the drugs, wouldn't it be easier to put guards on Kurt? Or arrest him, for that matter?"

She shifted uncomfortably. The ease of mind she had allowed herself to drift into began to be disrupted by the old suspicions. "Why do *you* think the guards are here?"

He lowered his voice. "To make us prisoners. You, me, and Hugh. They're here to watch all of us, and make sure we don't leave the chateau." He raised his hand. "I know you think I'm high again. Except I'm all out of pills. I haven't had anything for two days. I have to hoard what little pot and hash I've got left because the goons aren't letting me meet Kurt. So I'm really not making this up." He paused. "I know you think of my old man as some gentle, sweet granddaddy who wouldn't hurt a fly . . ."

"I don't think that by a long shot."

"Gentleness is not his bag. He paid me the three thousand to get me here, knowing I'd buy hash with the money and sit in my room and not give him any trouble—which was exactly what he wanted; except he made it *look* as if he's all uptight about my being a head, which is a crock. Then when I busted out and started making waves, he had to change tactics and hire guards.

But the reason's been the same all along: to keep me here in the chateau with as little fuss as possible."

"But Martin," she said. "Why?"

"I don't know. But my father never does anything without a reason. And you may not like to think it, but I'd bet your husband's been doing the same thing to you."

He was right: she didn't like to think it. But his verbalizing her recent fears gave them renewed strength. She closed her eyes a moment, fighting off the panic that seemed to crouch in the corners of her mind, ready to spring. "All right, Martin," she said wearily, "maybe you're right." She opened her eyes. "I've been trying to find out what happened to us while we were in the Aquadorme tanks—"

"So you don't believe what Mentius told us?"

"Do you?"

"No. . . . Is that why you asked me about those red marks?"

"Yes, it is."

"Is there some way we can find out what really went on?"

"There's someone I'm pretty sure knows, someone I'm trying to get to. Meanwhile, I think probably the best thing to do is seem to go along with them. Mentius already knows I'm suspicious, but I'd just as soon he didn't think I'm asking questions among the staff. Besides, it won't hurt you to cut down on your drugs."

He thought about this a moment, then nodded reluctantly. "Maybe you're right. You know, if nothing else, this past month I've been able to sort of think a little about what passes for my life, and believe me, it's beautifully screwed up. Anyway, for a long time now I've wanted to break away from my old man. It's not just that we don't dig each other personally; I don't dig his whole life, you know? I don't suppose it's anyone's fault, really. But I'd love to bug out and just wander around Europe and try—" He stopped.

"Try what?" she asked gently.

"Well, I know you'll think this sounds dumb, but I write poems."

"Why should I think that sounds dumb?"

"Oh, everybody does. People think poets are freaks."

"I don't. And I'd like to read some of your poems."

He looked horrified. "God no! Take my word for it, they're awful! I may not have much talent, but I do have some taste." He hesitated. "Still, I'd like to try, you know? At least try. That so crazy?"

"I don't think it's a bit crazy."

"You're the first person who hasn't laughed at the poet," he said, standing up and actually smiling.

"There's no reason to laugh. I wanted to be a ballerina once, but I gave it up. The important thing, though, is to be able to say you at least tried."

"Yes, that's true, isn't it?"

For the first time since she had met him, Ann thought Martin Hirsch looked relaxed and even happy. He put his hands back in his pockets. "Well, I guess I'd better get back to my room before the goons blow the whistle on me."

They returned to the bedroom and went to the door of his room. He paused for a moment and looked at Ann. "It's odd, isn't it," he said, "thinking of my father and your husband as 'them'?"

"Very odd," she agreed.

Then he went into his room and closed the door.

❧

By the next night, the summer weather had returned and it was warm and clear. Again Ann waited till Michael was asleep in the cryogenic capsule. Then, feeling somewhat like one of the Twelve Dancing Princesses, she put on her bathing suit, threw a sweater around her shoulders, and hurried down to the lake to try again. When she arrived at the pier, she found that not only was Dr. de Villeneuve there, but he was already in the water.

"Good evening," he said.

"Hello," she replied. "Is the water cold?"

"A little. But it feels good. Come on in." He spoke with a French accent, and his voice seemed friendly enough. She took off her sweater. "Is it deep enough to dive?"

"Yes. It's about four meters here."

She dived cleanly off the end of the pier, feeling a slight shock as she hit the cool water but quickly accustoming herself to it. After swimming in a lazy circle, she began to tread water. "Do you swim here often?"

He didn't answer for a moment. When he did, his tone was lightly sarcastic. "Come now, Mrs. Brandywine. You've been down here before, obviously waiting for someone since you didn't take a swim. Now, with all of Lake Windischgratz available for you to swim in, I don't think it's just a coincidence you've come here. So I assume you know I swim here often."

She laughed. "Caught. All right, I confess: I've been hoping to meet you."

"I'm flattered. I trust the reason is not a medical one?"

"Of course not." She hoped she wasn't overdoing it; then she turned on her back and floated. It's your move now, Doctor, she thought, rather enjoying this phase of her detective work. De Villeneuve made the move.

"Doesn't your husband know you're here?"

"Do you think I'd tell him I've been coming down to the staff quarters trying to meet an attractive young doctor? Really, I'm a bit smarter than that." She allowed herself to drift closer to him. "Besides, my husband's sealed up in his icebox for the night." There was no moon, but her eyes were accustomed to the darkness and she could see him watching her a few feet away.

"Do you make a habit of chasing young doctors?" he asked in an amused tone.

"Oh, I don't care if they're doctors, just so they're young. And interesting." Not too fast, she thought. "After all, it gets terribly dull here if you're not taking the treatment. Don't you get bored sometimes? I mean, trying to rejuvenate antiques?"

"I don't think of it as furniture restoration," he said rather stuffily. "But sometimes I get bored."

"Well then." She made little ripples with her fingers. "You won't tell on me, will you?"

"Are you afraid of your husband?"

"A little. He has a bad temper."

"I won't tell."

"That's nice of you. What's your first name?"

"Claude."
"I'm Ann."
"I know."
"What's that out there?" She pointed to a dark object about thirty feet offshore. "A float?"
"That's right."
"Race you to it."
She turned on her stomach and started toward the float. He followed. A few minutes later she pulled herself up on the wooden planking and leaned back, catching her breath. He climbed up beside her.
"You're a good swimmer," he said.
"So are you."
He knocked some water out of his ear. "Your husband's looking very good, wouldn't you say?"
"All three of them are. The Mentius Mafia's doing quite a job."
"Oh? You've heard our nickname?"
"I'm told you're very secretive."
"We have to be."
"Why?"
"If for no other reason, to protect Dr. Mentius. The details of the treatment—the extraction of Mentase, for instance—if others knew how it was done, they'd do it themselves. There's no real patent for something like this."
"I'm not very intelligent about patents, but couldn't he patent the formula for Mentase?"
"There's no formula. It's an enzyme. You can't patent an enzyme."
"I suppose not."
"It will be bad enough once the announcement of the discovery is made public. It will be like announcing the discovery of a genuine cancer cure, only more so—and you can imagine the uproar that would cause. That's one reason the doctor is nervous about this party of Lady de Ross's. If people see the change in her, some of them are bound to start rumors about a miracle drug for aging. Of course, she maintains they'll see when she leaves the chateau anyway, and I suppose she has a point. The existence of Mentase can't be kept a secret too much longer. But its nature—its molecu-

lar structure and where it is found—well, if that ever became public knowledge, then others would start producing it, which would be disastrous."

"Because of overpopulation?"

"That, and other things. Can you imagine what would happen if no one in the world died for even one year?"

"I suppose that's why Mr. Hirsch and the others are so interested in controlling the distribution of it?" she said.

"Definitely."

"In a way, then, the man who controls Mentase would be a very powerful person, wouldn't he?"

De Villeneuve didn't answer.

"Wouldn't he?" persisted Ann.

"He will obviously become one of the most powerful men of all time."

The Société Gérontologique. International distribution deals with top government figures. Only those "qualified" would get it. Slowly, the scope of the Mentase "conspiracy" began to form in her mind.

After a strained moment she felt De Villeneuve's hand on her knee.

"This isn't a very romantic conversation, is it?" he said.

She gently pushed his hand off her knee. "Romantic enough," she said casually. "Are you going to Lady Kitty's party?"

"No. Mrs. Mentius is giving the staff the weekend off. I'm going to visit my parents in Zermatt. In a way, I wish I were staying."

"Why?"

"So I could see more of you, of course." He put his hand back on her knee.

"You're not exactly shy, are you?" she said.

"Neither are you." He leaned over and took her in his arms. She let him kiss her. Then he pressed her down on the float and moved his powerful body on top of her, kissing her again. She felt his manhood pressing against her midsection.

Slow down, she thought. Slow down. My God, he's an absolute bull!

"Doctor?"

"Um?"

"I hope you didn't do this to me while I was asleep in the Aquadorme tank?"

"I thought about it." Now his hands were trying to undo the top of her bathing suit. She pushed them away as his lips kissed her neck.

"Were you the one who carried me upstairs to the Infirmary?"

"No, we put you on portable beds. . . ."

As gently as possible, without actually shoving him, she pushed him off and sat up.

"I think that's enough for tonight," she said.

"Why?" He sounded angry.

"I know what you're thinking: another teasing American bitch."

"Absolutely," he snapped.

"It's just that I want to whet your appetite. After all, I want to keep you interested." She stood up and prepared to dive back into the water.

"Where are you going?" he asked.

"To my room. I'll be back tomorrow night."

"And what if I'm not?"

"Well," she said, rising on her toes, "you'll never know what you missed."

She dived back into the water and started swimming for the pier, thinking what a dreadful bitch she sounded, and sort of relishing it at that.

❧

As she walked back to the chateau, Ann thought about what she had learned; De Villeneuve had been more enlightening than she had hoped, and surely more than he had intended. The key word had been "extraction." If the Methuselah Enzyme had to be "extracted," what was it extracted from? Humans? Like the RNA? Young humans, presumably.

In fact, herself?

Shivering slightly from the night breeze, she tried to remember what she had learned. Mentius said he'd discovered an enzyme in the human body that destroyed the cross-links between the DNA molecules until around the age of twenty-five. At that point, as he had said, the enzyme starts to disappear from the body, throws things out of balance. The cross-links multiply faster than what's left of the enzyme can break them up. The result is cell mutation and aging. Assume Mentius had discovered the enzyme, but couldn't synthesize it—needed funds for research to perfect the method. He went to Michael for money, who took him to Arnold Hirsch, who promised to finance him if he would give the Mentase to him. But Mentius said he couldn't: he had no way to produce it yet. Arnold persisted. He had no time—at any moment he might have a second, fatal stroke. Then someone—perhaps Arnold? —asked if Mentius might not be able to "extract" the Methuselah Enzyme from the bodies of young persons, people under twenty-five whose bodies were still producing Mentase. Mentius was shocked: the suggestion was ghoulish.

But he must have said it might be possible.

That would have been all Arnold needed. He would provide a young person—and who more convenient than his son? His son, whom he already hated for killing his wife. And Lady Kitty had no doubt volunteered her gigolo, Hugh.

And of course Michael didn't have to look far. He had his *young* and attractive wife.

It was monstrous, but it seemed the only explanation. And once Mentius had agreed to the proposal, the actual extraction of the enzyme would have to be done in secrecy. After all, this wasn't the sort of thing a respectable doctor would want to get around. Nor would anyone in his right mind volunteer for such an operation. So he used the elaborate deception of the Aquadorme tanks. And while they were asleep those three days, presumably undergoing sleep therapy tests, Mentius must have fitted that damned stereotaxic cage on her head and burrowed into her brain with the electric needle to draw out the precious Mentase—it must be produced somewhere in the brain. The extraction must have been done neatly and without her later realizing it. . . .

She was almost at the terrace of the chateau when she stopped and put her finger up under her wet hair, gingerly exploring the left side of her scalp. Then she felt it. A tiny square, no more than a half inch on each side, where her hair had been carefully shaven. Much too small for her to have noticed, and the hairdressers in the Cosmetarium had probably been instructed to say nothing about it. Then she felt the scab in the center of the square. A tiny scab. Almost healed now, for it had been there a month. But there, nevertheless.

"Good God," she whispered.

Someone stepped out of the shadows of the terrace into the light spilling from the windows of the chateau. It was a man dressed in a dark blue suit, a big man with a nondescript face.

"Good evening, Mrs. Brandywine," he said in a light, accented voice.

It was one of Arnold Hirsch's detectives. She climbed the steps to the terrace. "Good evening," she said, trying to appear calm. "It's a lovely night, isn't it?"

"Very nice. Been for a swim?"

"Where else would I have been in a bathing suit?"

Thinking that it probably hadn't been too smart to be so flip with him, she entered the empty chateau and hurried upstairs to her suite. Once there, she didn't even bother to dry off, but instead went to the desk, pulled out some of the light blue chateau stationery, and began a long letter to her brother Bob.

She was afraid to tell Michael she knew the truth. Afraid because, perversely, she couldn't stand the thought of his admitting it to her. It meant that her marriage had been a terrible deceit. The man she had loved and who, she assumed, had loved her, had cared so little for her that he had allowed Mentius to perform what must have been an extremely dangerous operation on her. Every time she thought of it, it chilled her. And yet the thought of confronting Michael with the truth made her so deeply miserable she said nothing the next morning, though she was sure he suspected something was wrong with her; the tight, drawn look on her face must have given away her state of mind.

When Mentius and the three patients had left the Salle d'Hercule to go to the lab for the day, Ann turned to Martin Hirsch, who had made one of his rare appearances in the dining room.

"Martin, I thought I'd go to the Infirmary and say hello to Hugh. Would you like to go with me?"

"Sure," he said unenthusiastically.

"I think Hugh's getting released this morning," said Sally Mentius. "It's been a week since his operation, and I hear he's feeling very spry, particularly with his nurse."

Ann and Martin were led into Hugh's room by the pretty nurse. "Monsieur Barstow has recovered most remarkably," said Yvette, smiling at Hugh who, in fact, looked in excellent shape. When she left the room, Hugh said, "Yvette's the best back-scrubber I've ever met. I'm beginning to see what Kitty digs in those bathtub scenes."

"Does Lady Kitty have scenes in bathtubs?" asked Martin, impressed.

"She spends so much time in tubs, she's got a ring around *her* middle," said Hugh. "So how are things, Ann?"

"Not nearly, I'm afraid, as good as you seem to be." She pulled a chair up beside his bed. "Martin was right. We weren't just brought here to keep the 'old folks' company."

"Then why?" Hugh asked.

"*We* are the Methuselah Enzyme."

She proceeded to outline to them her thoughts of the night before, to which they listened attentively, Martin interrupting once to ask why his father had wanted to take the Mentase treatment before Mentase could be synthesized. "Because he has arteriosclerosis," explained Ann. "And the treatment was really his only chance of surviving. Besides, I'm beginning to think you were also right about your father's interest in the political aspects of Mentase."

Hugh said, "So the three of them decided the three of us would make a dandy source of supply for Mentase?"

"That's right. If nothing else, we were conveniently handy."

"And Mentius took the Mentase from us those three days he zonked us in the Aquadorme tanks?"

"No," said Ann, "he took it from *me*. I'm sure he was frightened about doing it, and he probably wanted to wait to see how I recovered from the operation—that is, if I recovered. He must have used the stereotaxic cage, which left the red marks on my forehead and yours, Hugh—"

"But why not mine?" interrupted Martin.

"Because he hasn't operated on your brain yet."

"My brain?" Martin looked horrified. "You mean, Mentase comes out of our *brains?*"

"Yes. Look." She held up her hair and showed them the small shaven square with the tiny scab in the center. "See? Fortunately for Dr. Mentius, I have long hair, so the chances were I wouldn't notice the scar, which is small anyway. And, also very conveniently for Dr. Mentius, Hugh's hair is long, too, so he wouldn't notice the scar."

Hugh looked confused. "I don't dig. You mean he operated on me too when we were in the Aquadormes?"

"Yes, but he didn't extract any Mentase from you then. He apparently only set you up for the next operation if it looked as though I was going to survive the first one."

"What do you mean, 'set me up'?"

"I'm only guessing because I don't know that much about the brain, but it seems to me he could have planted something inside your head that later on would give you headaches. Naturally, you'd go to him when the headaches didn't stop—"

"Mrs. Mentius *told* me to go to him!"

"And he diagnosed a brain tumor . . ."

"You mean I *didn't* have a tumor?"

"Not if I'm right."

"That son of a bitch! That dirty son of a bitch!"

"That's pretty damned unethical, isn't it?" said Martin.

"No shit!" snapped Hugh. "Christ, do you think doctors are supposed to carve people up without telling them? What do you think they've all been so secretive for? And we've been sitting here, fat and happy, letting them get away with it!"

"Hugh, I feel the same way you do about it," said Ann, "but please let's hold off doing anything until—"

"The hell with that! I'm going to yell cop and have them all put in jail for goddamn life!"

"And how would you prove it?"

He looked surprised. "Well, for starters, I'd show them this damn scar . . ."

"And Mentius would say he operated on you for a brain tumor, which you can't prove you *didn't* have. And my scar is almost healed. So it would be our word against a world-famous scientist, plus his staff, plus Michael and Arnold and Lady Kitty, who I'm sure would back him up. They've gone about it awfully cleverly, and they've got us in a corner. Besides, we don't want to push Arnold Hirsch into getting ugly, with his six private detectives."

"Who look like they can get pretty ugly," said Martin. "But Ann, I'm not going to sit here and let them carve *me* up."

"Yeah, what about Martin?" said Hugh.

"Martin's in no danger, at least for a couple of weeks," replied Ann. "They waited a month between operating on me and on Hugh, and they just operated on Hugh last week. So it seems unlikely they'll try anything for at least a week or more. And by that time my brother will be here."

"And what's he going to do?"

"He's a lawyer. I wrote him a letter last night and told him everything. I asked him to fly to Lausanne as soon as he could. And when he gets here he can tell us what sort of legal action we should take, if any, or what we *should* do. I really think we shouldn't do anything until he gets here, and we shouldn't let any of them know we're on to it. That's why I didn't try a phone call—too risky. Anyway, it's your decision as well as mine."

The two men looked at each other, told Ann they didn't like it much but would go along for a couple of days—no more.

"Good." She got up and replaced her chair. Hugh was watching her. "Have you said anything to your husband?"

"Not a word."

"If you're right, he pulled one pretty crappy, unhusbandly trick on you, didn't he?"

"I think," she said quietly, "that's a bit of an understatement."

❧

But she didn't hear from her brother for four days. And, by the fifth day, Friday, she was becoming concerned. As she walked toward the Salle d'Hercule for lunch that day, Hugh took her aside and whispered, "What's happened with your brother?"

"I don't know. If I don't hear from him by tomorrow morning latest I'll have to risk calling him and tell him everything on the phone."

Hugh nodded. "That makes sense. You know, since I got out of the Infirmary I've been thinking over what you told us. And I've pretty well decided I ought to blow this scene. I mean, I'm so damned cheesed at Kitty-baby I could, like, strangle her every time I look at her. And I've managed to save a little money in the past two weeks, so why should I stick around this joint any longer? I think I'm going to tell her to shove it and then fade."

"Hugh, please don't leave till tomorrow, at least," said Ann, thinking how much she needed his support, not to mention how lonely she would be if he left the chateau. "Wait till I talk to my brother."

Hugh hesitated. "Yeah, okay," he said. "I guess I couldn't just walk out on you. But I'm getting very itchy."

She smiled. "Thanks."

"But keep me away from *her*," he added, glancing at Lady Kitty who had just come out of the Salon de Vénus accompanied by Michael. As they crossed the corridor to the Salle d'Hercule, they were too engrossed in each other's company to notice Ann and Hugh. When they had gone into the dining room, Hugh said, "How are you getting along with your husband?"

"How do you think I'd be getting along?" she replied. "I'm co-existing. I suppose that's the best way to describe it."

They started toward the Salle d'Hercule. "Has he been coming back late to your suite from the lab lately?" asked Hugh casually.

She looked surprised. "How did you know?"

"It was just a guess."

He led her into the red dining room, where Lady Kitty had already taken her seat and was talking to Sally Mentius about her Unbirthday Ball, which was scheduled for the following evening.

"The caterer will be moving in at eight tomorrow morning," she said, "so be prepared for the place to be turned into a madhouse. They'll be putting up the decorations and setting up the bandstands, and the decorator is an impossible neurotic, so he'll be screaming at everyone. . . . Have you rented your costumes yet?"

"Oh yes," said Sally. "Herbie and I are coming as Columbus and Isabella of Spain."

"How quaint," said Lady Kitty unenthusiastically. "And here's dear Ann," she continued, smiling a glucose smile as Ann took her seat next to Michael. "Who are you coming as, Pollyanna?"

"No, I'm coming as Marie Antoinette. And who are you coming as, Lady Kitty, Jezebel?"

Lady Kitty's lids lowered. "I assume that's supposed to be what we used to call, in bad plays, 'cutting dialogue.' In fact, I'm coming as Léonide Leblanc, or Mlle. Maximum as I believe she was called: the original owner of this place. Mrs. Mentius showed me lithographs of some of her gowns, and I've had one of them copied. It's quite spectacular, and I'm having my Paris banker send me my rubies; so, without seeming unduly immodest, I think I should look quite sensational." She smiled. "And Michael? Who will you be?"

"Louis XV."

"Charming! The philandering king." She looked sweetly at Ann. "Ah, and here's dear Arnold. But it looks as if he's already in his costume."

Arnold Hirsch had just walked into the dining room in a mod cut double-breasted suit that was such a radical departure from his normal conservative style that it did indeed look like a costume. It was light gray flannel with a four-button overlay, high lapels, and a nipped-in waist. With it he wore a deep blue Bengal-striped shirt and a flowered tie. With his sandy hairpiece and luxuriant sideburns, his newly trim figure and ruddy face, he looked like a forty-five-year-old Madison Avenue account executive on his way to the Sanctuary for a night of acid rock. His physical transformation was startling, and he knew it. He smiled with pleasure at their reaction.

"Do you like it?"

"Absolutely stunning!" gushed Lady Kitty. "I adore it!"

"I ordered it from Pierre Cardin. It's not exactly Wall Street, but since we're all getting younger it seemed to me we ought to try out some of the younger life-styles."

"I couldn't agree more," she continued. "Michael, you ought to buy some mod gear."

"Don't you like the way I dress?" he asked.

"Dear boy, you have superb taste. But you're looking so radiantly young, it would be fun to see you in something different. Don't you agree, Ann?"

She looked down the table at Ann, who shrugged indifferently. "Perhaps."

Lady Kitty laughed. "Hardly what I would call enthusiastic agreement. Oh, well. Wives never like their husbands to change. In that respect, dear Lord de Ross was the model husband. He was an insufferable bore when I married him, and was an insufferable bore when I buried him. Such constancy of character! Admirable. But speaking as a dropout from the marital wars, I can only say that men become so much more interesting when they experiment. Variety, after all, is the spice of life."

"Then yours sure as hell is overseasoned," said Hugh, chewing a carrot.

Lady Kitty blinked at him. "I'm not quite sure I like that."

"Very sorry. Not bad threads, though, Mr. Hirsch. Wouldn't mind having one of those Cardin suits myself."

"You have far too many clothes already," said Lady Kitty. "Don't be a pig."

"I didn't say I was going out to buy one. I said I'd like to have it. There's a difference."

"Not with you. When you want something, you give me no peace at all until I buy it for you, and I'm in no mood to indulge your gluttonous appetite for clothes. You're costing me a bloody fortune as it is."

Hugh was burning. "Hey Kitty baby, I just said I was looking, not buying. And like if you don't want to pay the rent, I'll be more than happy to take the next shuffleboard out of Retirement Village."

"Don't be an ass. And don't make a scene."

"You're making the scene. You've been hocking me about money ever since we got here. Like, I've told you a hundred times I'm ready to blow this place, right? If you think I get my kicks sitting around in this morgue listening to you and the playmate of the moment splash in your tub, forget it."

Lady Kitty was red in the face. "Hugh, dear, that will do . . ."

"No, it won't do!" He pushed back his chair and stood up, glaring at his suddenly nervous employer. "To you I'm nothing but a goddamn stud, but it's just possible I might groove in show biz if I could ever get away from this frigging mausoleum. . . ."

"Hugh, dear, you are the veritable answer to a producer's prayer. Now please sit down."

"Why should I listen to you yapping about how expensive I am and how you're not getting your money's worth, when I'd like to know how in hell you could work me in between tub sessions?"

"*Will* you shut up?" she blazed.

"No!"

She took a deep breath and forced a patently phony smile. "Dear Hugh, I shan't say a word more about money. You know this party is costing me a good deal, and if I fret about finances . . ."

"You've got more money than freaking God, so don't give me that crap. Now, are you going to lay off?"

"I said I would."

"That's better." Looking somewhat pleased at his triumph, he tossed the remainder of his carrot on the table and sauntered out of the room. Lady Kitty glared at him as he walked out. Then she looked at Arnold Hirsch and Michael and, with superb sangfroid, picked up her fork.

"Well, you can tell he's from Secaucus."

Lifting a forkful of shrimp salad to her mouth, she practically bit off the tines.

❧

"Hugh, you were magnificent!" said Ann a few minutes later as she joined him on the terrace. He was leaning on the stone balustrade smoking a cigarette.

"The old bitch," he growled. "She's a royal pain in the ass—always has been. Anyway, I feel better having let off some steam." He inhaled deeply. Then he said, rather bitterly, "They all looked so damned smug, didn't they?"

"Very smug," she agreed. "And by their lights they have good reason."

He nodded. "Yeah. Mentius may not win the Kindly Family Doctor Sweepstakes, but he sure as hell has proved his point. They *have* grown younger."

After a moment, Ann said, "Hugh, who is Lady Kitty's tub-mate, now that Bill Bradshaw is gone?"

Hugh shrugged. "I don't know. Probably the dishwasher. She'll bang anything in pants."

"No, you do know," she said quietly. "It's Michael, isn't it?"

He looked at her, started to deny it, then changed his mind. "Well, it's not the dishwasher."

She looked up at the gleaming white façade of the chateau. Of course. Hugh had tried to warn her before lunch. "Late from the lab"—what a laughable excuse *that* was! And of course, Lady Kitty's heavy-handed remarks during lunch. . . . But Lady Kitty? That hag? Except she wasn't a hag anymore. She had become quite beautiful. But still, Lady Kitty? Disgusting, nymphomaniacal Lady Kitty? She didn't know which hurt more: Michael's infidelity, or the woman she had lost him to.

Hugh flipped the cigarette into a stone jardiniere.

"I'm sorry," he said. "But I guess it's better you know."

"I appreciate your telling me." She tried to smile. "I really loved him. Once. I guess I'm the number one idiot of all time."

But now, she thought, *now* at least it's simpler. Now I know what to do when the time comes.

❧

At eight the next morning the army of caterers and decorators invaded the Chateau Mirabelle to prepare for Lady Kitty's Un-birthday Ball, and the building resounded with the whack of ham-mers and the yells of the workmen. By nine thirty, the mail had been delivered, and since there was no word from her brother, Ann went into her bedroom and, trying to sound casual, rang the switch-board operator to place a call to her brother in Larchmont.

"It will take me a half hour to clear a circuit, Mrs. Brandywine," said the operator.

"All right. I'll be here in my room."

She hung up, then went over to the bed where her costume and Michael's were laid out, having been delivered from the costumer in Lausanne a few minutes earlier. She held her dress up in front of her, then looked in a mirror to inspect it. It was an eighteenth-century court gown made of pale blue watered silk, and looked so beautiful she decided to try it on. The enormous skirt made it difficult to get into, but she struggled until it was on, then adjusted the towering white wig that had come with the dress. Again she looked in the mirror. It was impressive but something was missing. After all, Lady Kitty had probably been right when she said she would look sensational, and nothing would give Ann greater pleasure than to outshine Lady Kitty. So she went to the small wall safe, dialed the combination, and removed the black velvet case which contained the anniversary present Michael had given her. She opened the lid and looked at the magnificent turquoise and diamond necklace inside, with the matching pendant earrings fitted with the circle of the necklace. She remembered the thrill she had felt the night he gave her the jewels. She had never had anything remotely like them, and when he had put the necklace around her throat, she had felt like Cinderella. She picked the earrings out of the box and attached them; then she put on the necklace and looked at herself again. The splendid jewels made the costume. But how differently she felt about them now, only a few short months since they had been given to her.

Her spirits were depressed even further when she looked closely at her reflection. There were dark circles under her eyes, and her fair skin had acquired a pallor beneath her fading tan. Obviously, the strain of the last twenty-four hours, and in particular the strain of learning about Lady Kitty, was doing her no good. Lady Kitty! When she thought of her, she could howl with bitterness and envy. Envy? Yes, paradoxically, envy of a woman three times her age who had so casually stolen her husband away from her. It was bizarre to resent that, when there was so much else to resent. But nevertheless, she did.

She spotted Michael in the mirror, standing in the door behind her. She whirled around and looked at him almost guiltily, as if he had been reading her thoughts. "You might knock," she said irritably.

"Sorry, I didn't mean to frighten you."

He came into the room.

"Why aren't you in the lab?" she asked.

"Mentius gave us the day off because of the party. Schlessing and De Villeneuve are taking a long weekend, and there didn't seem any point in continuing the treatment till Monday. By the way, the switchboard operator asked me to tell you she's had to cancel your call."

He had picked his costume from the bed and was examining it. She stared at him, trying not to show her fear.

"My call?"

"The one you placed to Bob. The switchboard's been closed."

"Why?"

"Well, you might say the switchboard operator is taking the long weekend, too, which is partially true." He looked up from his costume. "I'm afraid your letter didn't get through either. It's amazing how sloppy the mail service can be in Europe."

She could hardly believe his incredibly casual attitude. But her amazement quickly gave way to anger.

"Why, *damn* you!"

"Now Ann, that's not a very pleasant way to talk to your husband."

"You go to hell! How dare you stop my letters?"

He looked at her coolly, unimpressed by her anger. "Well, you see, Ann, you have a bad habit of making things sound worse than they really are."

"Oh? I suppose I should have written that the operation you so lightheartedly let Mentius perform on me was all for the sake of humanity? Or maybe the impoverished aged, whom you were wailing about when we first got here?"

"No, it was hardly done for the impoverished aged."

"It was done for the *rich* aged, which makes it even worse! Might I ask how in God's name you could have been so insensitive, so selfish, so perverted as to ever have agreed to this . . . this *putrid* scheme?"

"Keep your voice down!"

"I'll yell my head off! And I want an answer."

"My motivation was very simple: self-preservation. And while I'll admit it was, as you say, insensitive, once Arnold decided to take the treatment and volunteered his son as a potential source, it seemed logical for me to volunteer you."

"A 'source'? What a wonderful way to be described! It makes me feel like an iron mine, or an old cow waiting to get milked! My God, to do something like this to your own wife—"

"Look, Ann, I'm not going to get in a brawl with you. I'll only say there was no alternative if we wanted the treatment, and Mentius said that though it was a tricky operation, there'd be very little risk to your health."

"If I survived! But that must have seemed a pretty small 'if' to you and the others! What if I died? What would you have said then? 'Poor Ann, she gave her life so we might live—forever!' What a charming epitaph!"

"As I said," Michael remarked impatiently, "there seemed little risk—"

"Even if there was no risk at all, you had no right to give that permission without asking me! No one has that right over anybody."

"Let's say my right is around your neck."

She put her hand up to the necklace and felt the jewels. "You *bought* me?" She looked disgusted. "Come on, Michael."

"In case you've forgotten, you didn't have a cent when you married me. You were an anonymous little secretary, lost in the gloomy canyons of Manhattan. I've given you a rather luxurious year—"

"Topped off by a glamorous vacation to picturesque Switzerland, where I have my head cut into by the famed Dr. Mentius!"

"Come now, Ann," said a voice at the door. "Let's not descend to a sordid domestic squabble."

She looked over to see Arnold Hirsch standing in the doorway. "May I join you?" he continued, not waiting for an answer. "Michael told me about the phone call you tried to place to your brother, and I thought it might be helpful for me to be here. Sometimes family difficulties are settled more quickly with a third party present, don't you think? Might I add that you look beautiful in that costume? Somewhat as I imagine Marie Antoinette must have looked."

"Marie Antoinette only had her head chopped off," said Ann. "My head has been excavated. I'm not sure Antoinette didn't get the better deal."

"But you survived the operation, which, of course, is more than she did. And I must say you look healthy enough. That was a very unfair letter you wrote your brother. Understandable, of course, but there is another way to think of what we've been doing."

She fingered her eardrops. "And what's your suggestion?"

"Well, I think you could consider your participation as a contribution to a scientific adventure. After all, the risk you took wasn't as great as the risk the three of us have taken."

"An interesting approach."

"And I don't have to spell out to you the benefits Mentase is going to have for, well, humanity."

She laughed. "Dear God . . . one for humanity! Arnold, I know perfectly well how you intend to use Mentase for the benefit of humanity. The people you approve will be given the treatment, and the people you don't, won't."

"But what alternative is there to controlling the distribution of Mentase? Surely you don't expect every person on earth to be given the opportunity to live forever? Even the most woolly-minded humanitarian wouldn't be that stupid."

"But that isn't the point. The point is, why should you be allowed to decide who gets it?"

"Because I own it," he said simply.

"*We* own it," corrected Michael.

"All right, we own it."

"Then Martin was right," said Ann. "You *are* some sort of Fascist."

Arnold smiled. "My son, with the simplistic certitude of the young, labels me a Fascist because I am over thirty, rich, and believe that society should not be handed over to drug-besotted children who think the answer to all the world's problems is love, or brotherhood, or casual copulation. I admit I believe government is impossible without centralized authority. But if that makes me a Fascist, it also makes Thomas Jefferson a Fascist, as well as Lincoln, Roosevelt, Churchill, Kennedy—any effective leader, for that matter."

"It's surely a matter of degree," she said. "You're playing with semantics."

"Then I'll play with ideas instead. Man is created unequal. A responsible government should offer him equal opportunity for advancement, but only an idiot would think all will advance equally. What we intend to do is offer those who advance the most chance for immortality—if they wish it. For that minority of each generation which is superior in brains and talent, death is an enemy which cuts them down just when they have reached their prime. Why shouldn't they be given the chance to avoid it? And wouldn't it benefit all humanity? I don't think you'd argue that mankind is doing a fairly rotten job of governing itself at present—though I suppose it could be argued that in some countries there has been a slight improvement over the past. But there is room for more improvement; in fact, there's a howling need for it, which the young point out to us with stupefying frequency.

"But the improvement won't come through vague, anarchic bromides about love. It will come through technology and science; order and planning. Mentase can remove power from the political hacks and put it in the hands of those best qualified to use it. Imagine the mind of a Mozart, a Plato, a Ch'ien Lung, a Buddha, a Jefferson, a Bacon, a Marcus Aurelius—imagine what these minds could have given the world if they could have been kept young, active, and healthy for centuries! But for every Aurelius, there are a hundred Neros. For every Beethoven, a thousand Spohrs. For every Lincoln, a million Millard Fillmores. History is a record of the fifth-rate because the first-rate are too rare and short-lived to exercise anything but a passing influence on society. Mentase, by offering the first-rate infinitely extended lifespans, can correct this."

Ann said quietly, "You're quite a salesman, Arnold. But who picks the Lincolns and the Beethovens?"

"They pick themselves, naturally. By what they achieve."

"Oh, so then the Mentase qualification committee—which I suppose consists of you two—"

"No. The Société Gérontologique will pick the committees, if you want to call them that."

"But you are the Société! You and Michael and Lady Kitty and Dr. Mentius. Isn't that right?"

"Yes. We will have ultimate control. The plan is simple. Once the synthesizing of Mentase is perfected—which Mentius believes will be in less than two years—the Société will build clinics in each of the major countries of the western world, operating within the framework of the national laws. A board of selection, chosen by us in conjunction with the government in power, will screen all applicants for the Mentase treatment. No one under thirty-five will be considered. That way, a man's abilities will already have been partially demonstrated. Besides, obviously, he wouldn't need the treatment till then. The rich will pay. But since the qualification is merit, not wealth, those who can't afford the fee will be subsidized by the clinic and, partially, by the government in power."

"You make it sound as democratic as apple pie."

"It will be selective, but democratically selective."

"And what happens once you're in the clinic? You get the treatment and keep coming back for the boosters?"

"Yes. That is, as long as you continue to qualify. Immortality, once earned, will have to continue to be earned. If the recipient goes sour, so to speak, the shots will be suspended."

"And what does 'going sour' mean? Doesn't it mean starting to rock the boat? Starting to have ideas the committee and the 'government in power' don't like?"

"To an extent. The greatest danger to the world today is permanent upheaval."

"Oh? And of course upheaval is the devilish creation of young people. So then, really, Mentase will be used as a sort of weapon against the young."

"Not a weapon. Weapons destroy society. Mentase is a tool to preserve it from anarchy—or, if you insist, the young who seem to be drunk with anarchy. Of course, by the time a man is thirty-five, he should have outgrown the puerile ideas he had in college."

"And if he hasn't?"

"Then he won't be given the Mentase."

"He'll be allowed to grow old and die? A painless sort of extermination, in other words."

"Let's say 'weeding,' to play at semantics again. Or better yet, 'cultivation.' The best are cultivated; the rest—" He spread his hands. "I admit there is a certain lack of sentiment involved. Selectivity implies rejection—the best clubs are the most exclusive, after all." He paused.

"Ann," said Michael, "certainly you're sophisticated enough to see that what the Société aims to do makes a lot of sense."

"Oh, I suppose it makes sense. Whether it's good sense or not, I'm not so sure."

"I can also understand your feelings toward me," he continued. "But the fact remains, you're my wife. And you have a vested interest in the success of the Société."

"And so," said Arnold, "isn't it more intelligent for you to join us, rather than work against us?"

She stood up and walked over to one of the windows overlooking the lake, the silk in her skirt rustling as she moved. They watched her as she looked out over the blue water. Then she turned.

"What you do with Mentase is your business. Or rather, the business of the Société and its four distinguished owners."

Arnold looked pleased. "That's a most reasonable attitude."

"I'm a most reasonable woman. However, it seems to me most unreasonable to remain Mrs. Michael Brandywine any longer." She looked at Michael. "I want a divorce."

He didn't look surprised. "All right," he said simply.

"I didn't think it would upset you too much. But this will." She looked coolly at both of them. "I want a large settlement."

Michael still remained impassive. "All of my wives have. You can keep the jewels, by the way."

"Thank you. But I want something a little more useful than jewels."

Now he looked curious. "What?"

"I want as my settlement all your holdings in the Société Gérontologique."

They both looked thunderstruck.

"What's the matter?" she asked. "Doesn't that fit into your plans for making earth a paradise of genius."

"I would say not," said Arnold.

"But why? Don't you think it's only fair to have a young person represented in the choosing of the qualification committees? After all, those of us under thirty-five must represent at least half the human race you're so eager to benefit."

"Ann," said Michael, "if this is your idea of a joke, it's a lousy one."

"It's a better joke than the one you've had on me," she said. "And in case you don't think I'll have colorful ammunition in court, then I think you'd better know I'm fully aware of the sudsy afternoons you've been spending with Lady de Ross."

Michael blinked. "How did you find out?"

"My divorce lawyer will fill in all the details in court."

Silence. Michael said in a quiet voice, "And what about your midnight swims with Dr. de Villeneuve?"

"All right. We can bring all the dirty linen out in court and see whose is the dirtier. And while we're airing the linen, everything else will get aired too, including what's happened here at the chateau, and all your fascinating plans for the future of the human race. The press and television will adore it! I can see the headlines now: 'Wall Street Financier Plans Master Race.' Or perhaps that's too unsubtle. How about 'Senior Citizens to Rule the World'? That would be a popular headline, especially with the young. Student radicals, for instance, would be ecstatic. Just think what they could preach to all those pink-cheeked sophomores who already have this curious skepticism about the morals of their elders. . . . Well, I'll leave the rest to your imagination."

No one spoke. Finally, Arnold Hirsch stood up. "You're rather ingenious, Ann. Really. I'm quite impressed. It never occurred to me you would be so, well, ambitious."

"I'm in ambitious company, aren't I? I guess it's catching."

"Yes, you are. Much too ambitious to allow an enormous investment of time and money to be jeopardized by a rather bright but unfortunately stubborn woman. Let me point out to you that Michael's shares in the Société are nontransferable."

"Arnold," she said, "after what Michael's done to me, there's nothing he owns I can't get—with a good lawyer, of course. And I intend to get a good lawyer."

"I'm sure you and Michael can arrange an amicable settlement. But it's going to be arranged out of court."

"Don't you think you're getting a little over your head? You can't keep me out of a divorce court."

"I think you're mistaken."

There was a slight change in his tone that was unpleasant.

"How do you intend doing it?"

"You've noticed the private detectives I've hired to keep an eye on Martin?"

"They'd be hard not to notice. But you're not really going to try something as foolish as making me a prisoner?"

"'Patient' is such a nicer word," he said. "A 'patient' who is recovering from a severe emotional crisis. Oh, let's say even a nervous breakdown, for instance. Yes, I rather like that: a nervous breakdown. What do you think, Michael?"

Michael was looking uneasy. "I don't know, Arnold . . ."

"But you shouldn't worry, Michael. Ann's going to have a very quick convalescence, aren't you, Ann? And I understand that in cases of nervous disorders, a person's recovery depends very much on his will to get well—his, well, mental attitude, as it were."

She was watching both of them intently. "How long do you think you can keep me here?" she said.

"Long enough for you to realize your little bravura gesture isn't worth the trouble and inconvenience you'll be put to. You have a price—you've just overestimated it. When you consider the advantages of financial independence for the rest of your life, you'll come around to our thinking. As for your talking to the press, I'm sure you could embarrass us, but I'm also sure Michael can arrange that whatever settlement he makes would be canceled if you put out unfavorable publicity about any of his enterprises. These things are messy, but lawyers know how to arrange them. And you see, Ann, we have very good lawyers too. Michael?" He motioned toward the door. "I suggest we leave Ann alone to think things over. 'Wisdom flourishes in solitude,' as the Chinese say."

He started toward the door, followed by Michael. "By the way, you're free to go anywhere you want in the chateau; it's just that one of my men will be with you. If you try to talk to any of Lady Kitty's guests, well, someone will be there listening, sort of a human wiretap. And naturally if you start saying things you shouldn't, he'll have to explain about the uncertain state of your nerves. So it will probably be wiser if you just talk to us."

Nodding politely, he followed Michael out of the room.

❧

When they had left the suite, she took off her costume and put away her jewels. Then, after putting on a skirt and sweater, she went to the door connecting her bedroom with Martin Hirsch's and quietly knocked. After a moment, Martin opened the door, dressed in a weird white gown that covered him completely and dragged on the floor behind him. "What's that?" asked Ann.

"My costume for the party," he replied. "I'm going as St. Peter."

"Martin, please get Hugh and bring him to your room," she said. "Then both of you come in here."

He looked confused. "Why?"

"Because if there's a detective in the hall, I don't want him to think we're all getting together in the same place."

"Oh. Did you hear from your brother?"

"In a way. I'll explain the whole business. Hurry!"

She closed the door, then checked the living room of the suite to make sure it was empty, which it was. Returning to her bedroom, she closed the door to the living room, then waited. Five minutes later, Martin led Hugh in.

"There was a detective," he said. "He's the same one that's been watching me. Except now he's got himself a chair."

"Where's your brother?" asked Hugh.

"Nowhere. They stopped my letter, and then they stopped my phone call, and now they've got the guards watching me and they're going to tell everyone I've had a nervous breakdown."

"Jesus, they're not kidding anymore, are they?"

"Hardly. I think we should leave the chateau, tonight. If I'm a prisoner, I think it's a pretty good assumption both of you are too."

"What do we do?" asked Hugh. "Just call the bellboy and check out?"

"It's not going to be that simple," said Ann, "but Lady Kitty's costume party couldn't have happened at a better time. And Dr. Mentius doesn't know it yet, but I think he and Sally are going to help us too."

❧

Sally Mentius was on her knees in the living room of her private quarters pinning the baggy seat of her husband's Columbus costume. Her Isabella of Spain costume had fit her; but Columbus's pantaloons had drooped, so she had been forced to do an alteration. "Stand still, Herbie," she said.

"I *am* still."

"No you're not. You're fidgeting. And Jeremy, stop that!"

Her two sons were firing suction-tipped darts at the Claes Oldenburg vinyl toilet.

"Why?" complained Jeremy. "I like to shoot darts at the toilet."

"It's not a toilet, darling," said Sally patiently. "It's a work of art."

"It's a comment on civilization," added Mentius wearily.

"It looks like a toilet to me. Except I don't understand why it sags."

"That's the comment," said his father. "Now, why don't you two answer the doorbell and then go outside and play?"

Whooping loudly, the two boys raced to the door and opened it, admitting Ann, who looked none too pleased when Jeremy bumped her as he rushed by her into the corridor. She closed the door and came into the living room. "Ann," exclaimed Sally, "you're just in time. What do you think of Herbie's costume? Does it show where I fixed the pants?"

"No," said Ann, taking a chair.

"I'll be so glad when this party's over," continued Sally. "Lady Kitty's crew have just taken over the chateau, and they're all fighting . . . God, it's a nightmare. Would you like a cup of coffee?"

"I think I'd rather have a drink instead," said Ann. "I need one."

"In the middle of the day?" said Mentius curiously. "That's a bad habit to get into, Mrs. Brandywine."

"I think you've gotten into a few bad habits yourself, Doctor."

Mentius didn't miss the edge in her voice, nor did Sally. She stood up, and for a moment there was an awkward silence. Then she said, "I'll get that drink . . ."

"Get me one too," said Mentius.

Sally looked surprised at this; then she said, "I think I'll make that three. Scotch?"

"Please."

As Sally went to make the drinks, Mentius watched Ann. Then he said quietly, "What's happened, Mrs. Brandywine?"

"I've had a very interesting talk with my husband and Arnold Hirsch," she said. "I suppose you know they've been stopping my mail?"

Mentius frowned. "No, I didn't know."

"Well, now you know. I also tried to place a trans-Atlantic phone call to my brother this morning. Your switchboard operator has obviously been instructed—or more likely, bribed—to tell them, so the call wasn't placed. Now, for such a luxurious place as the Chateau Mirabelle, and for the prices we're paying to be here, this strikes me as rather unusual treatment. However, not nearly as unusual as the rest of what's been going on here."

Sally Mentius put down the Scotch bottle and said to her husband, "You see? I knew this was—"

"Sally, please," said Mentius. He turned to Ann. For a moment, she was almost tempted to laugh at the doctor, who seemed somehow ludicrous in his velvet brocade jacket and sagging Renaissance pantaloons. Columbus and Claes Oldenburg toilets didn't mix comfortably. But when she looked at his face, her impulse to laugh faded. The doctor looked defeated. For the first time, she almost felt sorry for Herbert Mentius.

"Mrs. Brandywine," he said, "I had no idea Arnold had gone this far. I'll instruct the switchboard operator to place any calls you wish . . ."

"The switchboard's being closed this afternoon," interrupted

Sally. "The operator's getting the weekend off, like everyone else."

"That's beside the point . . ."

"Doctor," said Ann, "I'm not interested in making the call now. It's gone beyond the point of making phone calls. But I would like you to answer a few questions for me."

"All right," he said. "I'll answer anything you want to know. Sally, where's that Scotch?"

He sat down. Sally brought their drinks, then sat down next to her husband. "Ann," she said, "we'd never have gone through with this if it hadn't been for Arnold. He insisted on having the treatment now—"

"Sally," interrupted her husband, "don't put all the blame on Arnold. I agreed to it. What is it you want to know, Mrs. Brandywine?"

"Well," said Ann, "I've managed to piece together what I think happened, but there are still a few things I'm vague about. Why did you put Martin Hirsch in the Aquadorme tanks with Hugh and me when you didn't do anything to him then?"

"We thought it would look odd to you if Martin *didn't* go in the tanks. And the three-day sleep didn't hurt him."

"Then how do you plan to operate on him? He knows the whole thing too, now, and I can assure you he won't volunteer."

"Obviously, no one would volunteer. But we aren't planning to operate on Martin. He was brought here only as an alternate source. You see, I wasn't sure how much Mentase I could get from two sources, and I told Arnold I'd need a third if we needed more. As it turned out"—he was looking increasingly pale as he talked, Ann noticed—"we got enough from . . . you and Mr. Barstow."

"I'm glad to hear it," said Ann, with more than a trace of sarcasm. "And exactly where does the Mentase come from?"

"It's produced by the pineal gland."

"What's that?"

"A small appendage directly behind the pituitary gland on the underside of the brain."

"I've never heard of it."

"Not many people have. In fact, the pineal has baffled science for centuries. Descartes thought it was the seat of the soul. It's also been conjectured that it's a vestigial third eye, and lately it's been demonstrated that it is in fact affected by light, which reaches it via the sympathetic nervous system." The doctor seemed to welcome the chance to lose himself in the subject that obviously meant so much to him. "Now we know the pineal secretes a hormone called melatonin, as well as the enzyme hydroxyindole-O-methyl transferase, which regulates the synthesis of melatonin. It also regulates hormonal responses involving the gonads, the thyroid, the pituitary, the hypothalamus, and several other regions of the brain. It's what is known as a neuroendocrine transducer—"

"Wait a minute," interrupted Ann. "None of this makes any sense to me. Speak English."

"I'm sorry," sighed Mentius. "The point is, when I became interested in the pineal, when I was at Harvard, it was still a mystery. I had been working on the aging process, and had become convinced there was something in the pineal that caused it. It was similar to Tombaugh postulating that the planet Pluto had to exist, and then going ahead and finding it. At any rate, during a series of experiments which were actually involved with something entirely irrelevant to that, I stumbled on the fact that the pineal was somehow involved with the aging process. And after four years of work, I finally isolated an enzyme secreted by the pineal, which I named Mentase."

"Which, as you told us, breaks down the cross-linkage between the DNA molecules?"

"Correct. And the production of which, at around the age of twenty-five, the pineal gradually begins to slow down, which in turn speeds up the aging process. I learned later on, from my experiments on rats, that it was possible to extract a tiny sliver of the pineal and from this derive Mentase—rat Mentase, that is. So it was logical to assume the same thing could be done with humans. I hadn't contemplated doing this until Arnold Hirsch insisted on the treatment. I needed time and money to be able to synthesize the equivalent of human Mentase in the lab; but the only way I could get the time and money was to give Arnold what he wanted, and that necessitated deriving Mentase from humans, which in turn necessitated all this elaborate deception."

"And I was the first one?"

"Yes. Fortunately, Mentase is an extremely potent enzyme,

effective in one part to ten million. So I needed relatively minute amounts from you to prepare a series of shots for the patients. The Mentase from you lasted almost a month."

"Then it was Hugh's turn?"

"That's right. While he was in the Aquadorme tank, I implanted a harmless electronic device, something I designed myself. It's very much like the pacemaker, which is used to maintain a regular heartbeat in heart patients. When I activated it, it caused him headaches, which I diagnosed as a tumor. This gave me the excuse to operate on him for the second supply of Mentase." He paused. "I know what you must be thinking. What I've done violates most of the ethics scientists are supposed to honor. Believe me or not, I'm not proud of any of it." He reached over and took Sally's hand. "My wife has been against it from the start, and we've both gone through hell these past weeks. I'm not foolish enough to think this mitigates what I've done, and I'm fully aware I've left myself open to legal action from you and Mr. Barstow. I won't contest it if you bring charges against me. In fact, it will really be a sort of relief to admit it. But to be perfectly frank with you, I think if I had to do it all over again, no matter how miserable it's made me, I'd repeat the whole process."

"*Why?*" asked Ann.

"Because I'd do anything to make Mentase a reality."

"But, Herbie," said Sally, "that's Arnold Hirsch's excuse."

"No, it's not," corrected her husband. "Arnold wants Mentase for something else."

"Then he's told you what he wants to do?" said Ann. "The clinics he wants to build, and the tie-ins with the governments?"

"Yes, he's told me."

"And it doesn't bother you?"

"It's not that it doesn't bother me; it's just that I don't believe he can do it. Arnold has a fanatical side to him—I might say almost a megalomaniacal side to him. And because of his son accidentally killing his wife, he's developed an obsession about the young. Since he has so much power in the financial world, I believe he thinks he can manipulate people the way he manipulates money. I've listened to his theories—they're rather fascinating, but I'm skeptical about his ability to translate theory into fact."

"You may be underestimating him," said Ann. "How much of the Société Gérontologique stock do you own?"

"Five percent."

"How much does Arnold own?"

"Fifty percent."

"Why didn't he keep controlling interest? He put up most of the capital, didn't he?"

"Yes, and he wanted fifty-one percent. But I refused to go forward on that basis. There was quite a fight over it, in fact. Finally a compromise was reached by his taking only fifty percent. But I'm certain he agreed because he was sure your husband would vote with him in case of a deadlock."

"How much does my husband own?"

"You mean you don't know?"

"My husband isn't exactly the confiding type."

"He owns thirty-five percent."

"Do you know that Arnold has hired private detectives?"

"Yes. He told me they were to keep his son away from Kurt Oetterli, whom he's been buying drugs from."

"It's a little more than that. About an hour ago, Arnold told me that I was, in effect, a prisoner here in the chateau, and the detectives are my, well, let's say 'keepers.' He's got detectives watching Hugh and Martin too, so that the three of us can't leave the chateau until he lets us leave. As I told you, he's stopped my phone calls and my mail. Now I don't know how far you're willing to stretch your rather flexible ethics, Doctor, but it seems to me Arnold's going pretty far. If you don't believe me, go to your door and look outside. You'll see one of the detectives in the entrance hall, waiting for me. Unless, of course, you believe he's a strayed tourist."

Mentius got up, opened the door of the apartment, took a look outside, then closed the door and came back into the room.

"Is he there?" asked Sally.

"He's there."

"Then don't you think it's about time we did something about Arnold? He's talked you into jeopardizing your reputation, he's ruined your self-respect, he's frightened both of us and made life miserable for us, even though we cooperated with him. And now he has the nerve to threaten Ann. Do you want to end up in a real prison?"

Mentius was standing beside his chair, his hands behind his back, his shoulders slightly hunched over. He seemed to sag like the Oldenburg toilet. "Maybe if I talked to him—"

"Oh, for God's sake, Herbie, it's too late for that! You have to *tell* him you won't stand for this sort of thing! Ann is right. You're underestimating him! Maybe he means what he says he's going to do with Mentase, and is *that* what you want to happen to the thing you've devoted ten years of your life to? Are you just going to stand there and let the man pervert what you've worked so hard for? There's supposed to be some sort of nobility about science. There should be some sort of beauty in finding the truth about nature. But what's been noble or beautiful about what's gone on here?"

"All right!" he said angrily. "But what can I tell him? 'Arnold, take the guards away'? 'Stop bullying Mrs. Brandywine'? Suppose he says no, then what do I do? Call in the police to arrest my patient? Have the treatment stopped just when it's so close to being successful? Have every newsman and TV camera in the world here at the chateau, making a circus out of Mentase?"

"But you said you'd admit everything in court—"

"That's later! Later, I don't give a damn what happens to me. Later I can fight Arnold, for that matter. But right now is the wrong time. I *can't* get in a fight with Arnold Hirsch now."

And now Sally was angry. "Then you're going to let him get away with this? You're going to continue letting him degrade you?"

"Sally, the important thing is Mentase . . ."

"Mentase! You've used that as your excuse for everything. It's become an obsession with you. Is *any* discovery so important that it justifies becoming a criminal?"

"Excuse me," said Ann quietly. "But strange as it may sound coming from me, I think Dr. Mentius may be right for the moment. The damage has been done, as far as Hugh and I are concerned. The important thing is to avoid any more of it."

Sally looked at her. "But he can't allow Arnold to make you some sort of prisoner!"

"I know. But Hugh and Martin and I think we have a way around that."

"What are you going to do?"

"We're leaving the chateau tonight. Then I'm going back to New York . . ." She started to say, "and tell my brother what's been going on here," but she thought it would be better not to tell Mentius everything. Even though Sally Mentius was definitely on her side, her husband still looked as if he were wavering. "Then I'm going to divorce my husband," she continued aloud. "I've found out, along with everything else he's been doing, that he's been making love to Lady de Ross."

"Good Lord," said Sally, "does she sleep with *everybody*?"

"It seems that way," said Ann. "At any rate, I have plenty of evidence to use against him, needless to say, and I don't think I'll have any problem getting what I want in the settlement."

"What do you want?"

"His shares in the Société. That way, I'll be the second largest stockholder in the company. And it seems to me that may be the best way to fight back at Arnold Hirsch. At least he won't have control anymore, and it's even conceivable we might be able to buy out Lady Kitty later on. At any rate, it seems to me that's the best that can be done under the circumstances. The important thing is to get the three of us out of here with as little fuss as possible. I'm hoping that the two of you will help us."

Sally Mentius looked relieved. "Ann we'll do anything you want."

Her husband looked less enthusiastic. "But what about these detectives? And with all these people coming in here tonight—"

"Herbie!" said Sally. "We're going to help Ann. If there's trouble, too bad. We're through helping Arnold Hirsch."

Mentius started to say something, then changed his mind.

"All right," he said. "We'll help."

At eight that evening, as the setting sun splashed the sky with a gorgeous crimson, Ann stood at the window of her suite watching Lady Kitty's fantastically costumed guests swarming over the grounds of the Chateau Mirabelle. They were arriving from every capital of the International Set's private world: Tangier, Jamaica, Paris, Deauville, Sardinia, Malaga, Corfu, Estoril. They had come in private seaplanes, which landed on the lake, in private helicopters, a chartered jet; Mercedes, Rollses, Maseratis, DC-9's, an authentic restored Bugatti Royale, an Isotta-Fraschini, a Hispano-Suiza, and a spectacular yellow Duesenberg roadster. Within twelve hours they would all be gone again, for Windischgratz had no hotel, and it had been a tribute to Lady Kitty's drawing power that so many people would go to such inconvenience to attend her party. Of course, it was also a tribute to Mentius's reputation. The Chateau Mirabelle and its famed facilities were a magnet to those who could buy off everything in life except time. And now, as they gathered in their full plumage, waited on by the caterer's staff that had replaced the regular staff for the weekend, swilling the fifty cases of Dom Perignon Lady Kitty had ordered, along with the gallons of hard liquor, smoking Tijuana Gold and buzzing with gossip and rumors, they presented to Ann's eyes an eerie spectacle, rather like a gathering of bizarrely outfitted fiends to some Satanic revel.

Michael had moved out that afternoon, shifting his clothes and his sleep capsule to the empty corner suite at the front of the building across the rotunda from Arnold Hirsch's suite. His departure had been quick, quiet, and efficient. The presence of the footmen relieved both him and Ann of the necessity of saying anything to each other. She had watched him leave with silent relief.

Now she was alone, costumed in her elaborate French ballgown and wig, made resplendent by the necklace and earrings. She reflected it would probably be the last time in her life she would wear the jewels, and she had decided to make as good a show as possible. Even with the dark shadows under her eyes, she knew she looked attractive, which gave her some feeling of confidence even in these weird circumstances. But she was nervous, for reasons that had nothing to do with her appearance.

She heard the sound of the orchestra from the Salle des Fêtes and glanced at her diamond watch. Five after eight. The schedule was a little late, but not much.

Picking up her skirt, she started for the door, pausing in front of a mirror to take a last look at herself. She approved of what she saw. Then she raised the blue silk domino to her face, covering everything but her mouth and chin. Masks. Everyone at the chateau had worn masks but she.

Now it was her turn.

She let herself out into the corridor and smiled at the blue-suited guard. "Aren't you wearing a costume?" she asked.

He shook his head.

"Do I look pretty?" Rather coquettishly, she spun in front of him. He watched her with appreciation. He was chunky and simian, but young.

"*Schöen,*" he said.

"You don't speak English?"

"A little."

"Good. Maybe we can have a dance?"

He looked confused. "You and me?"

She shrugged. "Oh well. But you will take me downstairs? I've just run out of escorts."

"I'll *follow* you."

"That's better than nothing, I suppose."

She started down the corridor toward the grand staircase, saying loudly enough for the guard to hear, "'I have a little shadow that goes in and out with me. And what can be the use of him is . . .'" She looked over her shoulder and blew the surprised guard a kiss. "'. . . is very plain to see.'"

Smiling at his embarrassment, she started down the enormous circular stair to the brilliant scene below.

Lady Kitty had chosen "A Night in the Second Empire" as the theme of the ball and hired a Parisian decorator to "tart the chateau up," as she put it, though she admitted the place was fairly "tarty" to begin with. The decorator had done a restrained job. He had turned the rear terrace into the Café Tortoni, a famous restaurant of Louis Napoleon's Paris, erecting a gaily striped awning and filling the terrace with round tables. Little had been done to the Salle des Fêtes, which was already overly ornate, except that its heavily crystaled chandeliers and sconces were cleaned, and a huge net was suspended from the center of the ceiling; it was filled with balloons ready to be released later in the evening. A bandstand was set up at one end of the room, and the orchestra was costumed in frock coats from the period of the 1860s. The army of waiters were liveried, and an enormous buffet was set up in the Salle d'Hercule. The entire first floor of the chateau glittered with candlelight, for Lady Kitty had insisted no electricity be used so she could capture the "flavor" of the era. When her decorator reminded her the 1860s were the height of the gaslight era, she huffily informed him he was a pedant as well as a pederast, which did little to improve their relationship.

As Ann came down the staircase followed by the guard, she saw the hostess standing in the middle of the entrance hall greeting a throng of guests coming through the door. Everyone wore masks, but they all seemed to recognize each other. Cleopatra social-kissed Cardinal Richelieu, whose foot was stepped on by Theda Bara, who in turn was social-kissing the Empress Eugénie. Thousands had been spent on the costumes, and millions on the jewels. The press and paparazzi had been barred, but Lady Kitty had hired a photographer, whose popping flashbulbs accented the rock music blaring from the Salle des Fêtes like visual cymbal clashes. It was hot; the crowd was pushing; the noise was unbearable; Lady Kitty looked ecstatic.

It was the ex-actress's moment of triumph. She was wearing the copy of Léonide Leblanc's gown, a Second Empire ballgown in black velvet, the huge skirt of which was gored with slashes of crimson. The special messenger from her Paris banker had arrived that afternoon with her "working rubies," a ruby and diamond tiara with matching necklace and bracelet, the cabochon rubies, as big as small eggs, matching the crimson slashes in the skirt. The total effect of the jewels and the costume was undeniably spectacular, and Ann was forced to concede that Lady Kitty, radiating beauty, glamour, and health, outclassed practically every woman there, including herself. As she recalled the drunken wreck who had arrived at the chateau only weeks before, the metamorphosis was not only amazing, it was frankly galling.

When she reached the bottom of the stairs, she felt a hand on her arm. She looked around and saw a man with a black domino over his eyes, a black beaver hat, a black dress suit of the period of the 1830s, and a gold-tipped walking stick. Even before he spoke, she knew from his sandy hairpiece and sideburns that it was Arnold Hirsch.

"Mind if I be your escort?" he said. "It's quite a crowd, and young ladies shouldn't be allowed to go unescorted."

"Or unwatched?"

"Have it your way. I've got a table in the Salon de Vénus. Will you join me?"

"What if I say no?"

"I think you'll say yes. Come on."

He led her through the crowd to the Salon de Vénus, which was filled with tables, and seated her at a small table in the corner. There was a hurricane lamp at the center of the table; Arnold placed his hat next to it, then helped Ann into a chair. Signaling for a waiter, he sat down opposite her.

"What would you like?" he asked Ann. "Champagne?"

"Why not? It's on Lady Kitty."

"Why not indeed? Bring us a bottle, please."

The waiter nodded and left.

"Mentius told us absolutely no drinking tonight, but I'm breaking the rules. One should never turn down free champagne, particularly Dom Perignon. You really look quite beautiful."

"Thank you," said Ann. "Who are you supposed to be? Dracula?"

"The Count of Monte Cristo."

"The richest man in the world. Very appropriate." She looked around the room. "Where did my guard go? He's such a nice man, I hate to lose him. Oh, there he is." She spotted him leaning against the wall, watching them. He nodded and she waved a little salute to him. Then she turned back to Arnold, who seemed amused by her attitude.

"I understand you paid a visit to Dr. Mentius this morning after our meeting."

"That's right. Did it make you nervous?"

"There's nothing you could tell him he doesn't already know."

"He didn't seem too happy about having his clinic turned into a high-class jail."

"Oh, I'm sure that shocked the good doctor," said Arnold, leaning forward on the table. "Of course, the possibility that he might have killed you or Mr. Barstow while operating under somewhat unethical circumstances didn't seem to bother his finely tuned sensibilities. You see, Mentius, whom I admire in many ways, is a curious new breed, ethically. Well, I won't say 'new.' In a way, the scientist-cum-social revolutionary is as old, certainly, as Darwin, even older. They discover a revolutionary new truth; they may even fulminate publicly against the way society misuses their truth, but they do little about it. And they salve their own consciences by saying the discovery was inevitable, or that man is base and it's not their fault that their good intentions are twisted by despicable politicians or businessmen or whomever the current popular villain may be."

"You're being awfully hard on your benefactor."

"Am I? Take the current uproar at home about pollution. Aren't the scientists as responsible for the fact that the world is being polluted out of existence as the businessmen? Who started the Industrial Revolution, anyway? Wasn't it the scientist? Now, of course, the great revolution is in Mentius's field, biochemistry. The ability to control life and death has frightening ethical implications. The surgeon asks himself, when does the exact moment of clinical death occur? Is he justified in racing the clock a few minutes to remove an essential organ that might save another life? Then there's the whole field of genetic control. Is it moral to 'select' better genes? When Hitler tried to breed a master race, it was considered disgusting. But scientists are talking about doing the same thing in slightly less Wagnerian terms, and now the idea is becoming respectable.

"So Mentius comes along with a discovery that will enable us to control death, and the ethical flip-flops he's been performing have almost been laughable to an old cynic like me. I'm perfectly aware that he dislikes me and hates himself for in effect selling out to me—it's an unpleasant phrase, but an apt one. Yet he risked your life and Mr. Barstow's."

"And you've been willing to risk your son's. He also at least seems to feel guilty about what he's done, which is more than I can say for you."

"Oh yes, I'm sure he's had sleepless nights, thrashed about in a fine ethical frenzy. But he *did* it. And he has no right to look down his ethical nose at me when I use admittedly strong-arm methods to protect my position. I'm running a considerable risk trying to force you into playing our game, and I don't like running risks if I can help it. But given your stubborn attitude this morning, it didn't seem to me I had any choice. You see, this whole project has been an interesting power struggle. The old against the young, of course, and vice versa. And now, Mentius against me—that is, if he had the guts to fight me. Pure science against those who apply it. It's an old game. And while I don't like force, it's a method I'm prepared to use if necessary, just as Mentius was willing to suspend his ethics to get what he wanted. It's all a question of who controls whom, which is what every human relationship pretty much comes down to, admit it or not. And ethics generally get kicked around a good deal in the process. And here comes the champagne; just in time. My throat is dry."

The waiter brought a bottle of Dom Perignon to the table and opened it. When the glasses were filled, Arnold raised his to Ann. "To the man who invented champagne. The one scientific discovery that has brought nothing but pleasure to humanity, give or take a few million hangovers."

Ann drank the toast, then put down her glass.

"I've been giving some thought to our talk this morning."

"Oh? Should I begin to be optimistic about your coming around to my side?"

She ran her finger around the rim of the glass. "The problem is, I'm not so sure your side is all that secure. Or rather, that your position couldn't stand improving."

"How?"

"You say everything is a question of control. What makes you think you can control Michael? You saw how he's treated me. Why do you think you can trust him any more than I could?"

"I don't particularly trust Michael, or anyone, for that matter. But I don't particularly *distrust* him at this point."

"Then you're not being as clever as you obviously like to consider yourself."

She took another sip of champagne, then leaned back and looked around the room.

Arnold was annoyed. "You're being singularly opaque."

"Lady Kitty and Michael are sleeping together. Now, Michael is a good game-player, and Lady Kitty is a whizz at it. Don't you think that to have two of the four stockholders of the Société being so chummy is rather dangerous to you?"

"Not particularly. The thought has occurred to me, but I'm not worried about it. They have no reason to be unhappy with the present arrangement."

"Still, with Dr. Mentius getting a bit squeamish, it might be possible for Michael and Lady Kitty to team up with him, and then where would you be?"

"Right where I am now—in control."

"Oh? Since when is fifty percent 'control'?"

Arnold refilled his glass. "What precisely are you suggesting?"

"In my humble opinion, when it comes to Michael and me, you're backing the wrong horse."

He nodded appreciatively. "It's a thought."

She turned and looked at the guard. "I wonder if he'd dance with me?"

"*I'll* dance with you," said Arnold.

She smiled prettily at him. "Now Arnold, don't feel you *have* to. I don't want to cause you any more trouble than I already have."

He laughed and stood up. "Come on, Marie Antoinette. The Count of Monte Cristo begs the pleasure. The Count concedes he may even learn a thing or two."

"That would be nice," said Ann, getting up. "I mean, for the Count to admit there is something he might possibly learn from someone else is, well, almost revolutionary, isn't it?"

"On the contrary. The Count is always learning from others. That, and Mentase, is the best way to keep young. And the Count is feeling very young tonight. Very young indeed."

He took her arm, and she glanced at his masked face.

"I do believe your horns are showing under your hairpiece," she said.

He smiled. "After fifteen years, it's about time."

They started toward the Salle des Fêtes.

❧

"Come now, Kitty: tell us the secret."

Lady Kitty and Michael were drinking orange juice at a small table on the terrace. They were surrounded by a crowd of six: Countess Zoë von Strelitz-Langendorff, a fading German beauty dressed as Jean Harlow, who was standing beside Lady Kitty, looking enviously at her face. With the Countess was Prince Fabrizio della Brindisi, a young Roman who was dressed as a bird of paradise and was stoned on hash. Next to him was George Hicks, the rich American novelist, and his wife, and another couple no one seemed to know.

"Really," continued the Countess, "I haven't seen you for six months, but my memory can't be *that* wrong. I don't mean to insult you, darling, but there's such a fantastic change!" She lowered her voice. "Is it true Dr. Mentius uses monkey glands?"

"Elephants," said Lady Kitty. "He removes the testicles of elephants and shoots the sperm directly into our veins. It's a most unusual feeling."

Countess Zoë blinked. "I'd certainly think so! But why elephants?"

"Because they're so big, of course."

"I don't see what that has to do with making you young."

"I shan't give away dear Dr. Mentius's secrets. If you want to find out, pay the ten thousand pounds and take it yourself."

"But *elephants?*" the Countess said, making a face. "I don't think I'd want elephant sperm shot into me. One might begin to grow a trunk."

"Oh, no danger of that," said Lady Kitty. "But it's true I'm developing an absolute passion for peanuts."

Countess Zoë looked at her sourly. "Darling, I think you're putting me on. Don't you think she's putting me on, Fabrizio?"

"Definitely," said the Prince, swaying unsteadily.

"If you're going to be so secretive," continued the Countess, "I'll have to find out from someone else. I'll ask the doctor himself. Such a delightful man . . . elephants?" She rolled her eyes. "*Mein Gott! Andiamo*, Fabrizio."

The group moved on, and Lady Kitty chuckled. "Marvelous! I'm having the most marvelous time of my life! All these aging bitches *green* with envy—divine! The party's worth every penny it cost me. Michael, dear, you don't look happy? Is my oozums not having a good time?"

"Your oozums isn't feeling too hot," said Michael. "I think I'll have a Scotch."

"Ah ah ah—Doctor said, 'pas de booze.' What's wrong?"

"I feel dizzy. Not really dizzy, actually . . . things seem to be blurring periodically. I think it's my eyes. It's been happening on and off for a couple of days now."

"Poor darling. Perhaps it's the strain of leaving Ann."

"That's no strain."

"It's more than you think. Any big change in one's life causes a strain. But I'm so glad you've done it, and it's all over. It's been a strain on me, too, you know."

He forced a weak smile. "Kitty, you are the most delightful liar I've ever known. You've loved every minute of it, and you know it. Ann's been knifed by an expert."

"The best in the business. How long do you think the divorce will take?"

"I don't know. It's going to be sticky, judging from the way she talked this morning."

"Divorces always are sticky. At any rate, this time next year it should be all over and we can begin plighting our troth in earnest. I intend to send dear Ann an invitation to our wedding; that should warm her small midwestern heart. By the way, have you noticed whom she's spent the last hour with?"

"Arnold. He's keeping an eye on her tonight."

"I'd say it's more like dear Ann keeping an eye on Arnold."

"What do you mean?"

"They've been dancing almost an hour. I've watched. That little bitch is up to something."

Michael shook his head. "You're imagining things. And don't call her a bitch."

Lady Kitty lowered her lids to half-mast. "Loyalty? Come now, that's not your style. Besides, I'm not imagining it. And I don't like her getting too friendly with Arnold."

"Getting friendly with Arnold is like getting friendly with a puff adder."

"Admittedly. Nevertheless, the young Mrs. Brandywine is attractive, in her bovine way. And Arnold's hormones are pumping —don't ask me how I know: a woman can tell. *She* knows it too. I tell you, she's up to something, and I don't like it. Bootzie, darling! How are you?"

Barbara "Bootzie" Tcherkoffski, the fashion model, had just come up with her husband, Igor Tcherkoffski, the French film director. "Bootzie" was dressed as a Nubian princess and had nothing on above the waist but a huge Egyptian necklace which more or less covered her naked, makeup-smeared breasts. As she leaned over to kiss Lady Kitty, the necklace dangled, as did the breasts.

"Kitty, it's a marvelous party. Simply *marvelous*."

"Barbara, you're about to dip into Lady Kitty's drink," said her husband, pointing to her left breast which was only a few inches from the rim of the glass. Bootzie straightened, giggling. "I've already dipped into two Scotch mists tonight. It's the wildest feeling!"

"Dip into a bourbon on the rocks," said Lady Kitty, "and you can make a milk punch."

Igor sputtered with laughter as he led his wife away. Michael watched her go. "I wouldn't mind her dipping into *my* drink."

"Now oozums, don't be lecherous. But *revenons à nos moutons*, or however the hell the French say it. Ann's making me nervous."

"Why? What can she do? She and Hugh and Martin are all being watched like hawks."

"I'm not worried about *that*. That was one of Arnold's least imaginative ideas, though I suppose it's necessary. But don't you see that if Ann wants your shares in the Société, then the best ally she can have is Arnold Hirsch?"

"That's obvious. But it's also obvious the last thing he wants is for her to have them. Not to mention the fact that *I* don't want her to have them."

"But dear boy, what if Ann convinced Arnold to help her get the shares in the marriage settlement, in return for which she would sell them to him? Don't you think Arnold might be interested? He's always wanted a majority of the stock."

Michael set down his glass, looking rather nervous. "But why would Ann sell them to Arnold, even if she got them? She said she wanted them for—" He stopped.

"Precisely. She *said* she wanted them for some ridiculous altruistic reason. Now, dear Ann is a tedious moralist, I'll admit, but she's also no fool. She knows those shares are the most valuable things she can get out of you, and I'm sure she's as interested in their monetary value as she is in whatever she thinks they'll enable her to do to make the world safe for teen-agers. I think she merely wanted to take you in, darling. And I wouldn't be at all surprised if at this very moment she's leading dear Arnold down the garden path too."

Michael sipped his orange juice. "What do you suggest?"

"Keep an eye on them." She spotted another couple coming toward the table and lowered her voice. "It's important we prevent those two from doing the same thing we've done. Don't you agree?"

He nodded and got to his feet as Lady Kitty held out her arms to hug Franco Dinova, the Italian fashion designer who was dressed as Ferdinand VII of Naples. "Franco, you delicious piece of pizza, you! You've *made* my birthday by coming!"

As Franco kissed her, Michael made his way through the crowd into the chateau.

❧

Hugh Barstow had chosen his costume with some care. He had come as a guerrilla fighter, dressed in black pants and a black turtleneck sweater. Yvette Renard, the French nurse he had been sleeping with since his operation, couldn't afford to rent a costume, so she had come as a nurse. As they frugged on the crowded floor of the Salle des Fêtes, Hugh checked his watch.

"It's ten o'clock," he said. "Let's go."

Yvette nodded, and they wormed their way off the dance floor to the side of the room where Hugh's guard had been standing, watching them. He was a skinny French-Swiss with a long, not unpleasant face.

"Monsieur a un mal à la tête," said Yvette to the guard. *"Est-ce possible que nous montions chez lui pour une aspirine?"*

The guard grinned slyly.

"Je sais bien ce qu'il veut, et ce n'est pas une aspirine."

Yvette gave him a dirty look.

"Mais vous dites des saloperies."

The guard shrugged.

"Je m'en fiche de ce que vous faites. Mais je vous accompagne."

"Ça va sans dire, Monsieur."

Giving Hugh a look, she started toward the entrance hall. He followed her, winking at the guard, who whispered in Hugh's ear, "She is a cute portion of ass, no?"

Hugh nodded. "Cutest 'portion' I've seen in a month."

They made their way through the crowd to the elevator and got in. Hugh pressed "2" and the doors silently shut. As the elevator slowly started rising, the guard looked at Yvette. *"Peut-être quand vous et Monsieur sont finis, vous auriez quelques minutes pour moi, eh?"*

Yvette pursed her lips coyly. *"Peut-être."*

Hugh pulled from his rear pocket a small medical hammer Yvette had smuggled from the Infirmary. He raised it, then banged it down sharply on the guard's skull. He grunted and slumped to the floor. Hugh pushed the "Stop" button, which jerked the elevator to a halt. Then he pushed the bottom button on the control panel. The elevator slowly started down.

"This man has a dirty mind," said Yvette, kneeling to grab the guard's arm.

"Yeah, I noticed," said Hugh, taking the other arm. They pulled him to his feet. Hugh gasped: "Christ—!" The elevator had just stopped at the first floor, and the doors were opening. Hugh frantically pushed the bottom button again, but it was too late. The doors were open. Cardinal Richelieu and Ninon de l'Enclos started to get in the elevator.

"Sorry," grinned Hugh, pointing to the slumped guard. "I think he's about to be sick. Too much booze."

Cardinal Richelieu, who was drunk, stopped and hiccoughed. Then he made the sign of the cross. "*Pax vobiscum.*"

"Right," said Hugh, pushing the bottom button. "And Ecumenical Council to you, too."

The doors slid shut.

"Whew!"

They both leaned back against the wall of the elevator. The guard started to slip out of their grasp, but they propped him up again. The elevator stopped, the doors opened.

They pulled the guard into the damp basement of the chateau.

❧

Michael had been watching his wife and Arnold Hirsch for almost half an hour. In his white satin Louis XV costume, it had been difficult for him to remain inconspicuous, even in such a gaudily dressed crowd as this one, but he had managed it. Somewhat to his amusement, he had noticed the blue-suited detective, who was watching Ann, occasionally give him curious looks. The watchers watching the watchers—it was almost laughable. But Michael was too nervous and too ill to laugh.

Lady Kitty's suggestion that Ann might be playing up to Arnold Hirsch had caught Michael unaware, for he was long used to thinking of his wife as a child whose good humor could be bought by an expensive toy. He had made love to Lady Kitty with disregard for Ann's feelings. A selfish man, his self-centeredness had only been intensified by the miraculous rejuvenation accomplished by the Mentase, and the slowly dawning realization that apparently Mentius had achieved the impossible and had given him years—perhaps even centuries—of renewed youth had dissipated whatever restraints he'd felt before on his behavior. He had entered into the relationship with Lady Kitty primarily because he had seen the advantages of teaming with her against Arnold Hirsch. He had ended by becoming dazzled by the shrewd and once again beautiful woman. When the time came, he had told himself, he would break the news to Ann. She would shed a few girlish tears, and he would arrange an amicable divorce. Now, to his amazement, not only was Ann—far from shedding tears—demanding a divorce herself, she was also demanding his shares in the Société. And as he watched Ann dance with Arnold, who was obviously intrigued with her, Michael felt more and more nervous as he realized just how vulnerable his position was becoming.

At ten fifteen he saw Ann glance at her watch and say something to Arnold. Then they made their way off the dance floor, out of the Salle des Fêtes and into the entrance hall. Michael pushed his way through the crowd to follow them. He was stopped by two overweight men, dressed as Haroun al-Rashid and Grover Cleveland, who were engaged in a hot argument about the merits of the Turkish Riviera as a boom resort.

"Excuse me," said Michael impatiently, trying to get around them.

"I'm thinking of putting a hundred thousand in this private development corporation," said Grover Cleveland, ignoring Michael. "They're putting up a hotel near Smyrna and will sell off three-acre lots for houses. Strictly class stuff, like Layford Cay."

"I wouldn't invest a dime in Turkey," said Haroun al-Rashid. "It's unstable. The South Pacific's the place to invest. Samoa. American-controlled, happy natives, a good tax deal . . . Hey, watch out, dammit . . ."

Michael angrily pushed his way through them. "Get your fat stomach out of the way," he said.

"Don't push *me* around!"

But Michael was gone, shoving his way to the entrance hall. When he finally reached it, he looked for Ann and Arnold. For a moment he didn't see them. Then he spotted a blue dress at the top of the staircase. It was Ann, next to Arnold, who was leading her around the rotunda to his suite.

Suddenly the dizziness returned. But this time it was more than just dizziness. To Michael's horror, his vision split down the middle of his eyes. The left half of his view jerked upward violently as the right side jerked downward, like a television screen hit with distorting interference. He leaned against the wall and rubbed his eyes. Then he looked up again. Now the left side of the screen was expanding horizontally, stretching the staircase sideways as if it were made of silly putty. Simultaneously, the right side of the screen began to wiggle like jelly, jerking up and down as if trying to focus.

He broke into a sweat, shutting his eyes tight and shaking his head violently, almost like banging a television set to restore normal vision. What is it, he thought. What the Christ is happening?

Then suddenly, when he opened his eyes again, to his relief his vision was normal. It was as if some violent upheaval had occurred inside his brain and then, like an earthquake, it was over and done with. He pulled a handkerchief from the pocket of his satin breeches and mopped his face. It was soaking. Am I going blind, he wondered. Or am I going crazy?

He returned the handkerchief to his pocket. He was calmer now. He looked around the hall where the guests were milling, drinks in hand, babbling endlessly as the rock music screamed from the adjacent ballroom.

What was he looking for? Oh yes. A girl. A naked girl. No, no: a girl in an odd dress. A red dress? No, that wasn't it. A . . . a black dress. Yes, a black dress. Who was the girl supposed to be? It was someone he knew. He knew her well, he was convinced of that. And he was supposed to watch her, for some reason. But why?

He saw a girl in a black dress. It was a witch's dress, or more accurately, a mini-witch's dress. The girl had long, beautiful legs encased in black net stockings. She wore a peaked witch's hat and was talking to a young man dressed as Tarzan. The girl was gorgeous, radiantly beautiful, obviously an actress. Is that whom I'm supposed to watch? thought Michael. I don't remember seeing her before, but she's a knockout. What the hell: I might as well watch her. In fact, why not dance with her? Get to know her. Christ, she is gorgeous! Look at those breasts!

He made his way over to her and broke into the conversation.

"Excuse me," he said, "I couldn't help noticing you. You're the best-looking witch I've ever seen. What's your name?"

"Beatrice," said the girl in a soft, lyrical Italian accent. "And what's your name, signor?"

Michael thought. He stared blankly at her. He felt the sweat coming out on his forehead again.

The girl laughed. "Oh? You don't want to tell me your name?"

"I . . ." He hesitated. "I can't remember it."

The witch and Tarzan looked at him as if convinced he must be drunk. But the only thing Michael had had to drink all night was orange juice.

❧

The blue-suited guard had followed Arnold and Ann up the grand staircase, wondering why his employer was spending so much time with the woman he had been hired to watch. But when Arnold led her into his suite, the guard saw the reason, or at least thought he saw. Leaning against the wall of the rotunda, he pulled out a toothpick and began to work on his left bicuspid, listening to the rock music from downstairs and wondering about the strange love-making habits of Americans. To hire a private detective to watch the woman you were going to make love to? Very strange.

Inside the suite, Arnold set down a fresh bottle of champagne and proceeded to open it. "I'm getting a little tight," he said. "This champagne hit me more than I expected. I suppose it's because it's been so long since I had any."

"It will be good for you," said Ann, wandering around the room, casually looking through the open door into the dark bedroom of the suite. "It will relax you."

Arnold popped the cork and filled two glasses. "So you think you and I would make a good team?"

"Don't you?" she said, removing her mask and dropping it on a table.

Arnold carried the glasses over to her. "It's quite a switch from the way you were talking this morning."

"One has to be flexible to survive."

"But you're being *so* flexible. I'm not sure I trust you." He handed her one glass, then took a drink from the other.

"I don't expect you to trust me yet," she said, watching him. He was standing directly in front of her. She could smell a faint trace of his aftershave lotion. "But whether you trust me or not, all of your problems could be solved so easily, couldn't they? And mine too, for that matter."

"Tell me."

"Well . . . you want Michael's shares, and so do I. So, if we teamed up we could both get what we want, couldn't we? Besides, then you could dismiss those detectives and save yourself all that trouble and money." She smiled. "Doesn't that make sense?"

He set down his glass.

She watched him as he wiped his palms on his pants. He was obviously nervous, like a boy with his first date.

"Don't be frightened," she whispered.

"It's been fifteen years."

"Then think how much more exciting it's going to be," she said, putting her fingers on his shoulders. "There's been all sorts of interesting new developments in the past fifteen years."

He was trembling now. Hungrily, he put his arms around her and pressed his body up against hers, kissing her. She made no resistance. He moved his mouth from hers, around her cheek to her ear. "My God," he whispered. "My God . . ."

"Darling, let's go into the bedroom."

"Yes . . . all right . . ."

He let her go and took her hand, leading her to the door of the bedroom.

"Thank God for Mentase," he said, with an attempt at humor.

"Oh yes, thank God for Mentase."

He stepped inside the door and fumbled for the light switch. There was a soft thud, and he let go her hand. She heard his body as it hit the floor.

Hugh Barstow turned on the light and stuck the medical hammer back in his pocket. Martin Hirsch looked down at his unconscious father. "Good night, sweet prince," he said. "And flights of vultures sing thee to thy rest."

"Let's go," said Hugh. Quickly and efficiently, he and Martin stripped Arnold to his shorts, then tied his wrists and ankles, and gagged him. Then they lifted him and carried him to the cryogenic sleep capsule at the foot of the bed. "Open the lid," said Hugh. "I'll hold him."

He propped Arnold up as Martin opened the glass lid of the tubular capsule. Then they both lifted him inside it, Martin first removing his sandy hairpiece with the false sideburns. "Do you know how to work this thing?" said Hugh, peering at the control panel.

"I do," said Ann. Yvette, who was helping her out of her elaborate costume, followed her as she came over to the capsule and reached inside. "You just flip this switch," said Ann, turning on the left-hand switch, "then close the lid. The temperature goes down, the oxygen pressure goes up, and Arnold will stay in a nice deep sleep till eight tomorrow morning."

"Poetic justice," said Martin. "They zonk us, we zonk them. Good night, Daddy-O."

Hugh closed the lid of the capsule as Martin put on his father's hairpiece. "How do I look?" he asked.

"Let's hope you look like the Count of Monte Cristo," said Hugh. "Okay, get in his clothes. Yvette, how are you coming?"

"All right," said the nurse, who had gotten Ann out of her dress and was now wriggling into it herself, having taken off her own nurse's uniform. "But I think my waist is bigger than Ann's. This seems a little tight . . ."

"I'll help her," said Hugh, taking over the job from Ann. "You go into your room and put on a dark skirt and sweater. You can go through Martin's room."

"But I thought I'd put on Yvette's nurse's uniform?" said Ann.

"The white will show up in the dark. Put on something black. And hurry!"

❧

The guard outside Arnold's suite was half asleep when the door opened some twenty minutes later and Marie Antoinette and the Count of Monte Cristo emerged, their masks in place. The Count nodded to the guard, then led Marie Antoinette to the stairs. The guard followed them, thinking that his employer was a fast worker to have made love to the woman in less than a half hour. It should have taken at least ten minutes for him just to get the enormous skirt off her. As he looked at the Count, it occurred to him he looked taller than before, but he decided he was imagining things.

Martin saw the guard following them and thought that so far

the deception was working beautifully. As he led Yvette down the stairs, he wanted to shout with joy as he thought how furious his father would be when he woke up and found himself bound and gagged in the cryogenic hyperbaric sleep capsule. By that time, the three of them would be gone, which would make him even more furious. Let him rant and rave, thought Martin. What do I care? I'm free.

They reached the bottom of the stairs and headed through the crowd to the rear terrace. How perfectly it was all working out! Sally Mentius had given Hugh the key to the speedboat and arranged to have the boathouse left open and empty. Ann Brandywine had telephoned Ernst Stahling in the village and asked him to meet them at the dock and drive them to Lausanne, to which he had agreed. And after Lausanne? The future spread endlessly before him, beautifully free of complications. He had almost fifteen hundred dollars left of the three thousand his father had given him; that would keep him alive for months if he lived cheaply, and he intended living cheaply from now on. He was even considering giving up the blackbirds and the hash; it wouldn't be easy, but they were becoming a burden and Martin wanted nothing to hinder him. Being unencumbered was going to be as intoxicating as hash. And bumming around Europe trying to write poetry was going to be a much better high than he could get from the blackbirds. Better yet, there would be no more of those painful downs after the ups. The downs were beginning to clip the wings of the blackbirds. . . .

The main corridor was crowded, and they were having difficulty getting through, but he could see the terrace doors now. Once there, he was home free. He glanced at his watch: ten twenty-eight. Hugh and Ann should be out of the chateau. While he and Yvette had decoyed the guard, Hugh and Ann had let themselves out the window of Martin's room onto the roof of the service wing, using the aluminum ladder Hugh had taken for the second time from the garage. Then they had taken the ladder to the end of the wing and climbed to the ground, making their way through the park to the lake, then to the boathouse where they were to meet Martin. If everything worked, they would be in Lausanne by two. If everything didn't work—but Martin decided not to think about that.

They were almost to the terrace when he saw Lady de Ross coming through the door. He tried to duck behind another couple, but she had seen him. He froze as she hurried up to them.

"Arnold . . . Ann," she whispered, "help me find Mentius."

Martin stared at her, afraid to speak. But even in his shock he realized something was wrong with her. She looked as afraid as he did.

"Don't just stand there!" she said. "Help me find him! Michael is out on the terrace, wandering around like a vegetable. I think he's lost his memory!"

Neither Martin nor Yvette dared move. Lady Kitty gestured angrily. "Michael has gone completely blank! For God's sake, help me!"

Shall I run for it, thought Martin, glancing nervously at the terrace door. No—Christ, there's one of the guards right outside!

"Come on!" insisted Lady Kitty, grabbing his hand and tugging him back toward the entrance hall. "Don't you realize what this means? If Michael's lost his memory, it can happen to us too! We've got to find Mentius! Look for Columbus and Isabella!"

Martin glanced helplessly at Yvette, then followed Lady Kitty through the crowd.

In the boathouse, Ann and Hugh waited impatiently by the door, watching the rear of the chateau.

"Damn him," said Hugh. "Where is he?"

"What time is it?"

"Quarter of eleven. He's ten minutes late."

"Do you think the guard saw him?"

Hugh didn't answer, but it was obvious that was what he was thinking. They waited three more minutes. Then he muttered, "I'll give him till ten of. Then we fade."

"We can't leave him," said Ann.

"We're not going to do him any good if *we* get caught, are we?"

She didn't answer because she had seen something.

"Hugh, look!"

Four men were running towards the boathouse from the terrace. They were wearing blue suits. Hugh grabbed her arm and pushed her toward the boat. "Let's split."

"But—"

"Ann, don't argue!"

She climbed in the boat as Hugh untied the single line and pushed the boat out of the slip. Then he jumped on the bow and climbed in beside her. There was a loud roar as he turned on the motor. Then he shifted in reverse and backed out of the boathouse into the lake. Turning the wheel to port, he pushed the gear forward and gunned the throttle. The engine thundered, jerking the boat forward as the prop bit the water and lifted the bow. Shooting a plume of spray, they circled and headed out into the lake.

"Shall I turn the spotlight on?" shouted Ann over the noise of the wind and the motor.

"No. They might try and shoot."

They sped through the darkness, at one point narrowly missing one of the seaplanes whose pilot was asleep and who had stupidly left his running lights off. Ann looked back at the rapidly diminishing Chateau Mirabelle. Someone had turned two floodlights on and they glowered angrily from the roof, silhouetting the four guards on the pier. The guards were talking to each other animatedly. Then they turned and started back toward the chateau. She could still make out the guests on the terrace of the building, watching the little drama and undoubtedly buzzing over the cause of the excitement. The tall windows glowed with soft candlelight, which contrasted with the harsh candlepower of the floods on the roof. Inside the building the other guests would still be dancing, oblivious to everything but the music, the champagne, and their own pleasure. The chateau was a magnificent sight. But in a way she thought it looked like some ugly, malevolent jewel, glowing in its dark setting. Or was it the heat-lightning that was beginning to flash in the skies behind the chateau, heralding the approach of a summer storm? Whatever it was, she felt an intense relief to be away from the place.

They crossed the lake in twenty minutes. When they tied up at the town pier, Ernst Stahling was waiting for them with his VW. As the three climbed in the tiny car, Ernst said, "Would someone mind telling me what's going on?"

"Just get us to Lausanne, and, like, *fast*," said Hugh.

"No, wait," said Ann. "I have to call the chateau first."

Hugh groaned. "Call the chateau? Are you crazy? We just knocked ourselves out getting away from there!"

"Hugh, I have to find out if Martin's all right. I can call Sally Mentius. She'll tell me what's happened."

"Baby, those guards may be on their way here right now! They know we've come to Windy—whatever the hell the name of this burg is—there's no other place on the lake!"

"What guards?" said Stahling, totally confused.

"We'll tell you later," said Ann. "Please take me someplace where I can phone. I'll only take a minute."

"Jesus!" said Hugh, throwing up his hands.

"Hugh, I'm *worried* about Martin!"

"We can use my house," said Stahling, starting the car. "It's not far from here."

He drove off the quai and sped through the town, which was deserted and dark. On the outskirts, he stopped in front of a small chalet surrounded by a tiny, well-kept garden. They got out of the car and went up the walk to the front door, which Stahling unlocked. Entering a low-ceiling living room, filled with chintz-covered furniture and bad reproductions of Chagall posters, Ann saw the same young man she had seen come in with Stahling the night of the discothèque party. He was wearing tight leather pants and a leather motorcycle jacket, and was slumped in a chair slowly peeling an orange with a penknife, attempting to remove the curl in one piece. "This is my friend, Kurt Oetterli," said Stahling. "Lisl's brother."

"How do you do?" said Ann.

Kurt nodded as Stahling led Ann to a phone and she called the chateau. Then he looked at Hugh. "And how are you, Mr. Barstow?"

"Living."

"And Martin Hirsch? How's he?"

"Yeah, he's okay. We hope."

Ann had gotten someone on the phone; she asked for Sally Mentius, then covered the mouthpiece and said, "I forgot the regular staff's off for the weekend, including the switchboard operator."

"Who answered?"

"I think it was one of the guests. He sounded drunk."

"That figures."

Stahling looked at Hugh. "Who are you running from? Mentius?"

"No. Arnold Hirsch."

"Why?"

Hugh told him. When he finished, Stahling said in an awed tone, "Then the project Mentius has been working on all this time was this—what do you call it? Mentase?"

"That's right. And it works. Lady Kitty and the other two look forty. You wouldn't recognize them. But like, the problem is they've been a little casual about how they get the stuff."

"But they could manufacture it eventually?" said Kurt.

"So Mentius says. As soon as they figure out how to synthesize it."

Stahling and Kurt exchanged looks. Then Kurt smiled.

"Would you believe that Martin Hirsch told me all this six weeks ago, and I thought he was crazy?"

"I'd believe it," said Hugh.

"Hello, Sally?" said Ann. "We're in Stahling's house . . ." She stopped for a moment. Then she closed her eyes. "Oh no . . ." she whispered. "When? A half hour ago? Oh God . . ."

"What's wrong?" said Hugh.

She signaled him to keep quiet. "What should we do?" she said to the phone. "Come back to the chateau?"

"Like hell!" exclaimed Hugh.

"Yes, all right. We will. No, I understand. Tell the doctor I authorize it. We'll be there as soon as we can."

She hung up and turned to the others.

"I'm not going back to that hole!" said Hugh. "Not after all the crap we went through to get out!"

"The detectives have been dismissed," said Ann quietly.

"Says who?"

"Sally Mentius. She and her husband decided to get rid of them while Arnold was unconscious."

"I'm still not going back, detectives or no detectives. Arnold will just bring them back in the morning."

"I have to go back, Hugh," said Ann. "You see, my husband is dead. I just authorized an autopsy, but they think he was killed by the Mentase."

As the others watched, she sat down on a wooden bench by the phone. She couldn't cry for Michael.

But oddly enough, she still felt a terrible hurt.

part four

THE storm that had been threatening when they crossed Lake Windischgratz broke with surprising fury, sending down a torrent of rain and causing Stahling to delay their departure for the chateau. The road around the lake, he said, was prone to mudslides during heavy rains; it was safer to wait. He made coffee, and the four of them sat in the small living room listening to the rumble of the thunder and the pelting rain.

Ann wondered why Kurt Oetterli didn't go to bed. He seemed a surly type who barely spoke a word to either Hugh or herself. Something about him rather frightened her. It wasn't that he was Stahling's lover; it was more that he looked like the worst sort of male hustler, and the knowledge that he peddled dope didn't make her feel any more comfortable. On one occasion he disappeared into the kitchen for almost fifteen minutes. When he returned, she was sure he had taken either an uppie or some sort of fix, for he looked unnaturally excited and began pacing around the room with the restlessness of a caged tiger. But he said nothing and seemed to be lost in his own thoughts, whatever they were.

Stahling said little either; whether it was the storm or the lateness of the hour Ann couldn't tell, but something was making him nervous. He made desultory attempts at small talk, but his eyes were on Kurt, and when he went into the kitchen a second time, Stahling made a feeble excuse to join him. Ann could hear them whispering. Hugh was listening too, but he gave up. "They're talking German," he said.

"Kurt's rather odd, isn't he?" said Ann.

"Yeah, he's bad news. Rough trade plus narcotics. He looks like a mainliner to me."

"Heroin?"

Hugh nodded. "Most dealers are."

They said nothing more. But when Stahling emerged from the kitchen, Ann noticed he looked even more disturbed. Kurt followed him out and leaned against the fireplace, watching Stahling as he went to the window and looked out at the rain. Several times Stahling glanced nervously at Kurt. Then he turned back and stared through the streaming windowpanes at the darkness.

❧

At three forty-five, the rain finally let up sufficiently to allow them to make the trip to the chateau, although the deep puddles forced them to travel so slowly they didn't reach the chateau until six in the morning. The ground floor was brightly illuminated now, by electricity, not candlelight. But the cars had all gone and the place looked strangely deserted. As Ann and Hugh climbed out of the VW, Ann shook Stahling's hand.

"I appreciate all the trouble you've gone to."

"It was no trouble," he said. "And I'm sorry to hear about your husband. Kurt and I will wait in the car for a while in case you need us."

"You really don't have to."

"I'll feel better if we do. After all, I feel sort of responsible for you now."

"Then why don't you come inside? There's no point staying out here."

Stahling looked at Kurt, who shook his head. "We'll wait here. We'd just as soon not run into the Mentiuses."

As he rolled up the window, Ann and Hugh hurried up the steps of the entrance and went into the front hall of the chateau. Sally

Mentius was waiting for them. She had replaced her costume with a dress, and she looked as exhausted as Ann.

"Have they finished the autopsy?" Ann asked as Sally joined her.

"Not yet, but Herbie should be done soon. I . . ."

She started to make a customary expression of sympathy, but Ann stopped her. "Please don't say anything, Sally. Not now."

"Well, as I told you on the phone, we decided to leave Arnold where he was. It gave us a chance to get rid of those damned detectives; then we had to get the guests out, which was a mess, since a lot of them were drunk. . . . God, it's been a night! Then Lady Kitty was so upset thinking *her* memory was going to go that she got drunk . . ." She sighed. "Anyway, she and Martin and I have been waiting in the salon."

"There's no chance it was something else beside the Mentase that killed him?"

"We don't think so."

She took Ann's arm and led her into the corridor to the rear of the chateau. The decorations from Lady Kitty's ball were still up, although they now had a tattered look that added to the gloom of the occasion. A few empty glasses that the caterers had overlooked stood as forlorn mementoes of the party. Here and there, balloons and streamers had dried on the floor: the Salle des Fêtes was dark and silent. Their footsteps echoed on the marble floor as they walked down the corridor, and in spite of, or perhaps because of, the funereal atmosphere of the place, Ann couldn't help thinking of the Poe story where the prince's brilliant ball was visited by the Masque of the Red Death, who replaced the gaiety of the party with the silence of the tomb. When they entered the Salon de Vénus, Ann saw that here, at least, the tables had been removed and most of the remnants of the party were gone. The electric lights blazed in the crystal chandeliers, reflecting in the huge mirrors and illuminating the gilt cornices so that the room seemed gaudily brilliant after the dark hallway. But the atmosphere was no less heavy. Lady Kitty was standing by a mantel holding a drink. She still had on her black and crimson ballgown, but her face had become puffy from champagne and tears, and her beauty of a few hours before had been dissipated by the alcohol and tension. When she saw Ann, she fixed her bleary eyes on her and raised her arm in a drunken, pointing gesture.

"*There* you are!" she said. "Our little bird who flew the gilded cage so cleverly. . . . And there's dear Hugh, the pride of Secaucus. Welcome home, dear Ann and Hugh. Welcome home to the mausoleum."

Ann decided to try and ignore her, if possible. She glanced around the room. Martin Hirsch was sitting in a chair, glumly smoking a cigarette, still wearing his father's Count of Monte Cristo costume. He looked at Ann and said, "It didn't work out too well, did it?"

"Not exactly," said Ann, sinking into a chair.

"What a warm, heartfelt epitaph for poor Michael," said Lady Kitty. "Or doesn't the Widow Brandywine give a damn about her late husband? Her late husband whom, I might add, *she* killed?"

The remark stung Ann. "*I* killed him?"

"Did someone else force Mentius to stop making the RNA?" asked Lady Kitty. "Is my memory going too and it *wasn't* dear Ann who got all puffed up with midwestern self-righteousness and said—in tones not dissimilar to Moses on the Mount—'Thou shalt not grind up dead fetuses'?"

"Hey, Kitty," said Hugh, disgusted by her performance, "why don't you lay off? Ann's just lost a husband, such as he was."

"And while he was dying, where was his wife—such as *she* was? Running off in a speedboat with *you*."

"There was a good reason for us to run and you know it," Ann said.

"Oh, I know," said Lady Kitty, dismissing her remark with a wave of her hand. "And I don't give a damn. The point is, Michael loathed you. He thought you were an insipid little bitch, which you are. He was going to marry *me*. You didn't know that, did you? Michael loved me! And why shouldn't he? I have beauty and glamour and intelligence—all the things you lack. Now I even have youth! We were in love—and you killed him. The only man I've ever loved!"

"Crap," Hugh said. "You've never loved anybody but yourself, and you know it. That mirror in your room is so covered with kisses, you can't see your reflection."

Lady Kitty turned on him. "Shut up, you pimp."

"And as far as your beauty and glamour and intelligence go, it can all be summed up in one word: money. If you weren't so freaking rich, the only person you could land in the sack would be a drunk garbageman from Secaucus—like my old man. He digs boozy whores."

Lady Kitty's face became distorted with drunken rage. "You *toad!* You loathesome piece of industrial waste! You walking male organ! You're *fired!*"

"Hey, Kitty baby: there's a big news flash maybe you haven't heard? Like, I quit. Sneaking out of the chateau was my little way of telling you to go screw yourself. And if you don't shape up, I may slap a law suit against you."

"For what?"

"For breaking whatever law says you don't go around stealing slices of other people's glands."

She weaved in front of him like a baffled cobra, but the remark silenced her. She took another slug of her drink, then went over to a chair and slumped in it.

"The death watch," she mumbled morosely. "Except he's already dead."

"For God's sake, be *quiet!*" exclaimed Ann, whose nerves were ragged.

Lady Kitty glared at her, then took another drink.

"Look," she said, pointing to the French windows. "The rosy-fingered dawn is coming up. All the dawns around here are rosy-fingered, like some cheap postcard. I wonder if by the next rosy-fingered dawn here at the lovely Chateau Mirabelle, my memory will have gone too, and dear Dr. Mentius will be performing an autopsy on me?"

No one answered. She drained her glass.

❧

An hour passed before Mentius came into the salon followed by Dr. Zimmermann, the only member of Mentius's medical team who had not left the chateau for the weekend. They both wore surgical gowns; Mentius wore, as well, a look that showed he was physically exhausted. He came up to Ann and said, "Mrs. Brandywine, I'm afraid you'll consider me a rank hypocrite if I tell you how sorry I am about your husband. But I am. I've only lost two patients, and I genuinely believe they had no chance for survival. In your husband's case, though, I feel I must take full responsibility."

"A beautiful little *mea culpa*, Doctor," said Lady Kitty, sitting up. "And if I hear another from you, I may possibly vomit. What we're interested in is what killed him? Was it the Mentase?"

"Indirectly, yes," said Mentius, who looked too tired to take offense at Lady Kitty's sarcasm. "We took out a section of the brain and examined it. Apparently, there was a sudden and severe disintegration of the RNA in the brain cells."

"Like the white rats?" said Ann.

"Yes, except even more precipitous. I was totally unprepared for such a swift and massive reaction. We gave him all the RNA we had left, but I'm afraid it was too little and too late."

"But why," said Ann, "would a loss of memory have killed him?"

"Because the disintegration of the RNA not only destroyed his conscious memory, it destroyed his subconscious memory as well, by which I mean the motor centers of the brain that control the heartbeat and breathing. Michael's brain quite literally forgot to instruct his heart to keep pumping. It went into fibrillation, then stopped."

Lady Kitty got to her feet. "And is my brain going to be equally forgetful, Doctor? I'd hate to think I might be so absent-minded as to forget my pulse!"

Mentius turned angrily. "Lady Kitty, we're all under a strain, and your rather clumsy attempts at wit aren't helping matters."

"You're under a strain? What about me? I'm the one who may die at any moment! Are you going to get more RNA to protect me? Or are you going to wring your hands in moral anguish and do nothing, because dear Mrs. Brandywine is shocked by the way you obtain it?"

"I'm going to call the maternity clinic in Lausanne and try to make an arrangement with Dr. Bernhardi." He glanced at his watch. "If he's not at the clinic yet, I'll call his house, because I think it's important we get the two of you the booster shots as soon as possible."

"You mean," said Ann, "you're going to ask him to give you some of his stillborn babies?"

Mentius gestured helplessly. "I really have no choice, Mrs. Brandywine. In fact, I have no choice but to stop the Mentase treatment. I don't think I have to tell you that I'm hardly happy about stopping it, but your husband's death forces me to. I'll refund the entire payment to all of you and continue to treat Lady Kitty and Arnold with the RNA boosters until we're all satisfied there's no more danger of what happened to Michael happening to them. But as far as Mentase is concerned, I have to go back to what I first told Arnold. In its natural, insufficiently tested state, it's too dangerous to use."

He went over to a phone and picked up the receiver.

"Wait a minute," said Lady Kitty. "I think I have something to say about whether you stop the treatment or not. We knew it was risky before Michael died, but if you can give us the booster shots, I see no point to stop it."

"Jesus," said Hugh, "you mean you still want to go on taking that stuff?"

"Of course I do! It works, doesn't it? I'm young, aren't I? And if he stops the injections, I'll grow old again."

Mentius was staring at the phone. "What's wrong with this thing, Sally?"

"Nothing. Why?"

"It's dead."

His wife looked confused. "We closed the switchboard, but the outside lines are still working."

"No they're not, Mrs. Mentius."

The voice had come from the door to the corridor. They all turned to stare at the two men standing in the doorway. Both were holding guns. "We cut the phone lines."

Mentius looked at his former physical therapist. "Stahling, what the hell are you doing here with the gun?"

"I decided you didn't give me enough severance pay, Doctor."

"We've come for Stahling's bonus," said Kurt.

As they moved into the salon, both pointing their guns at the small group, Ann remembered their odd behavior in Stahling's house several hours earlier. The whispered conversations in the kitchen, the guarded looks, the overly eager insistence on waiting at the chateau in case she needed their "help." And of course this was the "help" they'd had in mind all along.

"Who is this lout?" said Lady Kitty.

"I'm Kurt Oetterli, the brother of the girl who bore the baby that Dr. Mentius pureed to save your memory, Lady de Ross. So in a weird sort of way, you might say I'm your memory's uncle."

"Are you insane?" she said wonderingly.

"Oh, a little, probably. Isn't everybody? Doctor, Ernst and I want the Mentase. Not all. We won't be pigs. Just a test tube of the stuff. Enough for the research lab of one of those nice big rich German drug companies to analyze."

"The Mentase is of no value whatsoever," said Mentius, staring at the revolvers. "So you might as well put away those guns. If I haven't been able to synthesize it yet, nobody else will."

"That's your opinion, Doctor. My opinion is that any number of drug companies would gladly at least like to *try* to synthesize it. Or cosmetic companies, for that matter. After all, Mentase would be the face cream to end all face creams, don't you think? Ernst and I figure they'd pay at least four million francs for a sample of the miracle drug that can make people young. And four million francs invested at, say, a nice safe five percent, would be just enough for us to retire to Algeria, where the sun is warm and there are ever so many Arab boys to wave away the flies."

"You're crazy if you think anyone would pay a million dollars for a test tube," said Mentius, wondering if they might actually use the guns.

Kurt smiled. "Perhaps, but I don't think we're going to have any trouble finding a customer. Now, why don't you take us to the lab? And I think it will be better if we *all* go. I wouldn't want anyone trying to contact the police until we're through."

Mentius said simply, "You can't have the Mentase."

"Doctor, these guns are loaded."

"I don't care. You can't have it." He *did* care. And he was frightened.

Kurt glanced around the room. "Stahling tells me you and your wife spent a lot of time and money collecting the original furniture to this place. I see he's right. It's very impressive. There are very beautiful things here."

He aimed his gun at one of the large gilt mirrors and fired. There was a soft "pop" from the silencer followed by the crash of shattering glass. Sally Mentius screamed. Kurt turned and fired at a large Chinese vase on a marble stand. The vase shattered.

"Stop it!" Sally said.

"Give us the Mentase."

"Give it to him, Herbie. *Please*. Give it to him!"

"Sally, I can't! Mentase is lethal in its present state! I can't let them sell it to a company that wouldn't know about the RNA—"

Another "pop" and a second vase exploded. There was something especially terrifying about the destruction of the inanimate furnishings, as if it were a dress rehearsal for the inevitable destruction of a living thing. Mentius's face was sweating, and Sally looked as if she were near hysteria. Only Lady Kitty seemed unafraid; oddly enough, she looked angry. "These idiots," she said to Mentius disdainfully. "We outnumber them. Call the staff! They can't shoot twenty people."

"There's no staff to call," said Hugh. "They're all off till tomorrow because of your party."

Lady Kitty turned to Kurt and Stahling. "How much will we have to pay you to get rid of you?"

"We want the Mentase."

"Come now, be practical. As the doctor said, it's lethal as it is now."

"You're alive. And your face is the best guarantee that it works. For an old woman, Lady de Ross, you look remarkably good."

"At least you have taste. How about ten thousand pounds?"

Kurt gestured with the gun. "I'm not bargaining."

"Five thousand apiece? You can take your money and consider the morning well-spent. I can assure you that five thousand pounds can buy you all the Arab boys you could possibly want."

Kurt laughed. "I take it you're an expert on the subject?"

"I am."

"If you'll pay ten thousand pounds, then some company will

pay a hundred times that. So you can keep your money. Doctor, I'm getting tired of waiting. The next thing we shoot won't be an antique—unless it's a refinished one like Lady de Ross."

He raised the gun and aimed it directly between her eyes. Now even she looked frightened.

"Well?"

Mentius half believed they were bluffing, but he didn't dare risk Lady Kitty's life on the gamble. He nodded. "All right. You can have it."

"Good. You lead the way, and the rest of us will follow."

Stahling took a position directly behind Mentius while Kurt placed himself behind the others; then Mentius led the group into the corridor. By now the chateau was bathed in pink light from the morning sun, which cast long shadows on the marble floor as they walked slowly toward the cross-hall that led to the lab wing. When they reached it, they turned to the right and went to the stainless steel doors. Dr. Zimmermann held them as the others filed through into the lab wing. As Ann entered the modern white hallway with the Lucite ceiling, she wondered at the almost placid way she and the others were giving in to the ugly authority of the gun. Yet there seemed to be nothing else to do except give the two men what they wanted, and certainly the Mentase wasn't worth risking more lives for. In fact, when she thought of the awful toll Mentase had taken on all of them already, she wondered if perhaps it wouldn't be better if Kurt took all of it and got it out of their lives: the pulverizers in Pathology . . . the embryos floating in the alcohol like rubbery dolls . . . Michael's brain disintegrating . . . the clandestine operations on her and Hugh . . . Arnold's Société, and his private detectives . . . She wished Mentius had never come to Michael. In fact, she wished Mentius had never discovered the Methuselah Enzyme.

They had reached the end of the corridor now, and Dr. Zimmermann opened the door to the laboratory. As they filed inside the big room with the slate-topped table running down the center of it, Ann was assailed by the odor of formaldehyde. Then, when everyone was in the room, Kurt pointed his gun at Mentius. "Where is it?"

The doctor went to a large refrigerator whose handles were

chained and padlocked. Pulling a key from his pocket, he unlocked the padlocks, removed the chain, and opened the door. He reached in and pulled out a steel strongbox which he carried to one of the slate-topped tables. Setting it down, he unlocked the box and opened the lid. Inside were two stoppered test tubes filled with an amber liquid. He took the tubes from their fitting and held them up, one in each hand, staring at them with what struck Ann as an odd expression on his face.

"This is the last of the Mentase," he said to Kurt.

Then he smashed one of the tubes against the slate.

"You bastard!" yelled Kurt, leaping at him, trying to grab the other hand. Mentius ducked and threw the remaining tube to the floor, where it, too, smashed.

Silence, except for the heavy breathing of Kurt. They all stared at the liquid which was spreading over the white vinyl tiles.

Mentius was watching the liquid in what seemed a state of near shock, almost as if he was amazed at what he had done and was already regretting doing it. "I couldn't let you take it," he said. "I . . . it's too dangerous."

"Idiot." Kurt looked at Stahling, who was at the door. Stahling looked disappointed, but Kurt's mouth was tight with disgust. His blue eyes roamed slowly from Stahling to Lady Kitty, then to Martin Hirsch, Ann, Hugh, Sally Mentius, and finally the doctor. He seemed to have come to a decision.

"All right, Doctor," he said. "If there's no more Mentase, then you'll have to make us some more."

"What?"

"Mr. Barstow told me all about the interesting operation you performed on him and Mrs. Brandywine—without their permission. Well, this time Martin is going to give you his permission—aren't you?"

He turned to Martin Hirsch, who looked paralyzed.

"I said you're going to volunteer for the doctor's operation, so we can get some more Mentase."

"Are you nuts? If you think I'm going to volunteer for some freaky operation—"

"Don't worry, Martin," said Mentius. "It's out of the question in any case. I have no staff."

"You have Dr. Zimmermann," said Stahling.

"But I would need De Villeneuve. He's my anesthetist. He and Schlessing are both gone."

"Doctor, you're going to do it. You're going to do it now, in fact. If you insist on being difficult, then I'll remind you that you have two young children here in the chateau, unprotected." He paused to let the implications of this get home to both Mentius and his wife. Kurt was watching her. "Now, I don't like to make a threat and upset your wife, so why don't you just do the operation, and give us what we want, and then it will all be over? And if it's a question of your conscience, well, just pretend you're operating on Mrs. Brandywine again."

Martin suddenly lunged for the door. Stahling grabbed his arm with one hand, jerked him around, then brought down the butt of his gun on the back of his head. Martin crumpled to the floor.

"There, Doctor," said Kurt. "You've just found your anesthetist."

The silence in the lab was broken by the excited scampering of the white rats in the cage.

"Come on, Doctor," said Kurt, "let's get it over with."

Mentius shook his head.

"Ernst," said Kurt, "you know the way to the doctor's private quarters. Go check the children."

Stahling hesitated.

"Go on."

He went to the door and opened it. Sally said, "For God's sake, Herbie, stop him!"

"Sally, they're bluffing . . ."

"How do you *know?*"

Stahling looked at the doctor, who closed his eyes. "All right," he said. My God, he thought. Oh my God. . . .

❧

At the extreme end of the lab wing of the Chateau Mirabelle, separated from the rest of the wing by a lateral corridor, was the surgical suite. Kurt shepherded Lady Kitty, Sally, Ann, and Hugh through the two steel doors of the suite into a short hallway at the end of which two other doors led to the operating room itself. In the middle of the hallway, two doors opposite each other led, on the left, to a locker and scrub room, and, on the right, to a pre-op/post-op room. Dr. Zimmermann had placed the unconscious Martin Hirsch on a portable bed, and it was into the pre-op room she now rolled him, with the assistance of Mentius. Stahling went into the room with her, covering the two doctors with his gun, while Kurt went to the end of the hall and looked into the big, rectangular operating room. In the center of it was the operating table, illuminated by a cluster of surgical spots above it. Around the table was a variety of machines: an oxygen dispenser, a rolling instrument cabinet with attached sterilizer, a heart and lung monitor, a defibrillator. Dominating everything was a large computer, which would help guide the electric needle into Martin's brain.

"There's where you can sit," said Kurt, pointing to a small viewer's gallery opposite the doors. The gallery was elevated a dozen feet above the floor level of the operating room, and separated from it by a long plate-glass window. It was reached by a stairway, the door to which was in the left corner of the room. Kurt pointed to the door, and Ann, Hugh, Sally, and Lady Kitty crossed the operating room and climbed the short stair to the gallery, which was a six-foot-wide cement block aisle holding eight folding chairs. After they had taken seats, Kurt, who had followed them up the stairs, said, "I think you'll all be comfortable here. And I'll be watching you. So don't try anything that would disturb the doctor during the operation. We wouldn't want anything to go wrong, would we?"

He closed the door and locked them in the gallery. Then they heard him run down the concrete stairs to the operating room. No one spoke until they could see Kurt through the window, coming out into the operating room. He looked up at them. Then he strolled over to the computer and began examining it.

"Do you think he'd actually shoot someone?" said Lady Kitty, in an unusually subdued tone.

"Yeah," replied Hugh. "Kurt's a sickie, he's high and he'd shoot."

Ann glanced at her watch. It was quarter till eight. In fifteen minutes, she thought, the automatic timer on Arnold Hirsch's sleep capsule would decompress the machine and wake him up. He would have no way of knowing what was going on in the lab wing, of course. But there was at best a possibility he might find out and be able to contact the police.

❧

"Hard mother."

The two words swirled through Herbert Mentius's mind as, twenty minutes later, he and Dr. Zimmermann wheeled Martin Hirsch out of the pre-op room on a portable bed. The blow on the head that Ernst Stahling had given Martin had been expertly aimed: it had stunned but not hurt him. When he had started to revive in pre-op, Zimmermann had administered anesthesia; then she shaved the tiny square on the side of his head. They could overcome the procedural difficulties, he supposed; but still, operating under these conditions, with two guns pointed at him, coming, as it did on top of everything else, had left Herbert Mentius in a state of near hysteria. "Hard mother." Latin: "dura mater;" the anatomical name for the outermost membrane of the brain, the so-called meninges which cushion the brain from the surrounding skullbone. Medieval Arabs had thought the meninges were the mother of the other body membranes—hence, "hard mother." An absurd name, really. And why was he thinking of it now? Why were ancient diagrams from Gray's *Anatomy* flashing in his mind, muddling him at the very time it was essential he keep his mind absolutely clear? The two guns pointing at him. He had never had a gun pointed at him, and he was ashamed of the terror it instilled in him. The guns. Sally's finally outspoken indignation at his behavior. His own guilt, however rationalized, at what he had done. His worry over the future of the Methuselah Enzyme, his monumental discovery that now seemed to be slipping out of his grasp, assuming a chaotic life of its own as others tried to expropriate and control it. . . .

"Shall I crank him up, Doctor?" said Zimmermann. They had transferred Martin from the portable bed to the operating table. Mentius nodded. How cool she seemed, he thought. The guns. They wouldn't shoot, would they? True, they'd shot at the mirror and the vases, but to kill? Would they have carried out their threat to hurt Jeremy and Jeffrey? Oetterli was a drug addict and pusher, after all, and they weren't carrying guns for amusement . . . Maybe they'll kill them all after the operation? Wouldn't that be the smartest thing for them to do? Then no one would know who had the Mentase. They won't even know it was stolen. My God, could they do it? Who stole the Mentase? Who stole the tarts? Hard mother, soft mother . . .

"That's enough," he said to Zimmermann. Martin was now cranked to a seventy-five degree angle from the horizontal plane. Zimmermann placed his head on a steel support, then positioned it with padded clamps. Mentius attached four leather straps over Martin's body which would prevent him from slipping or moving in any direction as the needle went into his brain.

Hard mother. Ridiculous. Obscene, like subway graffiti . . . dura mater, pia mater—tender mother, the innermost membrane. That was nicer. Steel engravings of Harvey and a tintype of Paul Langerhans came to mind. How much gentler the old boys were! Tender mother . . . the islets of Langerhans; there was almost a romantic quality to the way they had named parts of the body, as if they had been in love with the beauty of the human anatomy, in love with the handiwork of God or of nature . . . tender mother. He had been in love with the brain once. Awed by this fantastic machine that he had studied for so many years, when he wasn't sneaking off to the U.T. on Harvard Square to satisfy his unscientific appetite for cinematic Westerns. Weren't the secrets of the brain the secrets of life itself? "The seat of the soul," Descartes had called the pineal. And Mentius had proved him right, in a way. The pineal produced Mentase, and wasn't Mentase the source of immortality? Or was immortality the soul? Was the soul the only immortality? Was immortality worth it for men like Arnold Hirsch or Kurt, or Herbert Mentius? Did anybody have soul anymore, or was that, too, an old-fashioned romantic notion? He didn't know. Hard mother, Tender mother, dura mater, pia mater . . .

"What's that?" said Kurt Oetterli, pointing to the aluminum cube Mentius was attaching to Martin's head.

"The stereotaxic cage," replied Dr. Zimmermann tersely. "And *please:* be quiet."

"Sorry."

Mentius tightened the rubber-tipped screws which secured the cage to Martin's head while Zimmermann programmed the computer with the coordinates of Martin's pineal gland in relation to the sliding carriage on the cage which held the needle. The needle would go through the skull, through the "hard mother" membrane; then through the delicately cobwebbed arachnoid membrane; on through the cerebrospinal fluid which floated the brain, countering the pull of gravity; then to the "tender mother" membrane, until it would be pointing at the outermost layer of the brain itself, the cerebral cortex, the bark, or gray matter. How beautiful, how beautiful the brain. How did it go? "What a piece of work is man! How noble in reason! How infinite in faculty!" And how crappy in behavior. Ann's brain, Hugh's brain. In an age of destroyed privacies, Herbert Mentius had destroyed the final and most sacred privacy by invading their skulls. He had made ugly what should have been beautiful. He had savaged nature for his dream, and though the dream had been good, was even Mentase worth the price being paid for it? Ann and Hugh might not be really damaged; they might even have forgiven him, but he was still guilty and he knew it. As guilty as Arnold Hirsch; even, in a way, more so, for he'd always had the option of saying "no" to Arnold, and he had remained silent.

Now the gun pointing at him a few feet away was forcing him into still another operation, an operation necessitated by his own quixotic smashing of the test tubes. It was the final perversion of his work and dream, the theft of Mentase, to be peddled to the highest bidder. He glanced at the steel muzzle . . .

"The computer is ready, Doctor," said Zimmermann.

"All right." He looked up from the gun muzzle to the face of Oetterli. Good God, he's fascinated, thought Mentius. Really fascinated, like some child glued to his television screen watching a medical soap opera. Perhaps—

"Doctor, ready for the drill?"

"Oh . . . yes . . ." Pay attention. Pay *attention*, for God's sake! Clear your mind. Clear it! Concentrate!

As Zimmermann gave him the power drill with the tiny bit, he placed it against the small square she had shaved on the left side of Martin's head. Then he turned it on. Zimmermann daubed the blood as the bit pierced the skin and began drilling the tiny burr-hole in the bone.

He had been wrong to smash the test tubes, for that was what was forcing him to operate on Martin. Yes, he had meant well but it was only a gesture. He couldn't really destroy Mentase. Sally, poor Sally; she had been almost destroyed by the elaborate deception they had perpetrated. She hated Arnold Hirsch. But it was too late to divorce Mentase from Arnold and the Société. Sally could say, "Get rid of them," but it wasn't that easy. If nothing else, he had a commitment to Arnold and Lady Kitty. They were still his patients; no matter how potentially lethal Mentase was, with sufficient RNA booster shots the possibility of a recurrence of Michael Brandywine's fate was highly unlikely. And he had to admit that there was the possibility of an even worse consequence than Michael had suffered if he did indeed stop the treatment. . . .

Slowly the drill bit through the hard skullbone. Then it was through, and inside the skull. Mentius withdrew the drill. Quickly he slid the needle's mount over the hole and locked it in place. Then Zimmermann switched to computer control. The needle slowly lowered itself through the hole, piercing the dura mater, the arachnoid membrane, traversing the cerebrospinal fluid, then again piercing the pia mater until it was poised at the brain itself, directly over the most prominent of all the sulci, or convolutions, that wrinkled the cortex: the lateral fissure of Sylvius. Bundles of nerves ascending from the thalamus deep inside the brain burst into sprays of millions of individual fibers at the cortex. To damage any of them, or accidentally cut them, would be to damage the brain permanently; brain cells were nonregenerative. So Mentius had programmed the needle to reach the pineal by the path of least resistance, which, with the possible exception of piercing the sinuses, was the fissure of Sylvius.

The path of least resistance—he had chosen the path of least resistance. The available money. The easy way to finance the research for the synthesizing of Mentase. The compromise which led inevitably to the betrayal of trust . . .

The needle was going through the brain now, inching its way to the pine cone-shaped reddish pineal gland that hung on the bottom of the brain like a minute teat.

He glanced up at the viewer's gallery. Their faces were white behind the window. He looked at Kurt totally hypnotized by the gadgets—the cage, the needle, the heart and lung monitor whose needle jiggled across the graph paper recording Martin's pulse and breathing. Maybe he could make use of this fascination. Did he dare do it? What if Kurt fired the gun? He might kill Martin or Zimmermann . . . No, *no:* you're rationalizing! What you're afraid of is he might kill *you,* Herbert Mentius, discoverer of the Methuselah Enzyme. Likewise its betrayer. You've risked other lives for Mentase, shouldn't you be willing at least to risk your own life? A nice question . . .

The needle reached the pineal gland and an impulse from the computer opened the end into a blossom of three tongs. Neatly, they sliced the very tip of the gland, holding it like a tiny sugar cube. Then the computer signaled and, like an obedient slave, the needle began its return journey back through the fissure of Sylvius, the meninges, through the burrhole out into the open air, where Zimmermann captured the prize in a waiting test tube.

"It's over," said Mentius, straightening and looking at Kurt. "I noticed you seemed interested in the equipment. Would you like a closer look?"

Kurt's face lit up with flattered interest. "You're sure it's all right?"

"Of course. Just don't touch anything."

"I must say you've got some extraordinary machines in here," said Kurt, coming up to the operating table and peering at the electric needle. "Machines have always fascinated me. . . . And *that* little thing went all the way inside his brain?"

Mentius's rubber-gloved hand had closed over the scalpel on the instrument table. Now he brought it swiftly down onto Kurt's right wrist, cutting as deeply as he dared without actually severing the hand. Kurt's reaction was a slow double-take, astonishment next, and then sick fear at the sight of the blood. The gun had clattered to the floor. Mentius scooped it up and moved quickly away, certain that any second he would feel the bullet from Stahling's gun enter his heart or spatter *his* meninges all over the wall. Instead, as he tried to steady the gun with both trembling hands, he saw that Stahling was as surprised at his sudden action as

Kurt had been. In fact, he hadn't raised his gun. Now, seeing the doctor's gun pointed at him, he dropped his arm and raised his hands.

To Mentius's amazement, it was over.

Lady Kitty de Ross stretched luxuriantly in her bed and rubbed her eyes. After her long nap, she felt delicious. The triumph of her party, the shock of Michael's death, then the further shock of those two louts, Oetterli and Stahling, trying to hold them up—it had all been exhausting, and she had been sure she would wake up with an elephantine hangover. But, to her pleasant surprise, she hadn't; she felt wonderful. And hadn't dear Dr. Mentius been inspired? she thought. So brave he'd been—much more than she would have ever expected from the sad-eyed scientist—though she had to admit he'd looked as if he could faint with relief when the police finally arrived to take charge and book Oetterli and Stahling. But all the disturbances were over now, thank God, and there was reason to hope that life at the chateau could return to some semblance of normality.

Her thoughts suddenly stopped. Michael. Michael was dead.

Feeling deflated, she got out of bed, casting a guilty glance at the sleep capsule she hadn't slept in, contrary to doctor's orders . . . oh well. She went into the bathroom, washed her face, brushed her teeth, and combed her hair. Then, feeling better, she glanced at the huge bathtub and smiled. Such wonderful times she'd had in it since arriving at the Chateau Mirabelle! Bill Bradshaw and Michael . . . poor Michael, it was horrible what had happened to him. Momentarily, she felt chilled as she remembered what had happened to Michael might happen to her. But no—Dr. Mentius had said he would arrange for the RNA booster shots for her and Arnold. Surely they would be safe with the boosters; it was only that stupid Ann Brandywine's meddling that had caused the trouble in the first place. But there was something more important: Mentius's saying he wouldn't continue the treatment. Could he possibly have been serious, or was it all a bravado show of righteousness to placate his tedious wife? He *had* smashed the test tubes, after all. . . .

Again, she felt a chill as she thought what might happen if the treatment were stopped. Glancing in the mirror, she ran a finger over her face, the skin of which had become so soft and smooth. The thought of it growing old again was terrifying, unbearable. She closed her eyes a moment to fight off the fear that had suddenly washed over her like a flash flood. Then she opened them again. There was nothing to fear. She and Arnold could handle Mentius; they had handled him before.

Michael, Michael, Michael . . . God, she wished he were there at that very moment, making love to her. . . . She wanted a man, wanted one intensely, wanted to climb into the tub for one of those long, delicious baths.

Returning to her bedroom, she went to the window and sulked. When Lady Kitty wanted something, she wanted it immediately, and she was accustomed to having it. Now she wanted to make love. But there was no one to make love to.

Except . . .

Her head turned slowly toward the door that led to Hugh's bedroom. The door she hadn't used for so long.

Well, why not? She was still paying the rent.

❧

When the police had taken Stahling and Oetterli away, Ann Brandywine had gone upstairs to her suite and collapsed on the bed. The strain of the past twenty-four hours had exhausted her. All she wanted now was sleep. She had to inform Michael's children of their father's death, of course, but she had been told it would be several hours before the telephone lines Kurt had cut could be repaired, so she profited from the delay by catching some sleep. When she awoke it was afternoon. The phones were repaired, and she placed a call to Michael's oldest child, telling him what had happened. The lugubrious but necessary details concerning the disposition of Michael's body were discussed, and it was decided that, since he had wished cremation, Ann should have it performed in Switzerland. And that was about all that could be said, for what else was there to discuss? She hardly knew his children. Could she tell them what Michael had done to her? The true circumstances of his death? What point was there to it now, except to upset them unnecessarily and damage their memory of their father? So she told them as little as possible, but when she hung up, she felt an intense depression. It was, she supposed, a natural reaction to what had happened, but that was little comfort. More than ever she wanted to leave the Chateau Mirabelle, which was haunted now with so many terrible associations. The gilt cupids, the crystal chandeliers, the swirling nymphs of her luxurious suite suddenly seemed repulsive to her.

Getting off her bed she went to the closet, pulled out her suitcases, and began to pack.

"You're leaving?"

Arnold. It was his quiet voice at the door. She looked up from her packing.

"Unless you're going to try and stop me again?" she said.

"No. Since the Mentiuses dismissed my detectives while I was sleeping so peacefully in my capsule, there's not much point in my rehiring them. Besides, they really weren't very competent, were they?"

"What do you mean?"

"Well, you escaped, didn't you?" He smiled. "May I come in?"

She wished he would go away, but she nodded and continued her packing. He came into the bedroom and stood in front of one of the windows, his hands behind his back, staring thoughtfully out at the lake. He was wearing one of his Cardin suits and had retrieved his hairpiece, so that again Ann was struck by his remarkable youthfulness. She wondered what he wanted.

"How's Martin?" she asked.

"Mentius says he's recuperating as well as can be expected."

"You haven't gone to see him?"

"I tried. He didn't want to talk to me." He paused. "He's informed me through Mentius that he's leaving the chateau too."

She continued packing.

"And what will you do?" she asked.

"Complete the treatment, of course."

She looked up.

"Does that surprise you?" he asked.

"It surprises me that Mentius would continue it after what he said last night. Before he operated on Martin, he told Lady Kitty he thought Mentase was too dangerous to continue using."

"On the other hand, it would be more dangerous to stop using."

"Why?"

He turned and looked at her. "Because Lady Kitty and I would grow old again."

She tucked a pair of shoes in the corner of her suitcase, thinking of Arnold and Lady Kitty again, wrinkling and shriveling like dying leaves. She supposed Mentius couldn't subject them to that, no matter what Arnold had done. On the other hand, it seemed wrong, somehow, that after all the brave words, all the animosity and scheming, things would continue fairly much the same way as before, that Arnold and Lady Kitty would complete their desenescing this time using Martin as the source rather than herself and Hugh.

"Well, I won't bother you," said Arnold. "I know you're probably anxious to leave the chateau. But I wanted to say good-bye to you." He started toward the door. "What do you intend doing with yourself now? I mean, when you get back to New York?"

"I don't know."

"New York can be a fairly depressing place for someone who's all alone."

"Hardly more depressing than here."

"Perhaps." He ran his finger over his chin, the chin that once had supported a jowl but which was now youthfully firm. "If you'd let me, I'd enjoy taking you out to dinner sometime. I have no illusions about your opinion of me, but I was enjoying myself last night—until Mr. Barstow sledgehammered me, that is—and I'm foolish enough to think perhaps you were enjoying yourself more than you thought you would. So since I'll be alone too, perhaps we could keep each other company."

Now she knew what he wanted. Of course. It was typical of him. "Arnold, you really do have gall. You're also rather transparent. In case I haven't made it clear enough before, I'll now spell it out to you. I really think I'd rather go to dinner with Martin Bormann."

His expression didn't alter.

"Well, I think you're overstating the case against me. And as you pointed out last night, we would make a good team."

"As I'm sure you now realize, I was putting you on."

"Nevertheless, it's something we should consider."

"Why? Because suddenly I'm the second biggest stockholder in the Société? You're not very subtle, Arnold."

"Oh, well, there's that—yes, I won't deny that makes you more interesting. But it's more than that. You're beautiful. You're intelligent. You have a sort of moral straightness that's frankly intriguing to an ethical corkscrew like myself. You get along well with Martin, which I've never been able to do. On my side, I offer you certain advantages. I'm wealthy. Of course, Michael left you well fixed, but money going with money has its advantages. I flatter myself that, thanks to Mentase, I'm not physically unattractive; someday soon, I'll even have my own hair. And no matter what you think of my character, I have a genuine love of beautiful things which I think you share."

She closed the suitcase. "I'm *really* not interested."

"But you *may* be in time," he insisted. "All I'm asking is for you to keep an open mind for a while."

"Arnold," she sighed, "you may never admit this to yourself, but the only decent thing about you is your son."

He nodded his head slightly. "I suppose I deserve that. But I still can hope that you may change your mind."

He walked out of the room.

When Hugh heard the knock on the door connecting his room to Lady Kitty's suite, he stopped his packing, turned down the Dutch rock station he had been listening to on his radio, and went to the door to open it. Lady Kitty was standing on the other side, dressed in a filmy pink peignoir, her face carefully made up, her hair tied in a pink ribbon. He knew immediately what she was after. Whenever she put on that pink ribbon, it meant her furnace was rumbling.

"Hugh dear," she said smiling. "I wondered if you'd like to join me for a drink. Orange juice for me, of course. But it's been such a hectic twenty-four hours, and I'm finally feeling halfway human after sleeping most of the day, and, well . . . it's been some time since we talked."

Silence.

"Like, Kitty baby, I'm off the payroll, dig? So go pick up one of the bellboys."

She didn't take offense. "You *do* seem to boil everything down to the lowest common denominator. Every time I ask a man into my suite doesn't necessarily mean I want to make love."

"Oh yeah?"

"You're being tedious," she pouted. Her eyes spotted the suitcase on the bed. "And why are you packing?"

"Well now, guess."

"You're not thinking of leaving?"

"Oh no. I'm going to stay around so you can cut out my liver."

"You're behaving like a child. Now come in my suite and let's talk things over. There's no point in your being angry with me just because I let the doctor operate on you."

He shook his head. "Jesus, you really don't see anything wrong with it, do you?"

"Of course not. It wasn't as if you were *using* your pineal gland. You probably didn't even know you had one. Now come in and have a drink."

"Kitty," he said, "I'm through being house stud."

She saw he meant what he said, and her temper began to show. "I find it somewhat absurd to have my ethics attacked by someone with the morals of a programmed tomcat."

"Kitty baby, I come across as a goddamn saint compared to you."

She simmered over this a moment, then looked at him curiously. "And just what do you intend doing with yourself?"

"I'm going back to New York to take some acting lessons. I mean, I've got a real gimmick now: the only actor in show business with half a pineal gland. *That* should sell tickets."

"It's not your pineal gland that will sell tickets," she said disdainfully. "And if you think your face will, you haven't looked in a mirror lately. Oh, I'll admit you used to have a certain animal charm that was attractive in its crude way, though whatever gave you the idea you might be able to act is beyond me. But look in the mirror. You're getting wrinkles, dear boy. This heady existence at the top of the heap has been too much for you. You're wearing down." She smiled.

"Yeah, sure," he said. "Now do you think we could be spared the bitchery, just shake hands and say good-bye without a lot of crap?"

"Why not?" She held out her hand. "I'm not a vindictive person. I'll even wish you good luck. Frankly, I think you'll need it."

He took her hand and shook it. "You're all heart, Kitty."

"If you send me your address, I'll forward your clothes from Tangier." She looked at his hand and pointed to the skin. "Where did you get the freckles? You never had them before."

He retrieved his hand and looked at the back of it. It was covered with a dusting of light specks. He shrugged. "I must have gotten sunburned," he said.

"You mustn't get too much sun," she remarked, with an undercurrent of smugness. "It ages the skin." She ran her eyes up his body from his feet to the top of his head, as if giving him one final inspection. "Not bad," she said. "But definitely Secaucus." She turned and went back into her room.

He closed the door, relieved to be rid of her, and returned to his packing. But something she had said bothered him, and after a moment he stopped and looked at his hands. Both of them were covered with the freckles. It was undeniably odd. He went over to his bureau and looked in the mirror, checking his face.

To his surprise, there were frown lines on his forehead, and the skin around his lips looked strangely dry.

He heard a knock on the door that led to the corridor and went over to open it. Ann Brandywine was standing outside. "Hugh," she said, "could you come down to see Martin Hirsch with me? There's something I want to discuss with you."

❧

It was five thirty when they all gathered in Martin's room in the infirmary: Ann, Hugh, and Dr. Mentius and his wife. Martin was sitting up in his bed looking pale, but otherwise alert after the operation. The others stood around the bed looking at Ann, who had gotten them together.

"Doctor," she said to Mentius, "I understand you've decided to complete Arnold's and Lady Kitty's treatment."

He nodded. "I have to," he said. "Oh, I know what you're thinking. I suppose we're all thinking the same thing. There are excellent reasons why the treatment should be stopped, and God knows I'm not happy about continuing with Arnold Hirsch. I wanted to stop it last night; I suppose my breaking the test tubes was a belated attempt on my part to try and stop something that's become increasingly distasteful to me and my wife, and the rest of you, for that matter. But when I had a chance to think about it a little more rationally, I realized I really can't stop the treatment."

"Because they'd start to grow old again?"

"I'm afraid it's not quite that simple. There's a possibility that by stopping the injections at this stage of the treatment, I might produce what I suppose could be best described as a sort of biochemical nightmare."

"If that's true," said Martin, "what would you have done if Kurt hadn't forced you to operate on me?"

"I'd probably have had to ask your permission to operate. And if you hadn't agreed, I don't know what I would have done. But I'd have had to get some more Mentase some way. Last night, I was frightened by the guns and I acted stupidly. But now, well, no matter what I think of Arnold Hirsch and Lady de Ross, I can't jeopardize their safety. After all, they're still my patients."

"How much of the stuff can you make out of what you took from me?" asked Martin.

"Enough to finish the desenescing process," replied Mentius. "In two weeks' time, they'll both be at the biological age of about forty. After that, the daily injections won't be necessary any longer. And I'll have enough Mentase left over to give them monthly booster shots to keep them at the age level of forty for the next two years—but *just* enough."

"What happens then?"

"Then, hopefully, we'll have been able to synthesize and test Mentase in the lab and we'll have an unlimited supply of it. None of these secret operations would have been necessary if we could have waited till then, of course. But as you know, your father insisted on going ahead with the treatment, and given my initial mistake of agreeing to do it, there seemed to be no other way to accomplish what he wanted." He looked at Ann and Hugh. "The three of you were the victims—I suppose that's about the best word to describe it. But overlooking the rights and wrongs of my behavior, do any of you honestly think any positive good will be accomplished by punishing Arnold and Lady de Ross now that the damage is done?"

"Yes, I think so," said Ann.

"What?"

"Let me say first that I was thinking along much the same lines as you, Doctor. There didn't seem much point in trying to get back at Arnold—or you, for that matter—for what had been done to us. I thought the best thing to do was to go home, and since Michael's shares in the Société are now mine, I assumed that I, or you and I, could at least try to control Arnold later on, when Mentase is ready to be marketed—if you use that word to describe what he plans to do with it. But then a little while ago he came in my room, and I changed my mind."

"Why?"

"Because he started being especially nice to me."

"I'm not following you."

"It's simple enough. Last night, when I was Michael's wife, he tried to bully me. Today, when I'm Michael's widow, he's all tact and patience, urges me to think over his rather obvious proposals."

Martin looked surprised. "You mean my old man is getting interested in women again?"

"That may be part of it, Martin," said Ann, "but I'm not conceited enough to think I'm *that* much of a femme fatale. It's just that he's after my shares in the Société. Before, he had counted on my husband to give him the controlling votes. Now he has to depend on Lady Kitty, and while I suppose she'd probably go along with him most of the time, I imagine he's not all that sure of her. So now he's coming after me. But it's all the same thing: how to control Mentase."

She looked at Mentius.

"Yesterday you said you'd fight Arnold later on. But I think if you really mean what you say about not wanting him to control Mentase, then I think now is the time to take a stand. Because now you have a weapon to use against him."

"You mean, threatening to stop the treatment?"

"That's right. I think you should use the threat to force control of the Société out of his hands. Tell him you won't continue the treatment unless he signs over half of his shares to Martin."

Sally Mentius smiled. "What a marvelous idea!"

"Yes, I like that," said Martin enthusiastically. "That way, between you and me, Ann, we'd own over half the shares, wouldn't we?"

"Yes, which is only fair. After all, we were the 'sources' and we're young. We deserve some say in the control of the company. What about it, Doctor?"

Mentius shook his head. "I see your point, but I can't do it."

"Why?"

"I told you. I couldn't endanger their lives."

"Oh come on," said Hugh. "You weren't so goddamn finicky when you chopped *us* up!"

"But the operations I performed on the three of you were something I knew how to do!" insisted Mentius. "I admit there was risk involved in them, but I was operating with *known* risks: I could control the situation. I don't *know* what will happen if I stop giving the injections now—or at least, I know what I think will happen, and I have no way of controlling it."

"For God's sake, Herbie," exclaimed Sally, "this is the perfect opportunity to stop Arnold! What are you afraid of? What's this horrible 'biochemical nightmare' you think will happen?"

"I think," he said, "they would disintegrate. Quite literally. And they would still be alive while it was happening to them. I think probably the only relief they'd possibly have would be to go insane before the disintegration progressed too far."

Sally looked confused. "Disintegrate? I don't know what you mean."

"I mean they would age at an incredibly fast rate. So fast it would almost be visible."

"But why would it happen so fast?" asked Ann.

"Because the intensive Mentase injections I gave them speeded up their biological clocks as well as reversing them. I halved their ages in two months, and it's possible the process could reverse itself in the same time if I stopped the injections. Nature phases Mentase out of the body gradually, from about the age of twenty-five to age sixty. But they have no Mentase of their own in their bodies; only the Mentase I've given them. Now if I stop the injections cold and they start to age again, it's possible their biochemistry will go on a rampage. There will be nothing to stop the cross-linkage from forming; the process might proliferate like a virulent cancer. I'm not saying it's certain, but I'm saying it's a definite possibility."

Hugh took a deep breath. "Jesus, does Kitty-baby know this would happen?"

"No. I saw no point in frightening them, because until last night there was never a question of stopping the treatment. But I can't take the chance now."

"But can't you bluff them?" asked Ann. "Can't you threaten to stop the treatment and scare Arnold into giving up his shares to Martin? That wouldn't hurt them, and I think it would be worth trying. Or perhaps," she added quietly, "you don't think it's worth trying? Perhaps you don't care how Mentase is used as long as people know Herbert Mentius discovered it?"

He started an angry retort, then backed down.

Sally Mentius said gently, "Bluff them, Herbie. Ann's right. You have to care what happens to Mentase."

He thought a moment, then nodded. "All right." He looked at Ann. "But if the bluff doesn't work, don't expect me to carry out the threat."

They decided to tell them at dinner that night—the dinner that would be Ann's last meal in the chateau. As she dressed for it, she wondered what Arnold and Lady Kitty would decide. She knew her suggestion had been cruel; it was what she supposed could be called biochemical blackmail. On the other hand, there was no feasible alternative except to let things slide, with the result being that the fantastic power implicit in the control of

Mentase would remain in Arnold Hirsch's hands. And she had no illusions about her own ability to withstand Arnold's will over a long period of time, even though she was now the second largest stockholder in the Société. She was no martyr, and she was no fanatic. Eventually she might tire of the struggle, or Arnold would convince her his "system" of selecting those who would receive the Mentase treatment was as fair as was possible under the circumstances—perhaps even inevitable. If he was to be checked, it had to be now.

She had put on a black dress in official consideration of her dead husband. Now, she looked at her reflection, again noticing how tired she looked. She would have time later on to worry about her looks, she decided. She left her suite and started down the grand staircase to the first floor.

The great marble entrance hall of the chateau was empty and clean, the last debris of the party having been swept away by the efficient staff when it returned, and the click of her heels on the stairs rang in the silence of the rotunda. The huge ornate chateau seemed like a monument to the naive but well-meaning dreams of Mentius, as well as to the vanity of Lady Kitty's desire for eternal youth and Arnold Hirsch's lust for power and control. When she thought of the elaborate quadrille of deception and maneuvering that had gone on in the chateau, she wondered again if Mentase weren't more a curse than a blessing. Certainly, whatever change had occurred in the personalities of those receiving the treatment could hardly be called a change for the better. If anything, the Mentase had brought out their worst traits, a far cry from the Olympian objectivity Mentius had claimed his discovery would bring to the human race.

She had reached the bottom of the stairs; now she walked down the corridor to the Salle d'Hercule, where the others were already seated at the great table. The candles in the tall silver candelabra glowed softly, casting their warm light on the red damask walls of the room and dimly illuminating Hercules on the ceiling above. Through the French doors another brilliant sunset splashed the sky with all the colors of the crepuscular palette; and as she took her seat at the table, Ann reflected that although she had come to loathe the Chateau Mirabelle, she would never forget the beauty of its setting.

The meal began in silence, as if they all sensed something unpleasant. Just off-stage, Lady Kitty was seated opposite Ann, who noticed that the ex-actress's eyes were on her as she lifted her cup of bouillon to her mouth, the candlelight flashing from the jewels in her enormous rings. Her striking rejuvenation, which the night before had made Ann envious, now left her without any feeling at all.

It was Sally Mentius who broke the silence. "We've had a meeting," she said.

"Oh?" said Arnold. "About what?"

"About you and Lady Kitty and the Société. Herbie, tell them."

They all looked to the end of the table where Dr. Mentius was sitting. He put down his cup of bouillon and said, "Arnold, Ann has made a suggestion that we all have agreed to."

"Which is?"

"That you assign half your shares in the Société to your son."

Arnold looked quickly at Ann.

"I see. And if I say no?"

Mentius put his hands beneath the table and began squeezing his knuckles. "I'll be forced to stop the treatment."

Silence. Arnold wiped his mouth with his napkin.

Sally prompted her husband: "Tell them what will happen if you stop it."

"Sally, I'm not sure—"

"Tell them," she insisted.

"We know we'd grow old again," said Arnold. "What else?"

"I'll tell you," said Sally. "He's afraid you'll grow old quickly, as quickly as you grew young. He said it would be sort of a biochemical nightmare, and he's not sure how your bodies would react to it."

"What's that mean?"

"It means," said Mentius, "that it may be painful and it may be lethal."

"That's the choice," said Sally. "And my husband means it. We both mean it."

Lady Kitty looked frightened. "You're bluffing. You wouldn't dare try it. It's nothing but extortion!"

"You're right," said Ann. "It's extortion and it's blackmail. But we want Martin to have the stock."

"But why?" said Lady Kitty. "What makes you think that pimply-faced teen-age addict should have anything to say in the running of the Société?"

"The most important thing," said Sally, "is that Arnold not have *everything* to say about it. Or you, for that matter."

"Oh I see," said Lady Kitty, glaring at Ann. "We're being altruistic again. The moral Mrs. Brandywine, who has done nothing but cause trouble since she got here with her damn ethical wailings . . ."

"And look what you did to *us!*" said Ann. "You didn't give a damn about us, as long as we made it possible for you to lose a few wrinkles."

"You killed your husband and now you're willing to kill us so that sometime in the distant future some vaguely democratic principle can be upheld—it's insane! I've never heard such perverted humanitarian idiocy!"

"It may be idiocy to you," said Ann, "but it's important. Ask Arnold. He knows how important it is. Am I right, Arnold?"

Arnold was toying with his soup spoon and looked, for the first time, edgy. "I think you're exaggerating what the Société intends doing with Mentase."

"No I'm not."

Her tone was effective. He put down the spoon. "Lady Kitty," he said, "my business is reading people. I don't think they're bluffing."

"Just a minute," said Lady Kitty. "Doctor, you say you think we would grow old quickly. Is that right?"

"Yes."

"I assume you mean that we would start to show signs of aging in, well, weeks? Just as we lost the signs of aging?"

"I think so. But I can't be certain."

"But, Doctor," she said, "you must have made a mistake in your calculations before. A serious mistake. Hugh dear, show the good doctor your hands. Show him those interesting freckles that have appeared on your skin."

Hugh looked at his hands. "Why?"

"Don't ask tedious questions. Show him."

Hugh, who was sitting at the doctor's left, held out his hands to Mentius to inspect. As he looked at them, Lady Kitty continued: "I knew what they were the moment I saw them, because I used to have them myself. They're not freckles, and they're not sunburn."

Ann, who was noticing the faint freckles on her own hands for the first time, said, "What are they?"

"But dear Ann, it's obvious. They're liver spots."

❧

The three of them sat up in the Salon de Vénus till well past midnight. It was the second night in a row that they had been kept up, and the strain was beginning to show. Lady Kitty was nervous and irritable, and Sally looked exhausted. Only Arnold Hirsch, who had had more than enough sleep in his hyperbaric cryogenic sleep capsule, looked reasonably fit. He sat in a chair leafing through a back copy of *Paris Match.*

At quarter past midnight, Hugh and Ann joined them. They had been in the lab with Mentius since dinner, and the exhaustive examination had left them as weary as the others.

"Is he done with the tests?" asked Arnold.

They nodded. Ann curled up on a sofa and put her head on her arms. "I'm going to sleep. Wake me up when Mentius comes out of the lab."

"How long will it be?"

"He said it would take him another hour," said Hugh, slumping into a chair and closing his eyes. "So we wait."

❧

At one o'clock Mentius and Zimmermann came into the room from the lab and woke everyone up. As Ann sat up on the sofa, rubbing her eyes, she said, "Have you figured out what's wrong?"

Mentius nodded. "All the tests seem to confirm the same conclusion," he said. "By cutting off part of your pineal glands, we seem to have inadvertently stopped their production of Mentase. So instead of Mentase phasing out of your body over a number of years, as it normally does, it's vanished entirely. And the result is, of course . . ." He hesitated.

"The cross-linkage is speeding up?" said Hugh.

"Yes. There's nothing to break down the links between the DNA molecules, so the process is running rampant."

"Like a cancer?" said Ann.

"Well, certainly with the speed of a cancer. The liver spots, the incipient wrinkles, the dry skin, the feeling of lassitude you complained about—these are the first signs of what I suppose we could call hypersenescence; or, in plain English, you are aging about a hundred times as fast as normal."

"So it's going to happen to *us* instead of them?"

"Please, Mrs. Brandywine, there's no reason for alarm—"

"No *reason?*" she exclaimed. "Are you crazy? Hugh and Martin and I are going to turn into corpses in a couple of weeks because of you . . . because of your damned meddling . . . and we're supposed to sit back and take it calmly? You were going to improve on nature! Is *this* your improvement?"

"Mrs. Brandywine—"

"I didn't mind growing old slowly! I didn't mind dying someday —what's wrong with dying *some*day? What's wrong with growing old *normally?* But now we're going to grow old in—what? A month? A week? Three days? How much longer do we have, Doctor? An hour?"

"Mrs. Brandywine," said Mentius wearily, "we can easily restore the balance in your system. All we have to do is give you Mentase injections."

"Martin's Mentase?"

"Well, yes . . ."

"How long is that going to last? You've got all of us now, Doctor—Martin, me, Hugh, Lady Kitty, Arnold. . . . We all need Mentase now. How long will Martin's last?"

Mentius shook his head. "I don't know."

"Then, Doctor," she whispered as the tears ran down her wrinkling face, "*where* are you going to get more?"

She stared at him. He didn't have an answer.

EPILOGUE

LOUIS Christophe Steiner, the Alsatian manager of the Casino d'Afrique in Tangier, looked around the elegant gambling room with satisfaction. It was a good crowd for the end of July, which was a few weeks before the city usually became inundated with the French on their August holidays. There were two cruise ships in port, and the Casino had attracted a large number of the well-heeled American tourists, who might drop a few hundred francs at the crap tables, but probably not much more than that. The cruise crowd didn't gamble too heavily. No, the big gamblers usually didn't arrive until later in the year when the International Set moved into residence. That's when the no-limit trente-et-quarante table was always filled, and a roulette table was considered slow if it didn't clear at least twenty thousand a night. But still, it was a respectable crowd, well-dressed, generally well-behaved. The new French rock combo was packing them into the discothèque room next to the Casino; the management would do all right tonight.

And there were even a few of the International Set on hand, even before their season. Lady Kitty de Ross had taken her usual seat at table three, though he had hardly recognized her when she came in the Casino, she looked so amazingly young. He had heard rumors of a cure she had taken in Switzerland, and they were obviously true. If anything, they had understated the change in the old bitch. It was more than a change, actually. It was a transformation.

That former rock singer he had fired earlier in the year and who had then moved on to become Lady de Ross's lover—he was here too. Except he had left Lady de Ross at the door and gone to the bar, where he was now buying a drink for a young Swedish blonde who had been drifting in and out of the Casino for a day or two, scoring with some of the businessmen types. What was the singer's name? Ah yes, Barstow. He hadn't seen him for a while. He wondered if he had gone to Switzerland with Lady de Ross. If he did, the cure obviously hadn't done much for him. He looked shockingly older—middle-aged in fact. Louis Christophe Steiner reflected that being a stud for Lady de Ross must be a debilitating way of life.

Then there was that middle-aged American woman that had come in with Lady de Ross and was sitting next to her at the roulette table. Whoever she was, she must have money. She was expensively dressed, and that turquoise and diamond necklace she was wearing must have cost a fortune. Poor woman, she probably was beautiful once, a wreck now. Her face had that hard, wrinkled look that Lady de Ross used to have, that look that came from too many martinis, too many cigarettes, too many lovers, too many years. Steiner guessed she must be close to fifty, though she might be a few years younger. She ought to get the name of the clinic in Switzerland; she looked like she could use a youth cure.

Ah, *voilà!* He knew it, he could spot it—the pattern was always the same. That young French boy—the good-looking one that he suspected was working the place with the Swedish girl Mr. Barstow was buying drinks for at the bar—the French boy had been hovering around the American woman for several minutes now, and she had just flashed him a smile. She was saying something to him now. What would her line be? Would he place a bet for her to change her luck? That was the usual opener. Yes, that was what she tried. She was handing him three chips, which he was placing on seventeen. Win or lose, he would be sitting next to her within ten minutes. And then . . .

Louis Christophe Steiner shook his head. The game was so old. It would be amusing to see someone think up a variation.

"Faites vos jeux, mesdames et messieurs. Faites vos jeux."

Ann placed fifty francs on twenty, then looked at Yves. "What number are you playing tonight, darling?"

"Twelve," he said, smiling. His teeth were incredibly white against his deep tan.

"Let's hope you do better than last night."

"I thought I did very well last night, Ann."

She shrugged, thinking how greedy he was, but he would do. She hoped Hugh and Martin were having luck. Hugh she didn't worry about, really; he was an old hand at this game, and he had that Swedish girl practically hypnotized. But Martin had gone to Deauville with his father, and Martin was hardly experienced at this sort of thing. But then, neither was she. She was learning, though.

"Mesdames et messieurs, les jeux sont faites."

The croupier spun the wheel and flicked the white ball. It landed on nine. Nine. The available Mentase had lasted only nine days when it had been split five ways. Nine days, and then it was gone and the terrible change in her face and body had accelerated. But Lady Kitty and Arnold were as afraid as she now. For though they had almost reached the end of their treatment, without Mentase boosters they would start to change also. They had all become addicts now, and what did it matter that Arnold had given Martin half his shares in the Société? Mentius's plans for mankind, Arnold's dreams for the Société—all had dissipated as her face and Hugh's—and lately Martin's—began to mummify, and they had all dispersed, fleeing the Chateau Mirabelle in a ravening search for Mentase.

"I'm out of chips," said Yves an hour later. Ann got up from the table.

"Let's have a drink, then we'll buy some more."

Yves accompanied her through the crowd toward the bar. What a ghastly life, she thought. What a ghastly, lonely life.

"Yves?"

"Yes?"

He's so polite, so available, so disgusting in his beautiful way.

"What are your plans for the next month or so?"

"My plans?" He smiled and spread his hands. "That's up to you, Ann."

"I'm leaving Tangier in a few days. I wondered if you'd like to go with me?"

"That depends."

"I'll make it worth your while."

Look how warm his smile becomes, she thought. How his eyes shine! Oh, this one is a professional, a real professional.

"Where are we going, *chérie?*"

"*Chérie*" yet! God.

"Switzerland. To a clinic outside Lausanne. A rejuvenation clinic."

"Oh yes, I've heard about them. Is this one of those places where they use the glands of goats?"

"I don't think they use goats," she said, opening her purse and taking out some money. "Get me a martini, darling. I'm feeling rather old tonight, and it's not a pleasant feeling." She looked at him. "I hope it never happens to you."

Yves laughed as he took the money and signaled to the bartender. "But we all get old sometime, don't we?"

LAKE

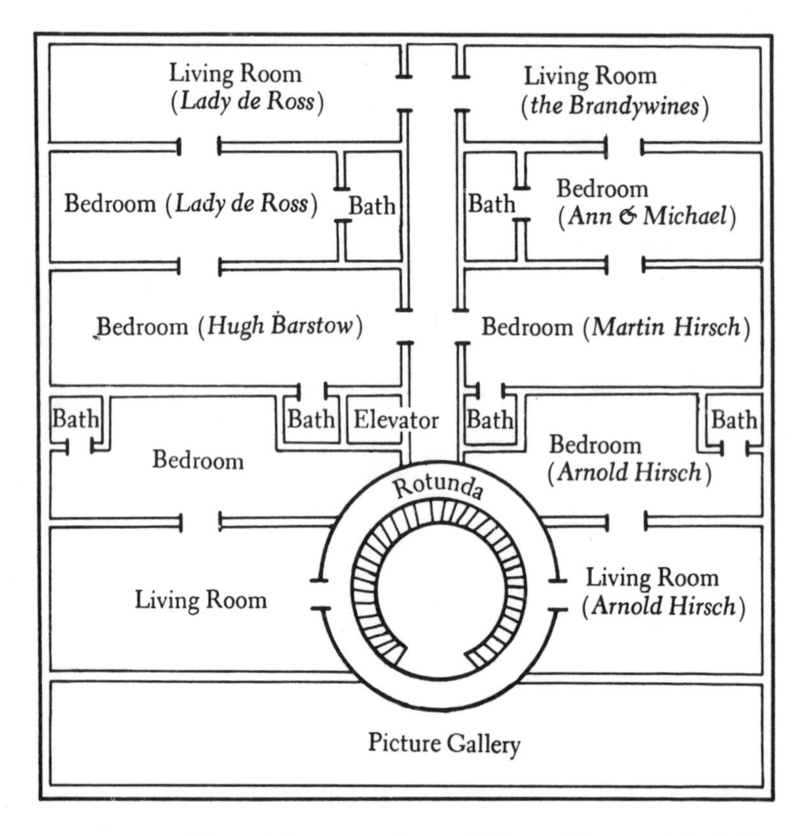

DIAGRAM C: *Plan of Suites on Second Floor, Chateau Mirabelle*